HOLLY WINTER MYSTERIES

BOOKS 1 - 4

RUBY LOREN

BRITISH AUTHOR

Please note, this book is written in British English and contains British spellings.

BOOKS IN THE SERIES

SNOWED IN WITH DEATH

THE DUNCE DETECTIVE

Holly frowned at the first flurry of snow when it splattered wetly on her windscreen. Her wipers soon cleared her vision of the road again, but the white stuff was definitely here to stay.

She bit her lip and wondered if she'd make it to Horn Hill House before the road became impassable. There'd been a weather warning for snow when she'd left her cottage in Little Wemley (a village in deepest, darkest Surrey) early that morning. She'd driven away sooner than she'd originally planned, but the bad weather had also been annoyingly punctual.

"A bit of snow won't keep me away," she muttered under her breath. Even if volcanoes popped up like pimples, and frogs started raining down from the sky, she was certain she'd still figure out how to get to Horn Hill House. The event she was on her way to attend was the chance of a lifetime. Nothing would persuade her to miss it. She could only hope that the other esteemed guests attending the convention were just as committed.

The competition win had been a complete surprise.

Even the most talented detective in the world couldn't predict blind luck. Holly had been thrilled when she'd received the email inviting her to the annual meeting of the greatest private detectives in Britain. During her time off - between occasional small-time mystery cases and her evening work as a professional lounge pianist - she was a coffee break 'comper'. This particular competition win had seemed like fate.

It's going to be amazing finding out what it's like working as a real private detective! she thought, turning down a narrow country lane and swerving to avoid a wandering sheep that had momentarily looked unnervingly like a walking snowman.

Holly had already investigated her fair share of mysteries.

She'd recently traced and recovered her next door neighbour's stolen dog. Her discovery had resulted in the prosecution of a group of exceedingly nasty human beings who'd been organising dog-baiting events. Holly had been incredibly relieved that she'd managed to solve the mystery and save 'Smosage' the sausage dog, before he'd been thrown into the ring as bait.

Well... sort of relieved.

The tiny dog had shown his gratitude by latching onto her ankle and refusing to let go when she'd tried to put him in her car. He'd topped off his thank you by being sick all over the upholstery.

Still... her neighbour Doris had been suitably grateful for his return, and Holly would never admit that she'd been very tempted to keep on driving when the silly dog had spotted a rabbit by the side of the road and launched himself through her unwisely open window. They'd been bombing along a dual carriageway at the time.

There'd also been the case of the mayor's missing chain. The Little Wemley mayor's chain was something rather special. It was an antique from the Victorian period and - for no apparent reason other than the decadence of whomever must have been the mayor at the time - it was encrusted with rubies.

In truth, it was rather unsurprising that somebody stole it.

It hadn't even been the first time that the chain was 'borrowed without permission'. Holly had been called upon to solve the mystery twice before.

In the case of the first disappearance, it had transpired that the mayor had only mislaid the chain. The missing village heirloom had turned up a few days later in a drawer. The second time, the mayor forgot that he'd asked his secretary to arrange for the chain to be cleaned.

On the third occasion the chain disappeared, it really had been stolen. Holly had searched for clues and managed to trace the thief's whereabouts to the local pub, where she'd found him loudly boasting about the success of his theft. It wasn't really a case worthy of Sherlock Holmes, but it had got her name in the paper again.

Holly had definitely started to build a reputation for solving mysteries. Or, if you asked her arch-enemy - sorry - *sister*, Annabelle: 'sticking her nose into other people's business'.

Holly brushed a stray strand of her dark brown fringe out of her eyes and vaguely wondered what to get Annabelle for Christmas. She couldn't remember if she'd already given her a lump of coal...

The strand of hair fell back down and tangled with her eyelashes. Holly huffed a breath out, blowing it skywards. She knew she should have had a haircut before leaving for Scotland, but there hadn't been time. Her schedule in the run-up to Christmas was always packed - as was her pianist's brain with every Christmas song ever written. There hadn't been time for a trim.

She frowned at herself in the rearview mirror, wondering if it was worth risking a quick snip with the nail scissors she'd packed in her suitcase. The last time she'd cut her own fringe, she'd ended up with a patch of stubby hair sticking straight up above her forehead, but then, she had only been five-years-old at the time. Haircutting ability was something you naturally developed with age... right?

Her preoccupation with her infuriating fringe almost made her miss the turning. The signpost was already half-crusted with fresh snowfall. It was only some extra sense that turned her gaze and revealed the words: 'orn Hill Hou' - the other letters already concealed by feathery flakes.

She slammed the brakes on and then remembered how important it was to not do anything sudden (like slamming the brakes on) in icy weather. "Fudgecicles!" she said (or at least, something that *sounded* similar) when her car slid around the bend and gently bumped against a hedge. The branches immediately shed their full-load of snow onto her roof.

Holly twitched her head from side to side and was relieved to discover that no one had witnessed her little bump. She didn't want to appear anything less than competent when she met her professional idols. She'd already researched each of the seven detectives who were attending their annual convention at the house. She'd even made a fact file. They were so well-known it had been easy to read up on all of their greatest cases. She only hoped that they might see some spark of the same potential in her...

"This has to be it..." she muttered under her breath when she turned a corner on the long driveway. The imposing outline of Horn Hill House loomed over the bleak landscape, silhouetted on the brow of a hill against the curiously orange sky.

Holly drove onwards, her wipers furiously swiping the snow away. Every time her car's wheels skidded a little on the settling snow, her heart jumped in her chest. She hoped that the seven detectives had shared the same foresight and had chosen to arrive early. It didn't seem likely that the drive up to Horn Hill House would be passable for much longer.

Please don't let me be the only one here! she suddenly thought and wondered (in a slight panic) what would happen if she was stuck in the middle of nowhere, without any way of getting into the house? Visions of her having to break-in popped into her head. She crossed her fingers on the wheel. It wouldn't come to that.

She drove into the gravelled car park, her wheels making squeaking noises against the snow. Six cars were already parked. Holly suddenly wondered if she was late after all... before realising that the detectives were one step ahead of her. She shook her head in amazement and felt a thrill of uncertainty. Holly suspected that she was already out of her league, and she hadn't even met the seven, yet!

The snow blew straight into her face when she opened the car door and stepped out into the arctic landscape. With an almost audible 'ping', Holly's fringe sensed the cold weather and curled up of its own accord. She swore and desperately patted the rest of her now-maniacal hairdo.

So much for first impressions.

Holly felt a swirl of emotion twist in her gut when she looked at the bright lights that shone from within Horn Hill House. In the midst of the snowstorm it should have been an inviting image, but her hands shook with the same stage-fright she always suffered from whenever she played the piano at big events.

These detectives were already on their way to becoming

7

legends. She'd found a lost dog and a chain - stolen by a man who was more 'village idiot' than 'master-criminal'. Why would any of them give her the time of day?

A little voice in her head whispered that even the greats had to start somewhere... She didn't even have any serious aspirations to be a professional, right? She was perfectly happy solving mysteries in her spare time and being a professional pianist by night.

The little voice inside her head laughed at her transparent attempt to convince herself that she lacked ambition. Holly pretended not to hear it. She also ignored the stab of unease that grew in the pit of her stomach - putting it down to a fresh attack of nerves.

But it wasn't just a bad case of the jitters. It was a ghostly premonition of a terrible future that was lying in wait within Horn Hill House.

The next twenty-four hours would be a deadly dance with death.

And not everyone was going to make it out alive.

LET THE GAMES BEGIN

Six heads turned her way when she walked into the living room.

The front door had been open a crack, so Holly had let herself in. She'd patted her hair down as best as she could, being simultaneously grateful and regretful that there'd been no mirror in which to check her reflection. She wasn't particularly vain, choosing to dress in clothes that suited her, rather than the latest fashions. She also never did anything fancy with her hair and makeup; but extreme weather conditions tended to transform her from Little-Miss-Normal into the swamp beast from the black lagoon. She hoped that the detectives would use their famed powers of deduction to deduce that she didn't always look this terrible.

The smile jumped onto her face a couple of seconds too late when she realised they were all staring, waiting for her to say something. "Hi, I'm Holly," she supplied, pleased that her voice sounded pretty level. "You must be the detectives. Although, there are only six of you..." She'd looked around and had picked up on the obvious.

"Ah, yes... Holly Winter - our lucky competition winner. I'm glad you made it through the bad weather." A woman clutching a large and ornate organiser got to her feet and flashed Holly the brightest smile she'd seen in a long time. Pale-pink stained lips, a hint of blusher, and natural honey blonde hair - that seemed unfairly neat and tidy - completed the other woman's perfect first impression.

"You're not one of the detectives," Holly said and then bit her tongue. She was letting her mouth run away with her!

Fortunately, the woman didn't mind. She even laughed. The high, tinkling sound would have been more appropriate coming from a fairy.

"That's right. I'm not! Much like you, I'm a fan of these legendary private detectives' work. Every year, it's my job to select a venue and organise this event. This year, it was a bit of a challenge," she added, looking thoughtful for a moment. She shook her head, before sliding a pair of designer glasses up her nose and glancing down at her organiser. "I'm afraid that one of our number called me early this morning to let me know that he couldn't make it, due to fears about the weather." The woman looked sideways out of the window. "Regretfully, I may have hinted that he was being a little overcautious, but looking out there now... he had a point." The smile faded for a second, before it was renewed with an even more luminous one. Holly wondered if she'd be willing to part with the number for her dentist. "Still! We'll have a cosy time up here together, swapping exciting stories about what's happened during the past year."

Holly caught the two female detectives glancing at one another and flicking their gaze upwards. She got the message - this organiser was trivialising all of the work and risk they put into their jobs and their life. However, she also observed that the moment was over in a second. Some people were just sweet and fluffy by nature. These detectives bore their organiser no ill will. It was clearly just her way.

"Oh, how could I?!" the bubbly blonde exclaimed, looking so horrified Holly wondered what dreadful thing she'd done. "I haven't introduced you to anyone! My name's Miranda Louis. As I said when I was chattering away back then, I'm the event organiser. This gentleman is Jack Dewfall." She pointed to the man seated to her left. He was in his early thirties and sported an army regulation hair cut. His physique, however, was not regulation. He'd developed a strange soft paunch that seemed premature in relation to his age. Being familiar with his cases, Holly was a little surprised by his personal appearance - but she suspected it was a classic reminder that appearances are often deceptive.

"Next to him is Lydia Burns." One of the two other women present - a well-kept lady in her forties, with an enviable sheet of dark hair and perfectly applied red lipstick - inclined her head.

"You've probably heard about her cases," Miranda carried on. Holly nodded in what she hoped was a non-committal manner. She knew them all, but after Miranda's admission to also being a fan, and the almost-eye rolling that had passed between two of the detectives, she'd decided to keep that information close to her chest.

"And then we have Pete Black…"

"Adventurer, detective, and everyday hero at your service," the man finished with a slanting grin and a wink at Holly. His flashy blonde hair was decisively parted in a style reminiscent of a bygone era.

The sound of a hastily-stifled cough came from the other side of the table. Pete narrowed his eyes and shot daggers in the direction of the remaining female detective. She pretended not to notice his gaze and made a big deal of examining her deep-green, manicured nails.

"And this is Emma White," Miranda said with false brightness.

Holly could almost touch the building tension.

Emma smiled at Holly - the most genuine smile she'd seen so far. Holly couldn't help but like the other woman, who was in her late twenties - close to Holly's own age. She and Pete were the youngest detectives there, but they had both already achieved so much during their careers.

"Don't worry, I'll skip the entirely unnecessary introduction where I try to jump straight into your pants," Emma said airily, studiously ignoring the fist-clenching and head-shaking that took place on the opposite side of the table.

Holly risked a little smile back, privately wondering what had happened to make relations so frigid between the pair. She supposed it was the obvious, given Emma's larger than life dyed auburn hair, natural prettiness, and fast tongue. Team that with Pete's good looks and arrogance, and you had a perfect recipe for disaster.

"Anyway, this is Lawrence Richards," Miranda finished, visibly pleased to have completed all of the introductions without any physical fights breaking out.

The front door banged and juddered as it was thrown open, pushed by the howling wind. Heads turned again when a new visitor entered the room.

"Sorry I'm late. Can you believe this weather? I did not see it coming. I set out this morning in shorts and a t-shirt," the new arrival said with an easy grin.

All around the table, the detectives muttered their derision at this inexcusable lack of foresight, as the man - who could only be Rob Frost - sauntered inside. Holly felt a rush of exhilaration when she realised - with an odd kind of relief - that he wasn't the one who'd cancelled his invitation.

She was in the presence of the man who had solved every single unsolved robbery case he'd turned his hand to. Gold bullion, hidden for decades, had been dug up by him, and bounty worth millions was recovered and returned - no matter how smart the thieves had been. Rob was a personal favourite of Holly's. She even privately thought that his off-the-wall cases and style of investigation could easily be turned into their own book or TV series.

"Wow, Tom... you look different. But hey, I'm not judging," Rob said, grinning at Holly and raising his hands in mock defence.

Miranda cleared her throat and belatedly introduced Holly, who was already blushing under Rob's scrutiny.

She did the only thing she could think of doing and scrutinised him right back.

Rob was in his mid-thirties, and would definitely have looked more at home on an assault course than the army specialist, Jack. He was probably a little over six-foot-three tall, with broad shoulders and an easy way of standing that let you know he was completely at ease with himself. His hair was dark and trimmed close at the sides with some longer growth on the top. The only thing that really made him stand out as a detective was his dark eyes that seemed to be taking in a hundred observations to every one that Holly made. She felt like she may as well be standing naked in front of him.

The blush rose in her cheeks again and she finally broke eye contact - just catching a glimpse of the small smile that danced on Rob's lips, before he spun a chair around and plonked himself down on it.

"So, what's been happening guys? I want the real stories this time, not all of that PR spin your agents sold to the papers. Lydia, did it really take you three whole months to figure out that it was poisoned lipstick that killed all those supermodels, or were you just playing dumb to claim more on your expenses? Come on, you can tell me." He winked at the other detective.

Lydia sat back in her chair and made a huffing sound that let them all know this kind of taunting was beneath her.

Her superior silence didn't last for long. "You'd understand the magnitude of the challenge if you saw just how much gear those girls use to get ready!" she protested.

Rob's eyebrows shot up. "You're telling me they were all on drugs as well? Surely that was the first thing you told them to avoid?" He shook his head in amused disapproval.

Lydia reached a hand up - as if to tear her own hair out - but then thought better of it.

Rob just grinned. "Only kidding, Lyds. I wouldn't have cracked it that much faster than you. I reckon it would have taken me at least a week," he said, his tone serious.

Across the table, Pete spluttered out a laugh. "I could have done it in days..." he claimed, making Emma snort.

"I doubt you'd have ever solved it. You'd be too busy chasing tail to catch the killer," she sniped.

Holly noticed Miranda wincing. Confrontation was clearly something she hated.

"Let the games begin." Rob grinned, spreading his hands wide.

"How about we kick off the story telling? That way, everyone can have their say," Miranda suggested, like she was talking to a group of unruly school-children.

To Holly's surprise, the tension immediately diffused and the detectives mumbled their agreement. Miranda's overly sweet, patronising way of speaking to them, strangely had the desired effect on the highly-strung detectives.

"By the way... who drove into the hedge on the way in here? I thought all of you super-sleuths would have seen a little corner coming," Rob said, laughing at his own joke.

Holly subtly covered her face with her hand.

Great.

So, this was what it was like spending time with people who noticed every single detail. She had a feeling this weekend was going to keep her on her toes.

If she'd known what was waiting just around the corner, she'd probably have wished herself at a convention for bankers instead of detectives.

Then again... even death may be more preferable than that.

"Okay, let's do a little show-and-tell, shall we?" Miranda suggested, still in primary school teacher mode. After everything she'd heard during the last five minutes, Holly understood why. "Rob, you were the last in, so how about you go first?" Miranda asked, flashing the male detective a beautiful smile.

Holly's heart sank to the floor. She frowned and ignored the unwelcome sensation.

Rob sat back and ruffled his hair, somehow contriving to make it look even more attractive. "Well, I don't like to brag... but I've beaten you all again. I think it's only right that everyone else goes first." He grinned around the room.

Holly heard a couple of grumbles, from which she inferred that Rob made a similar claim every year.

Rob Frost just shook his head and raised his eyes heavenwards in mock exasperation. "Now, now, Jack... no need for jealousy. I know you work with the military to prove how tough you are, but some of us don't have to compensate for anything... if you know what I mean." Rob winked at Jack, who tried very hard to act as though he was above all of this.

Fortunately for everyone's sanity, there was someone in the room who was struggling to stay silent.

TROLLEY DASH OF TERROR

"Listen up people! Once you hear about my case, you won't be laughing about murderous schoolgirls any more," Pete began.

"Why? Is your story not about murderous schoolgirls? And if not, why mention them at all?" Rob asked, looking genuinely confused.

Pete's bottom lip jutted out a little. "Technically, there were murderous schoolgirls... but the case was a lot more intricate and deadly than it might initially have appeared, given the dismal way the press reported it."

"I seem to remember reading that you were obliviously dating the leader of the crime ring. I can't believe you'd sink as low as dating a schoolgirl. Wait... actually, I can, " Emma commented.

Pete was looking sulkier by the second. "She wasn't a schoolgirl! She just employed and influenced a gang of highly-violent, armed schoolgirls," he explained. It was with an effort that he managed to summon up a halfhearted slanted smile. "What can I say? I like bad girls."

Emma mimed sticking her fingers down her throat.

"You dated the leader of the entire operation without knowing that she was the leader of the entire operation?" Jack said, disbelievingly.

Pete looked like he might be about to explode. "Well, what may have started out as one thing, soon became the key to my undercover success…" he began again, but was cut off by another loud snort from Emma.

Holly was starting to wonder if she had issues with her sinuses as well as issues with Pete.

"I read that you were still hooking up with her until the day she was arrested. For some reason, the killer schoolgirls managed to evade every sting operation the police planned. Probably because you were blabbing about it to their boss. Then, when the game was up - after the police finally caught one of the little terrors - you happened to be staying at the leader's house and managed to overpower her, just before the police arrived. For some reason, someone was stupid enough to credit you with solving the case and being a big hero." Emma pretended to look thoughtful. "Seriously, who is your publicist? They really know how to work miracles." She flashed a cruel smile in the other detective's direction.

He sighed and looked towards the ceiling. "That's not how it actually went down, but you've basically ruined the story, and I really cannot be bothered to correct you. Believe what you want, but that was a tough case, and I got to the bottom of it. No more schoolgirls wielding sharp objects," Pete said, crossing his arms and sinking down into his chair.

Emma smirked around the room, but the other detectives were all pretending to be engrossed in drinking their various beverages. The rivalry between Pete and Emma was too much for any of them to stomach, and no one wanted to pick sides.

"Seeing as you're all so quiet, I think it's time for me to tell you all about my greatest case of this year. Pete, you might get bored. It doesn't involve any schoolgirls." Emma shot a look of mock concern across the table.

Pete pretended to be removing an imaginary spot of lint from his shirt.

"The case of the Tommy Gun murders wasn't one I was initially assigned. It was just a result of me being in the right place at the right time - something which does seem to happen a lot to me," she admitted with a great deal of false modesty.

"It's because you're always sticking your nose into other people's business," Pete sniped.

Emma pretended he didn't exist. "I was doing some shopping in Hull when I heard the gunshots. Naturally, I went to see what was happening."

"While *normal* people ran the other way…" Pete muttered.

"By the time I got there, the action had finished, but the man who'd been attacked was still there, lying in a pool of blood. I was just in time to hear his final words 'Tommy Gun'. I knew then that I had a case. I had to find out the meaning of the dead man's mysterious last words. Of course, I went on to singlehandedly bring down the mafia gang who'd been extorting money from Hull's businesses for years. Although, I had no idea that I'd achieve all of that back on that fateful, tragic day…"

"I heard that you neglected to mention to the investigating officers that the dead man had spoken to you before he died. Didn't the police nearly arrest you for withholding evidence?" Pete interjected.

Emma frowned. "If they wanted the evidence, they should have been there to collect it. I'm not responsible for lazy police work. Anyway, they thanked me in the end!" she said brightly, and then frowned, forgetting where she was in her story.

"We get it. You found out 'Tommy Gun' was a guy with a

stupid name. You stuck your nose into lots of people's business and made such a big noise about the local mafia that the police had to take action, or publicly lose confidence. Jolly well done," Pete said, his arms firmly folded.

Emma smiled at him. "Thanks Pete, that means a lot coming from you."

Pete opened his mouth to argue that he had definitely not meant it, but shut it again.

Emma smirked triumphantly.

"Hey, Lawrence, I never really hear about your successes. It's only the messy, messy failures that hit the headlines. What have you been up to this year?" Rob asked.

Lawrence's eyes darted around the room for a second. "You know I can't say what I've been doing. Everything is classified information!" he squeaked, his voice thin as a reed.

Rob nodded enthusiastically. "Sure, sure... Official Secrets Act and all that jazz, but what about hypothetically? Just make something up! If they're still alive, we'll know you did a good job - and hey, just hypothetically, right? Between old friends?" he wheedled, but Lawrence's lips were zipped shut.

"There are no secrets with my cases," Lydia began, flicking her dark hair back over her shoulders. "The case of the lipstick killers was my greatest success of the past year. It all began when..." Everyone around the table exchanged looks, and Lydia faltered.

"Sorry Lyds, you should be pleased... but that case was in practically every magazine and newspaper because of the models dying. I think I know every single detail inside and out. But you looked great in all the press shots!" Emma said, surprisingly tactfully.

Lydia's smile only wobbled for a second before it lifted again. "They were quite flattering, weren't they?" she said, and everyone breathed a collective sigh of relief.

Holly had also heard about the case back when it had all taken place. Emma was right to claim that it had been impossible to avoid. The press had flocked to cover the murders of the beautiful people and had reported the crimes in glorious, technicolor detail.

"I suppose that means it's my turn," Jack said, before launching into a story so convoluted and full of military jargon that Holly barely understood a word of it. If that wasn't confusing enough, half of the information was classified, so as well as jargon to contend with, there were also large holes in the plot. By the end, all she could figure out was that Jack may have averted a bomber from attacking a local supermarket by bundling him into a trolley and pushing him down a hill - so that he exploded away from innocent civilians.

"Wow, Jack… that was killer! I won't need to read any of the Andy McNab books I brought with me now," Rob said with a smirk.

Jack scowled at him. "Your turn, Rob. How many holes have you dug yourself out of this year?" Jack asked, trying to rile the other man.

"I think what you meant to ask was 'How many holes have I dug myself into?'," Rob corrected, a stupid grin on his face.

"I'm guessing the answer is a lot of them," Emma said, her mouth twitching up at one side.

Miranda glanced down at her rose gold and sparkly diamanté watch and gave a squeak of alarm. "Sorry, Rob. You'll have to tell us over dinner. You should all go and freshen up. We'll meet back down here in fifteen minutes. Otherwise, the roast will be ruined," she said, before rushing off in the direction of the kitchen.

"What a shame. I pity you all having to wait in such suspense," Rob said, doing his best to look truly concerned.

"Don't worry, Rob. That's fifteen minutes more you can use to make up something good." Jack's smile was frosty.

"Ah well… at least I won't have to be too creative this year to wipe the floor with your trolley dash of terror." Rob shot another grin at Jack, and then swiftly exited the room before the other man could reply… or throw anything heavy at him.

THE MURDERER IN THEIR MIDST

A rriving on time was apparently not cool.

While waiting for the others to arrive, Holly had ventured into the dining room to find it was decorated ready for the evening meal. Gold, bauble-adorned wreaths hung around the room, and even the mounted head of a roaring red deer stag hadn't escaped. Tinsel was woven through its antlers. Despite the big day still being weeks away, crackers were out on the table and candles were lit. The fireplace was disappointingly empty, but the room's heat was kept in by the thick, dark-blue velvet drapes that blocked out the snow scenes.

"Do you know what the roast for dinner is yet?" Emma White called, sashaying down the staircase in a beautiful beige dress with colourful flowers splashed all over it. Holly suddenly wondered if her white mini-dress and beige tights were a little plain. She wished she'd thought to pack something in a different colour. With so much snow around, she'd probably disappear if she wasn't careful.

"I don't know. It smells like something is being deep fat fried," Holly confessed, already wondering if this was some secret test. Could all proper private detectives pinpoint what was for dinner, just by smelling the air in the hallway? Emma tilted her head and then nodded in vague agreement.

"Whatever it is, I don't know about you... but I'd take Rob Frost over dessert any day. I think he's been spending more time in the gym than on the case recently, but I am not complaining about that." She flashed a conspirator's smile at Holly, who echoed it back, weakly, wondering if it was always like this in the world of investigating. Did everyone constantly swap partners? It seemed a little incestuous. The annoying voice in her head piped up to tell her that she was just jealous. She'd felt that familiar jolt of attraction when Rob had walked into the room for the first time. Her intuition hinted that the way he'd looked at her was a sign that the impressive detective had felt it too, but her knowledge of his great deeds wouldn't allow her to believe it. There was just no way she had a chance - especially with Emma, and perhaps even Miranda, as her rivals.

Fortunately, her tirade of self pity was cut short before she could make a fool out of herself by telling Emma what a perfect couple with perfect children she and Rob would make. Lawrence strolled down the stairs, nodding his thinning head in their direction, before walking straight past them towards the kitchen. Clearly, appetite came before manners. Next down was Jack, who made brief conversation, before heading straight over to the drinks cabinet. Holly rather unkindly reflected that this affection for alcohol must be the reason for his curious physique. She swallowed the thought as soon as it appeared in her head, remembering that out of all of the detectives, this military specialist had probably seen harrowing scenes that were enough to drive anyone to drink.

"Oh, well, that's just typical," Emma muttered under her breath. Holly turned to see what she was talking about.

Lydia Burns was dressed in a floor-length gown that was so deep a shade of red, it almost looked like it had been stained with blood. Despite her more senior years, Holly knew she was currently outsmarting them all when it came to fashion. Her own white dress now seemed positively plain.

"What did I miss?" Rob appeared at the top of the stairs just behind Lydia. She couldn't help but wonder if...?

Emma tutted under her breath. Holly imagined they'd both made the same leap of inference. Perhaps there was hope for her as a detective after all!

Rob grinned some more. "Oh, you girls... you make me laugh," he said and walked down in a subtle haze of *Jean Paul Gautier* aftershave, leaving them all to wonder.

"Oh good, we're all here," Miranda said, appearing in the doorway of the kitchen. She was wearing a ridiculously ruffle-adorned, pink apron. It suited her.

"Uh, no... Pete's missing," Lawrence observed, his voice quiet, but carrying, in its thin way.

"Shall we get on before the food you've worked so hard to cook for us is ruined? I'm sure Pete just wants to draw out the moment for some extra attention," Emma said, and for the briefest of moments, her gaze rested on Holly.

"Ah, yes... well, it is ready," Miranda said, visibly torn between the compliment and the incendiary remark.

"Don't sweat it. I'll go back upstairs and drag him out of bed. He's probably fallen asleep. The man works too hard. What was his last case? I wasn't really listening earlier. Schoolgirls with steak knives, or something?" Rob shook his head, still smiling. "Tough crime, tough criminals."

"Just go and get him," Lydia said, most likely thinking back to Rob's cross-examination of her own case. *Or, perhaps she subscribes to the 'treat them mean to keep them keen' philosophy*, Holly thought.

"So, should we..." Miranda's hands fluttered over the

ludicrous flounces of her apron, as she hovered in the kitchen doorway. Holly wondered if Miranda really was the super fan she claimed to be, or if she was an events specialist who was paid - probably by the detectives themselves - to run the whole event and further bolster their egos by playing the part. She had a feeling she'd have figured out the answer by the end of the weekend.

"Oh my gosh, you cooked all this yourself?" Emma cooed when they entered the kitchen, sliding past a semi-protesting Miranda.

"Yes! Well, you know... it was nothing," the organiser said, slipping back into the room. She wasn't fast enough to conceal the flash of white wrapping that was sticking up from the bin. So, Miranda had her flaws, too!

Emma turned and raised an amused eyebrow at Holly, before they walked back into the dining room.

"Can I help you bring things through?" Holly asked, turning back.

Miranda stared at her like she had spoken a foreign language, before flapping a hand. "No, no. It's okay. There's really nothing to do," she said, before rushing off and making such a clattering sound, it made Holly wonder if their dinner had just ended up in the floor. Sometimes, it was better to not have an enquiring mind.

"I wonder where Rob is?" Lawrence asked, looking mildly concerned.

"I hope he didn't decide to tunnel his way into Pete's room," Jack said and guffawed loudly at his own joke. Holly opened her mouth to defend Rob, but then realised it was better not to join in the less-than-friendly competition and side-taking that was going on.

They were just about to give up waiting and start dishing up, when Rob reappeared. He looked a lot less cool and collected than he had done when he'd come down the stairs the first time.

"Pete's dead," he announced, his face pale. "Someone's killed him. There's a dagger in his chest and blood… lots of blood." What little colour remained in his cheeks vacated when he said the word 'blood'. A moment later, he pulled himself together. His mouth hardened into a determined thin line.

"I think we should all go up and take a look," Jack said, pushing his chair back. His drink and the food were forgotten.

"Maybe the ladies could wait here, and someone should stay with them…" Lawrence suggested, looking wistfully at his food.

Lydia rolled her eyes. "We've all seen our fair share of dead bodies, Lawrence. Even you don't have a perfect track record."

Lawrence stopped looking at his food. His light blue eyes sharpened behind his spectacles as he absorbed the insult.

"Well, I guess we're all going," Jack broke in, his eyes flicking up to the ceiling. Somewhere above them, Pete presumably lay dead with a knife in his chest.

"Is this some sort of a game, like a fake whodunnit to solve?" Holly whispered to Miranda, who looked horrified by the thought.

"Gosh, no! We would never trivialise…" She stopped talking. Holly wondered if she'd insulted the other woman, but to her surprise, Miranda's eyes were beading with tears. "Oh, this is awful. Everyone here is just so nice! How could anyone kill Pete?"

Holly opened her mouth to point out that the six detectives they were sharing the house with probably had more enemies than the rest of the population of Britain put together - not to mention their fierce inter-rivalry - but it didn't seem the right moment to shatter Miranda's odd delusion.

"Yup, he is definitely dead," Lydia commented, rather crassly, when they walked into Pete's bedroom.

Holly bit her lip hard, as she came face to face with her first ever dead body.

Pete's neatly side-parted hair was still in perfect condition. He lay on his back with his arms by his side. His expression held all of the serenity of someone still asleep, but Holly could tell from the grey pallor and the lack of a pulse jumping in his neck that this was one micro-nap Pete Black would not be waking up from.

"Single stab, straight into the heart. That's why there isn't a lot of blood," Jack commented. Holly tried not to hear the hint of admiration in his voice. This was an efficient kill. Also, how was this classed as being 'not a lot of blood'? She supposed the walls hadn't been redecorated, but she shared Rob's opinion rather than Jack's.

All of the visitors in the room grew silent. They stared at Pete's body for such a long time that the tension climbed to a point where Holly was half-expecting the corpse to jump up and scream at them.

"Is anyone else staying here at the house, Miranda?" Lawrence finally asked, in his usual quiet way.

Miranda quickly shook her head, her eyes determinedly fixed on the light fixture at the centre of the room.

"So... it's one of us. One of us killed Pete Black," Rob concluded, sounding horrifyingly intrigued by the idea. "We have a murderer in our midst."

DINING WITH DEATH

"I suppose now wouldn't be the time to mention my record-breaking feat of solving a case in five minutes and putting myself forward for the role of lead detective on this case?" Rob asked, looking around at the ashen faces. "No, probably not the time. Maybe after coffee and mints," he concluded.

"We've got to call for help. The police will come," Holly said.

Everyone stared at her like calling the police was a completely alien concept.

"Oh yes… the police," Lydia conceded.

There was some collective eye-narrowing.

"It is the law!" Holly persisted. There was finally some grudging agreement, although, she heard a few 'wouldn't waste my time' mutterings. They walked down the hall as a group, collectively deciding not to loiter in the room where the smell of death lingered.

"Right… here we go," Holly said, feeling a sense of trepidation, as she dialled 999.

She'd never been in an emergency before, but this was a

real-life situation, wasn't it? Someone was actually dead. She blinked a few times and wished her head would clear. How could anyone think straight after seeing something like that? It was one thing reading about violent murders in a novel, but quite another in real life. Half of her still wanted to believe that this was all part of the event - a false death set up to challenge the other detectives. Unfortunately, she knew that Pete Black was no actor. He was a genuine private detective, whose short career had just come to a brutal - and very final - end.

"Er, do they usually take so long to answer?" Holly asked, feeling stupidly unprepared for this. The phone was making a noise, but she wasn't sure if it was ringing or not.

Lydia seized the handset and listened. "Dead. Whoever did this has also cut our lines of communication."

They all pulled out their mobile phones and berated the evil genius behind the absence of cell service, until Jack pointed out that it was probably their fault for picking such a rural Scottish location for their meet up. The phone lines being down could also be explained by the snow.

"This is probably all the work of someone who had an axe to grind with Pete. Someone who's been unusually lost for words since Rob came down and told us he was dead," Jack said.

Everyone turned to look at Emma, who didn't even have the good-grace to blush. "Oh, come on! I'm the last person who'd kill him. Seriously, when is it ever the obvious suspect who actually committed the crime?" she bit back, folding her arms.

"Well, statistically..." Lawrence began, but Emma carried on speaking.

"Pete and I had a love-hate relationship, sure. But if I'd killed that smarmy, cheating, good for nothing, I wouldn't have stabbed him. I would have planned something a lot nastier. He'd have known all about it, and exactly who had done it to him, when he finally got what he deserved." She looked around brightly.

"Okay, great!" Rob said, looking nowhere near as perturbed as Holly felt. "That sounds perfectly reasonable to me. Does anyone else have questions? No? Well, how about we all go down and have some dinner? We're all together, so the killer probably won't strike again. We've all seen those bad horror movies. If we stay together, then we live. Or, hey! Look on the bright side! If someone else gets murdered, it will be a cinch to catch the killer because we'll see it happen."

"What makes you think someone else is going to die?" Jack asked.

Rob held up his hands defensively. "What? I didn't say that, did I? I was just trying to lighten the mood. Dinner? Yes?"

Seeing as no one else had any better ideas, they followed Rob back down to the dining hall. It was fortunate that none of the food had been dished up, and that it was served on large, communal platters. However, there were a tense few moments after Rob took his first bite, where everyone pretended to be engrossed in pouring their drinks, or examining the Christmas crackers.

"Still alive! I told you it would be fine," Rob said, a second before all the lights went out.

They were plunged into darkness.

Holly shivered in the icy breeze, which had been enough to extinguish all of the candles a moment before. She nearly jumped out of her skin when a loud bang echoed around the room.

There was a moment of dead silence.

"I don't suppose that was someone pulling a cracker?" Rob enquired.

Someone near Holly swore - probably when they realised Rob wasn't the victim.

"I think it was a gunshot," Jack said.

There was another bang, not as loud or as fatal as the first. Holly suspected Rob had just hit his head on the table.

A SHOT IN THE DARK

olly heard Rob mutter 'Hey presto' under his breath when the lights flickered and came back on. The person seated next to her remained silent. That was because they were dead.

"Oh no, Lawrence..." Emma said, her voice emotionless. But then, during the very brief time Holly had known Lawrence, he had never inspired any particular emotion at all.

So, why would anyone want to kill him?

"I feel sick..." Lydia said. She pushed her chair back, sitting with her head between her legs and taking deep breaths.

Holly looked back at Lawrence and found that Lydia's reaction was not unreasonable. She was glad that she hadn't got around to eating her dinner yet.

She also wasn't going to be eating it anytime soon.

Her food hadn't escaped the event unscathed. She looked down in horror at all of the... bits.

Jack walked round the table to have a look. "Shot from behind..." he immediately said and then looked up and down the side of the table where Lawrence had sat. His eyes fell on Emma, who sat on one side of the dead man, and then they stayed fixed on Holly herself. "Have you got anything on you to prove that you aren't a psychopath who has come here to kill us all?" His voice was deadpan.

Holly didn't know if he was serious or not. "Uh... I..." She stumbled, wondering what she could possibly say or produce. An anti-psychopath ID card? These detectives had known each other for years. Wasn't it far more likely that it was one of them who was the killer? But then - albeit rarely - psychopaths did exist, so she understood the reason behind Jack's accusation.

She shook her head free from confusion. She knew she wasn't the killer!

"No way. I saw how pale she turned when she saw Pete. That was definitely her first dead body. She's not our killer," Emma cut in. Holly didn't know whether to thank her or throttle her.

"So... it's one of us. It must be someone on this side of the table. They had to get around behind old Lawrence and do him in," Jack said, his voice grave.

Emma glared at him. "*Do him in?* What is this... an Agatha Christie novel? You were on this side of the table, too. You're also a suspect and - much as I hate to admit it - you are the firearms expert. However... where you, or any one of us, have hidden the gun, I don't know," she finished.

Holly revised her opinion that Pete and Emma's rivalry was a big motive for murder. It would appear that Emma doled out her disdain in equal measures for all.

"Now... this might be a shot in the dark, but are we a hundred-percent sure that we're the only people here?" Rob ventured.

Everyone stared at him.

"What? It's a perfectly reasonable theory!" He frowned

and it slowly dawned on him. "Oh, right. It probably was too soon for that turn of phrase. Look, I'm sure Lawrence would want us to keep things upbeat. You know... if he wasn't dead."

"Maybe you're right," Lydia said, her voice sounding terrible and her face looking worse. Lawrence's death was clearly not sitting well with her. She raised her gaze to meet Rob's. "But, you know what? I'm not going to sit around here doing nothing. Your last theory that no one would die if we all sat together and ate dinner hasn't worked out. I'm going to conduct my own investigations. Alone. The way I always do." She winced. "Right after I've been sick." She stood up and hastened (surprisingly speedily, given the tightness of her dress) back towards the main stairway.

So much for safety in numbers, Holly thought.

"I don't really feel festive anymore," Jack grumbled, pushing himself away from the table and walking after Lydia.

"I'd better go and make sure he hasn't gone to kill her," Emma said. Her tone was sarcastic, but her expression wasn't. Trust wasn't particularly high amongst the professional private detectives.

Holly, Miranda, and Rob were left sitting alone in the dining room with the very dead Lawrence for company.

"What are we going to do with the body?" Rob asked, in the same tone of voice you might use to propose a post-dinner game of charades. Miranda blinked a few times but said nothing (her horror akin to an unsuspecting person being invited to play charades).

"We could put the bodies outside to stave off decomposition?" Holly suggested, wondering why she seemed to be thinking so clearly now. She was still seated next to some pretty gruesome remains, and her white dress had turned out to be a truly disastrous colour to choose, but all in all, she seemed pretty okay. She was alive. That definitely counted for something.

"Ah. I just meant I've got a Santa hat that we could use. I'd suggest a paper crown, but it probably won't cover much," Rob said, looking serious and thoughtful. Holly was starting to wonder if he was actually insane and somehow no one had noticed.

As if reading her mind, Rob spoke again. "By the way, I'm the sane one. It's the others you want to worry about. Also yes, yes I am very attractive," he said, with his fingers on his temples, staring at Holly with a smirk on his face.

She rolled her eyes, beginning to realise why the others in the group exercised their eyeballs so often. Of course, if they were very unlucky, they'd all be bouncing out of their heads and rolling across the floor soon. She gulped. Perhaps she wasn't thinking straight after all. "Er, we should probably…"

"Get dessert?" Rob finished. "Great idea!"

Holly looked from Lawrence to Miranda and realised they had to get the traumatised organiser out of the room. Or rather, she had to. Rob was already in the kitchen hunting for the next course.

"It hasn't been cooked yet," Miranda said, her voice a whisper when Holly half-walked, half-carried her out of the dining room, back towards the living room.

"The dessert… it was going to be warm chocolate fudge… cake." Between the words 'fudge' and 'cake' Miranda burst into tears. Holly was left with a dress that was not only plain and splattered with debris, but was now also wet and in danger of turning see-through.

"Found some cheese… no dessert, just powder. Even I'm not desperate enough to snort chocolate cake mix. See you girls later. Don't do anything I wouldn't do!" He hesitated in the doorway with an entire block of cheddar in his hand. "There's actually not a lot I wouldn't do. Try not to kill anyone or, you know… die. I guess we'll count up in the morning and then we'll try my suggestion. We'll search this house from bottom to top, because I'm smart, and I'm nearly always…" He paused, lost in thought. "No… wait. I'm always right. Yeah, that's it," Rob finished.

"Count up?" Miranda said, her face somehow turning a shade paler.

Holly forced a laugh, which came out alarmingly high-pitched. "He's kidding, aren't you, Rob? No one else is going to die." She shot him a meaningful look, but he wasn't even looking her way.

"Well, we are all going to die one day. Just… maybe some sooner than others," he concluded. Unsurprisingly, his reassuring speech did nothing to stop a fresh flood of tears from spilling down Holly's dress.

"I think you should go to bed now," she suggested, wondering if she could get away with outright telling him to get lost.

Rob cheerily waved the cheese at her. "All right. I'm going. Just a heads-up, don't come into my room tonight. There'll be numerous deadly booby traps set up, and don't take it personally, but I'm not telling you what they are. Heck, I probably won't even tell myself… just to make things more interesting." He wandered off down the corridor.

Holly turned to see that Miranda had calmed down a little. "On the plus side, there's a good chance he won't be down for breakfast," she told the organiser.

"I heard that!" Rob shouted from the corridor, before finally walking up the stairs.

"I must say, being snowed in with a bunch of people who keep getting murdered is not exactly what I expected my prize to be," Holly said to break the silence when she and Miranda were finally alone.

"Oh, I'm so sorry this has happened. I would never have

planned it here if I'd thought… " Miranda sighed, completely missing Holly's weak attempt at humour. "This is just terrible!"

"It's fine. Really," Holly said, trying to make the other woman feel better. Nothing about this situation was fine. "At least we still have… electricity. Most of the time," she added, reaching around for a silver-lining, before remembering what had happened earlier when Lawrence had been shot. "Come on, we're probably not in danger anyway, right? We aren't detectives!" In truth, Holly had no idea as to the motive behind the crimes, or if there was any pattern. One of their number could just be wiping the rest out for fun.

Holly's mind danced back to Emma's feud with Pete, and then Jack's logic that only someone sitting on the same side of the table as Lawrence could have killed him - and then had time to return to their seat without anyone noticing before the lights came on again. Jack had also been sat on that side of the table, meaning that he was a suspect too. Miranda had been standing when it had happened, so she was also under scrutiny. Although… Holly couldn't really bring herself to think of the tear-stained organiser as a brutal killer. *Appearances can be deceiving*, she reminded herself and wondered if she was sat alone in the room with the killer.

Where is the gun? the voice inside her head queried. She still couldn't figure out how anyone could have managed to conceal a gun after killing Lawrence in time for the lights to come back on.

"I… I suppose you're right. These seven detectives, sorry - six - have met for a few years. Maybe one of them has gone crazy. They are under such a lot of pressure," Miranda said - as if being under pressure excused violent murder.

"I'm sure no one could ever want you dead," Holly said to comfort the other woman, but was a bit miffed when the organiser didn't return the sentiment.

"You're right. I've nothing to do with any of this! At least we're in the company of great detectives. One of them will figure it out," Miranda said, brightening up.

"Yeah, you bet!" Holly said, privately thinking that if there was anyone she'd consider well-qualified to plan and commit the perfect crime, it would be a private detective. The way the deaths had happened... they weren't impulsive. This had all been carefully plotted.

And Holly was starting to wonder where she personally fitted into the deadly drama.

SCOOBY DOO

Holly did not sleep very well. A double murder has a way of making it hard to drop off into dreamland.

For the first few hours, she'd lain in her bed staring up at the ceiling, listening to the sounds of the old house creaking. Once or twice, it had creaked so much she'd wondered if there was a ghost somewhere up in the rafters. That thought hadn't made her sleep any easier - especially given the possibility that there were two brand-new ghosts running around the old house.

When she finally opened her eyes (after what felt like five minutes of sleep) and looked out of the window, the world was still white. It was only now the storm had been vanquished that she realised how much snow had fallen. Judging by a telegraph pole she could see in the distance, the entire bottom floor of Horn Hill House must now be under several feet of snow. She tried not to think about the state her car would be in. Her insurance might not cover galavanting off to Scotland in ridiculous weather conditions.

She was just thinking how muffled everything sounded

when there was snow on the ground, when a scream cut through the air. The little voice inside her head whispered '*And so it begins*' but Holly was already running out of her room and onto the landing.

Emma White stood in the corridor, her hand still resting on the handle of the door she'd just pulled open.

Before Holly could reach her side, she turned and spoke. "I was just going to ask if she wanted breakfast. Miranda is downstairs making it. I offered to wake people up. I'd almost forgotten…" Emma finished, her voice getting quieter at the end until no sound came out.

Holly nodded understandingly. She inched towards the room, being careful to steer clear of Emma. Perhaps it was paranoia, but when you were staying in a house with seven other people, and they kept dying, one by one, exercising a little caution was a healthy attitude to hold onto.

"What happened to her?" Holly asked, frowning at the inert form on the floor of the bedroom. Lydia Burns didn't look nearly as polished as she usually did. Her hair was dishevelled and wavy, and her face - which was devoid of makeup and her trademark red lips - looked a strange shade of green. Holly stepped forwards for a closer look… and then retreated just as quickly when the smell hit her. It initially smelt like expensive perfume, with hints of spice and leather, but there was something off about it. Why was it present in such pungent quantities? Had Lydia spilt a container when she'd died?

"The perfume…" Emma said and started backing away in horror. She dragged a bewildered Holly after her, so they were both out of the room. "Poisoned perfume. Breathing it in directly must be enough to kill you! Whoever is doing this… they must have persuaded Lydia to use it, or smell it, or something. Remember when she said she felt ill last night? It could already have been happening then."

Holly tried not to let her knees shake too much. She'd just taken a big whiff of the very thing that may have been responsible for Lydia Burns' death, and she hadn't had a clue! "Thanks, I might have stayed in there too long, or even touched it, if it weren't for you," Holly said, wondering why something was jumping up and down in the back of her mind. She couldn't seem to catch hold of the unreachable thought.

"What the heck is all of the noise?" Jack Dewfall strode out his room, already dressed in a tailored military-esque suit. Holly wondered if he wore it to bed.

"Lydia's dead," Emma said without a trace of the emotion she'd displayed to Holly.

Jack just nodded in acceptance. "I assumed that would probably be the case. One of us was bound to die in the night. The killer is keeping this to a tight schedule."

Holly felt like smacking him around the head. If he'd had a theory, why hadn't he shared it sooner?

"Case... cases... this is to do with cases!" Holly said, thinking out loud, as her brain finally connected the dots. "Pete's most successful case of the past year was that knife-crime gang he stopped." Emma made a noise of derision and muttered something about them being harmless schoolgirls, but Holly ploughed on. "Lawrence's case was probably an assassination attempt of some type, right? And Lydia... Lydia solved the lipstick murders, where models were being poisoned by their lipstick. Now she's been poisoned by perfume. She may not have even worn it. Perhaps it was in her room already in a bottle designed to leak, or someone might have crept in last night and covered her mouth and nose with it while she slept, just to finish the job." Holly bit her lip, unsure if she wanted to analyse exactly how Lydia had met her end. It seemed all too likely that similar ends were planned for the rest of the detectives.

"Yeah, I was thinking that, too," Emma said, nodding like it was obvious.

Jack mimicked the movement. "Pretty clear when you think about it."

Holly felt crushed for a second, before she realised what they were doing. Despite a murderer picking them off, these detectives were still in competition and could never concede anything to anyone in their field of work. Holly tried not to sigh too loudly. It was probably partially due to their own arrogance that they'd been caught out. But the real question still remained: Who was murdering the detectives, and why?

She was about to open her mouth to put that question to them when Rob strolled around the corner, dressed in a fluffy rabbit-print onesie. On anyone else, it would have looked ridicu... Wait.

No.

It still looked ridiculous. Even with Rob Frost wearing it.

"Did someone say breakfast?" Rob asked, smiling benignly around.

"No one said breakfast," Jack corrected, his mouth set in a grim line of disapproval.

Rob frowned and scratched his head. "No, someone definitely said it approximately five minutes ago. It was before you all started talking about horrible Lydia's death?" He frowned. "Or is that Lydia's horrible death? It's too early for good syntax."

Rob looked around at the blank faces and fixed his gaze on Holly. "Nice work on the case theory. It seems to fit. It's so obvious that we all completely missed it!" He laughed in what seemed a genuine manner and headed for the stairs.

Holly frowned at the backhanded compliment. You couldn't win with these people!

"Come on, if we wait any longer, one of us will have died before we can dish up the scrambled eggs!" he called back.

The detectives standing on the landing shrugged and followed him.

Miranda's worried expression was immediately replaced by her usual sunny smile when they poked their heads into the kitchen.

"Good morning, I've already set the table in the, ah… main room," she faltered, her mind clearly flashing back to the violent demise of Lawrence Richards and his final resting place in the dining room - where he presumably still sat, face down in his stone-cold dinner. A different group of people would probably have moved him, or covered him as a mark of respect, but Holly suspected that these detectives had concluded that they wanted everything as untouched as possible. They must already be deep into their own investigations. It was just too bad that none of them trusted her enough to share their ideas, and with the way they were dropping like flies, it didn't look likely that their trust would be increasing anytime soon.

"Thanks Miranda," Holly deliberately said, after they'd filed into the room and crowded around the large, but rather low, coffee table. The blonde organiser looked startled for a second, and then shrugged, like whipping up a full English breakfast had been a piece of cake. *Perhaps it was,* Holly thought, remembering last night's packaging and wondering if there was such a thing as a re-heatable breakfast. She decided she'd rather not know.

"Great job everyone! We've made it through a meal with no one dying," Rob said when they'd all finished eating and were drinking the filter coffees that Miranda had again brought out all by herself. Holly wondered how much she was getting paid.

"Shut up, Rob," Jack said, without batting an eyelid. "We need to get to the bottom of this right here and right now. Yesterday, we were all tired and we ran out of time. Today is a new day, and it's not the day that I am dying." The heavy detective leaned forwards and spread his hands wide on the table. "I'm proposing a mission for help. The white stuff is pretty deep out there, but the blizzard has ended. I'll go for help while you all wait here. Then we'll get to the bottom of this matter." He eyeballed them each in turn, his thoughts visible on his face. *Whichever one of you is the murderer, you aren't getting me.*

He stood up and went to grab his coat, returning a few seconds later looking even more like the *Michelin Man* in his down jacket.

"You all hang tight and try not to kill each other. I'll be back before you know it," he said, leaving the other detectives, Miranda, and Holly no time to argue. He thrust open the large French doors, letting the snowdrift fall in, where it formed a big pile at his feet. Miranda squeaked in protest (presumably because of the venue deposit) but then stuffed a fist in her mouth. Jack turned around to grin at them all, one final time, the military genius about to go on another rescue mission.

"See you later, suckers!" he said and trudged up the hill of white powder. They could all just see his feet through the top of the glass doors, walking away across the snow into the distance.

The glass doors rattled when an explosion sent the snow, and whatever remained of Jack, high up into the air. When the white powder cleared, all they could see were Jack's boots, one still upright on the snow. The rest of Jack was gone.

"I did not see *that* coming," Rob said, his mouth the mirror image of the three other gaping holes in the room. Rob tilted his head. "With hindsight, it seems rather obvious, doesn't it? He's a military detective. Boom. Landmine." Rob glanced, nervously, at the boots in the snow. "Having said that, I'm not going to assume that there was just the one landmine that Jack happened to step on. I reckon we're stuck here until whatever happens, happens."

"So, we're all going to die," Emma said.

Miranda choked on her coffee. "There are only four of us left. One of us has got to be the murderer. Isn't that right?" she said, surprising everyone by having an opinion.

Holly resisted the urge to yell 'not it!', knowing that everyone would claim the same - whether guilty or innocent. "We still aren't certain that we're on our own here," Holly reminded them, remembering the creaking noises she'd heard last night. "Is there an attic? We should start there. If not an attic, the cellar…"

Emma and Miranda made sounds of agreement, but Rob just rolled his eyes. "Why does it always take someone else to make the same suggestion I've made for people to actually do it?" He shook his head.

Holly felt guilty for a second, before Rob flashed her a genuine smile. "Don't worry about it," he said, dropping out of character for once. "So gang, let's split up and solve this mystery! Daphne and I will take the attic. Shaggy and Scooby, you're down in the cellar. If there is such a thing…" he said, reaching out and pulling Holly to his side. Apparently, she was Daphne, although she'd always considered herself more of a Velma. She was the smart one of the group.

"Shut up, Fred," Emma said, before stalking out of the room with a baffled looking Miranda trailing behind her.

"Excellent! I'm sure absolutely nothing at all will go wrong with this plan," Rob said, his tone dry.

JUST LIKE NANCY DREW

"Any idea where the attic could be in a big old pile like this one?" Rob asked as they hiked up the stairs.

"Somewhere near the top of the house?" Holly offered, her mind still going through the deaths of the four other detectives. She was trying to piece together something - anything - that would give them a clue as to what was going on.

"No kidding, Sherlock," Rob commented, but Holly was starting to notice that even his usual humour seemed strained. It was as if he could sense his own death approaching.

Now that she thought about it, Holly wasn't feeling so great herself. So far, it had only been the detectives who'd been targeted, but without knowing the motive behind these murders, it could still be open season on them all. Perhaps the killer was just an exceedingly creative psychopath.

"Hey, I hope you didn't mind being assigned to attic duty. I just don't want to go anywhere that could be classed as underground right now," Rob said.

Holly nodded. At least one of them had figured a few things out. "None of this makes sense," she commented rhetorically.

"Welcome to my world. It always feels that way until you crack the thing open. Usually, you've got a bit more breathing space. This case is more along the lines of how many breaths do we have left? Ah-ha!" Rob said, when the broom handle they were using to check the ceilings finally knocked on something hollow.

"If that's a loft hatch, it looks like someone papered over it years ago," Holly observed, squinting up at the apparently flawless ceiling.

Rob rubbed his stubbly chin. "Or that's what someone *wants* us to think," he said, grabbing a sturdy looking - probably very valuable - antique table and placing it beneath the suspected entrance. "Hi-yah!" he yelled, jamming the broom handle up and tearing a hole through the thick paper. He ripped the rest apart. Then, with an admirable lack of hesitation, he pushed open the loft hatch. Rob placed it back down a couple of seconds later.

Holly discovered she'd been holding her breath.

"Yeah, uh… it probably was covered up for years. There is absolutely nothing up there. All I could see was a broken window, and it looks like birds or bats might use it as a roost," he said. Holly wondered if that was what she'd heard last night. It sounded likely.

Rob looked up at the rip in the ceiling. "Hmm, if we use a bit of sticky tape, they might not notice?"

Holly bit her lip but said nothing. If they all died at Horn Hill House, a ruined ceiling would hardly be anything to worry about.

"Look, I've been thinking some more," Holly said when they walked back down the stairs, hoping to find two not-dead people waiting for them in the living room.

"Thinking is a good thing to get into the habit of doing," Rob said, probably for the sake of hearing his voice out loud.

"Whoever has been killing detectives obviously knows you well and knows all of your cases, right? How many people can know all of that stuff?" she asked, and then realised how silly it sounded. She herself had found out tons just by searching for the detectives on the internet.

She blushed and carried on before Rob could tell her she was nutty. "I mean, I know there's general information out there, but how could they know that Jack would be the one to go for a rescue mission? Or that Pete was going to take a nap? Or even that Lawrence would be sitting at the table and not decide to move, or something like that?" She wondered if it could possibly be that - so far - the murderer had just had an unfair share of dumb luck.

The more she thought about it, the more it didn't feel right. It was as if everything had been planned and put in place before they'd even come to Horn Hill...

"Hey, Rob... How much do you trust Tom March?" she asked, remembering the seventh detective who had cancelled at the last minute.

Rob's expression immediately darkened. Holly wondered if she might have just hit the nail on the head. "Well, it's probably him, Miranda, or Emma... I took the liberty of excluding myself, because I know I didn't do it, and you, because I actually suggested the competition that you won. Hmm... I suppose you could be a genius at computers and have fixed it so you could win somehow, just so you could come up here and kill us all." He frowned. "Probably not, right? We were just alone together for ages and you didn't try anything. There was no hint of an evil mastermind speech at all. Unless I talked over it. Did I talk over it? I have a habit of doing that."

Holly shook her head, just to reassure him. "Why did you suggest the competition?" she asked, genuinely curious. She'd assumed it was Miranda's idea - probably in an effort to gain some sane company for herself over the weekend.

Rob shrugged. "I thought it would be nice to have someone come in from the outside world who might not pick holes in our stories the way other detectives do. That and I also thought that just in case someone decides to kill us all off, wouldn't it be great to add in an extra target to buy myself a little more time? I'm very forward thinking like that."

"Thanks a bunch," Holly muttered.

"What were you doing up there? You took forever!" Miranda greeted them when they walked back into the living room. The organiser suddenly dissolved into blushes. Rob grinned, enjoying every second of her and Holly's discomfort.

"Nothing but bats and birds and, ah... a slightly ripped ceiling to report," Rob said, deliberately avoiding eye contact with Miranda.

"We found nothing, too," Emma said, and then quickly added: "Miranda and I made cake," before the organiser could ask the questions she so clearly wanted to about the ceiling.

Emma held out a plate towards Rob, who took it eagerly.

"I needed something chocolate so badly. I'm afraid I couldn't resist," Miranda said, raising a plate containing her half-eaten piece of sticky cake.

The next moment, she was dead.

Rob dropped his fork a second after Miranda dropped to the floor.

"Of all things sacred and holy..." he muttered and stared longingly at his plate of cake. "Fudge!" he cursed... or

49

perhaps he was just identifying the type of cake. It wasn't very clear. Emma said a different word beginning with 'f' that was definitely not 'fudge'.

"Why would anyone want to poison Miranda?" Holly asked, hoping her curiosity wasn't callous.

Emma and Rob exchanged a glance.

"Well…" Emma grudgingly began, after Rob had shaken his head and mimed placing crosses in front of himself a few times to indicate he didn't want to speak. "Miranda wasn't exactly a detective, but she was a super-fan. You might have missed it…" Holly wasn't sure if that was sarcasm or not. "Anyway, we've allowed Miranda to put these little meetings together for us for a couple of years now. She loves hearing about our cases and we…" She cleared her throat. "…well, these meetings can be interesting for us, too."

Rob unhelpfully mimed being overcome with gratitude at the almost - but not really - complement.

"There was one case that Miranda cracked all on her own," Rob cut in, but Emma shot him a glare that clearly said he'd given up his right to tell this story.

"Being a super-fan, she was the only one who figured out that the mastermind behind seven different murders was actually the same person. It just so happened that we were each working on the individual murders in our own different ways. It was that case which brought us all together. Miranda solved it, and after she solved it, she made us a chocolate cake to celebrate. From then on, well… she's always made the cake," Emma said, starting to sound a little bit choked-up.

"So… it *is* someone who knows you really well," Holly deduced, feeling simultaneously alarmed and relieved.

There was no way a stranger would have known about Miranda's connection with cake. Someone with a personal grudge against the detectives was definitely targeting them, and she personally had no history with them. There was surely no reason for her to die. That didn't change the fact that two detectives were still alive, one of the seven was missing from the meeting all together, and it was pretty obvious that something was going to happen to reduce their number even further.

The silence stretched out as the others thought through the same facts.

"It's probably Tom," Emma said, voicing all of their growing suspicions aloud. "But why? And also... how? We've searched the house."

Holly had just opened her mouth to say something when they all heard a crash from upstairs. Emma's reaction was to sprint from the room in the direction of the sound. She was already gone by the time Holly shouted at her to stop.

There was a burst of machine gun fire and the sound of running footsteps was cut short.

"Tommy Gun mystery," Holly and Rob said together, exchanging a horrified look. They didn't want to go and see what had happened to Emma, but just in case... in case she'd somehow made it... they had to. They had to see what had happened and see if it got them any closer to solving this case, before it reached its very final conclusion.

"Where did the machine gun fire even come from?" Rob mused when they stepped out into the hall, both treading carefully to avoid the spreading pool of blood that surrounded the late Emma White - another detective mown down by the twisted fiend behind these murders.

Holly quickly glanced at the bullet holes and then back up in the direction she supposed they must have come from. All she could see was a wooden panel, much like any of the hundreds of other similar panels that decorated the interior.

"What if everything that has happened was set up in advance? What if someone's been watching us all along without actually being here at all?" she said, feeling the cold dread of realisation washing over her.

"Tom... Tom was always good with technology," Rob growled, his hands twitching nervously.

"I have an idea. Let's go back to my room while we figure out what to do next," Holly suggested. "I probably won't have been targeted, will I? Also, there aren't any tunnels or anything like bank vaults in my room... and how would anyone have predicted that you'd end up in there?" she finished.

Rob raised an eyebrow.

Holly just crossed her arms and gave him a death stare. Now was really not the time!

"You could have picked any room," she said and immediately blushed when she heard her own words. "I didn't mean..." She sighed and trailed after Rob, whose chest seemed to have puffed up to double its usual size.

They both sat on Holly's four-poster bed, staring out at the snow in the distance. The snow closer to the house featured a huge crater and rather a lot of staining. They didn't look at it.

"So... things are triggered, and we're probably being watched. Listened to as well, I guess," Holly said, glancing at Rob for approval. To her, this sounded way too much like being in a bad spy movie.

"Yeah... who knows, right? I don't do technology. I just get in the bad guys' heads and then get my spade out and dig," he said, miming digging. "Now Emma... she was great with tech! Always knew how to program my iPod. Jack, too. He was very into it with all the military stuff. And Lawrence... the sort of gear he had to track targets and isolate threats - well, it boggles my mind!" He sort of trailed off. "Come to think of it, everyone here - even Miranda - was brilliant at technology - apart from me. They'd probably have been able to figure all of this out a lot sooner, if they'd lived. That's probably why I'm still alive," he added brightly, and then frowned, remembering that while ignorance had kept him alive so far, there was still the big finale to come. "How are you with technology? Could you hack their system and turn it back on them, or something like that? I don't know what I'm saying. It just sounds good."

Holly gritted her teeth. "Nope. If you want a piano played, I'm the one to call. I can send email and do the usual everyday stuff on a computer, but not much more. I definitely don't know about any of this hi-tech surveillance stuff." She looked round at Rob, but he didn't even appear to be listening.

He was crouched in front of the bookshelf. "We should start checking for bugs. Having said that, I have no idea what one looks like, so we probably won't know if we find one. Whoops!" His hand had brushed the spine of one of the rather weathered books and it fell face-down onto the rug. There was a dull metallic thunk when it landed.

Rob and Holly looked at each other for a long, silent second.

"Nancy Drew," Rob said, reading the spine. "It looks like your name was on the kill list after all." He gingerly lifted the book. Holly looked down at the sharp metal barb, which was so firmly embedded in the floor, the rug was now pinned to the floorboards. If she'd opened the book, it would have fired straight into her face.

"They're all amateur detective novels," Rob noted, inspecting the spines of the remaining books.

Holly gulped, probably audibly. If they hadn't been running around the house, she'd almost certainly have picked one up to read. That sort of book was her favourite. Someone had either known it, or was a very good guesser.

"Why would anyone want me dead?" she mused, thinking wildly back to the dog-fighting ring and the mayor's stolen chain. Neither of those cases seemed worthy of a death vendetta.

Rob shrugged. "Maybe our killer wanted a clean sweep. By the way, it would be awesome if you could let me know if you see anything that looks threatening or deadly and at all related to my cases. Just a heads-up," he said casually, but Holly wasn't fooled by his cool act. She may have narrowly avoided death thanks to Rob's clumsiness, but his own ending was still imminent.

"We may have semi-solved the mystery. Your old friend Tom isn't really your friend. But we're still probably going to die," Holly concluded, chewing that one over.

The traps that had killed all of the other detectives may still be loaded. They'd need to watch themselves around the machine gun area and the room where Lawrence had been assassinated. And who knew? There could be more death traps hanging around the place - just in case any of the original attempts had failed.

"What do we do now?" Holly pulled out her phone and stared again at the tiny 'no service' message on the screen.

"I can think of a few things..." Rob said.

Holly shot him a warning look.

"Do you think that cake was a hundred-percent poisoned, or just the sponge itself? Maybe if I only ate the icing..." the last detective standing mused.

"Maybe there is no death trap for you because the person doing this to us knew that, if you were left alone for long enough, you'd eventually find a way to kill yourself with no help needed."

Rob frowned. "Now is not the time to flirt with me!"

Holly was about to protest, but he was already on his feet, looking out of the window. Not so subtly, his hand searched around the window pane edges until...

"Ah-ha!" he said, pulling off what looked like a blob of congealed dirt to Holly, but turned out to have little wires attached to it. "This is definitely a... something. What are the chances that it's the only one?" They searched some more, but found nothing further, except for the strong possibility that Holly's bathroom mirror contained a concealed camera - something which completely grossed her out.

"I guess that we should hope for the best and talk plans," Rob said in a low voice that they both prayed wouldn't carry. "I say we make a run for it."

Holly's eyes were immediately drawn down to the snow that surrounded the house. "Following in Jack's footsteps," she muttered.

Rob winced. "I know it's chancy, but we can't stay here forever, or that chocolate cake is going to start looking real good. I mean, it already does. But, you know - even better."

"No, I mean really follow in his footsteps. Until he hit the landmine, he was fine. Hopefully we will be, too," Holly explained.

Rob's face brightened a little. "Hey, that is a point! Too bad Jack only made it a few steps before 'boom'. But it is a start."

Holly chewed her lip, wondering if this really was the only way. But with decomposing bodies for company and no more poison-free food, they didn't have much choice. Unfortunately, she suspected that the perpetrator of this massacre would have realised as much.

"It seems as good a time as any to die," Rob said, pushing himself up off the bed and walking out the door.

Holly made to move after him and then sat down again.

He shot her a sympathetic look. "Take your time, I'll wait," he assured her.

She nodded absently, her eyes still fixed on the distant, perfect, undisturbed snow. She walked back over to the window and ran her hand across the spines of the books, lost in thought.

Rob looked up when she finally exited the room.

"I just had another thought," she told him.

LUCKY NUMBER SEVEN

Old houses tended to have their fair share of junk. Holly knew it was time to brave the cellar and go in search of it.

Rob waited nervously in the living room, trying to pretend that Miranda wasn't face-down on the floor. They'd both agreed it would be a pretty stupid idea for him to go into the cellar. Holly wasn't convinced it was one of her most brilliant plans either, but Miranda and Emma had visited and returned unscathed. She could only hope that the same would be true for her... and that she'd be able to find something that fit the idea she had in her head.

A few tennis rackets and strips of twine later, they had what they needed - makeshift snowshoes.

"Nice work, Miss *Blue Peter*, but how does this help? Beyond giving the forensics a good laugh..." Rob asked, looking dubiously at his feet. They were standing in front of the sodden carpet, where the snowdrift Jack had let in had since melted.

"Jack went out in his combat boots, right? The mines were either buried during the storm, or maybe even before it.

After all - the bad guy couldn't bank on there being snow to keep us all here. It's probable that they were laid right after we all arrived. So maybe they had to do it in the snow? I guess there's also a chance it was done before all the snow and then - I don't know - activated later? Is that a thing with landmines?" she asked and shuddered, half from cold, half from the thought that she may have already walked over a landmine that contained enough explosive to vaporise her. And she hadn't known a thing about it.

"My bet would be that they did all of this long before we arrived. This killer doesn't leave a lot to chance," Rob concluded, still frowning at his tennis rackets.

"The theory of the shoes is that they'll spread our weight. There's a chance we may be light enough to not trigger the mines. It probably won't work, but I just thought... every little helps," Holly said, thinking more and more that this had been a stupid idea. Actually, the whole wanting to be a real detective and driving up to Scotland for this convention had been a stupid idea, but there was no time to dwell on that.

She had an appointment with death.

They crawled up the steep incline of snow, both holding their breath after every movement. Eventually, they were standing on top of the white stuff, looking at the crater where Jack had met his end.

"Ladies first?" Rob heroically suggested. Holly glared at him. They both stared at the red stain on the snow for a bit longer, before they furiously played rock, paper, scissors.

Holly won.

"Best of three?" Rob asked, but Holly crossed her arms.

The first few metres went fine. Holly's theory about following in Jack's footsteps held out, and it was only when they reached the spot where Jack had died that things went a bit pear-shaped.

"I suppose we should go round," Holly suggested, trying

not to be sick from the smell of blood and... other things... which were starting to defrost, along with the snow.

"Into the unknown we go," Rob muttered and shuffled around the edge of the hole, casting nervous glances in its direction. Holly followed him.

They made it another two metres before it finally happened.

"Boom!" a voice shouted. They both nearly jumped out of their skin. A burst of maniacal laughter travelled across the snow and they looked back in the direction of the house, to see a man striding around the side towards them.

Where he'd come from, Holly didn't know, but she had a feeling that they really didn't want to stick around to find out.

"Run!" she hissed at Rob, but it turned out to be quite a challenge to do anything more than a steady waddle in their tennis racket shoes. Holly wondered if she'd slowed them down for nothing. The man was walking easily across the snow, like there was nothing to worry about. *Perhaps he just knows where all of the mines are*, she thought. She wondered if they could take him out and then follow his footsteps back to safety. Unfortunately, if he was willing to show himself to them, it probably meant that there was zero chance of their survival.

Just to prove her right, Rob made a strangled screaming sound and promptly fell to his death.

Or he would have done, if Holly hadn't been semi-expecting it and grabbed the back of his coat, swinging him a little to the left with a gargantuan effort.

"Unnngh!" said Rob, which might have translated into: 'Thanks for mostly saving me'. Alternatively, it might have meant: 'There are spiky things in this pit that just opened up, and I'm still hanging over it'. The latter was unfortunately true. While Holly had done enough to keep Rob from outright falling into the previously concealed pit, he was now braced over the abyss... and the snow around the edges looked like it could give way at any second. Holly hoped that he was as in-shape as he looked, because his core strength was about to be tested.

"Tom March, I presume?" Holly said, turning to face the newcomer, hoping that if she blocked his vision of Rob, Rob could quietly work on getting himself out of the sticky situation.

A gun glinted in the bright afternoon sunshine, looking dark and deadly. The man standing in front of her slowly clapped against the back of the hand that held the gun, the cruel smile not leaving his face. Holly looked at the person she'd assumed to be the face of evil and found he actually looked quite normal. His hair was pale and ashy and his face was quite pleasant, if it hadn't been for that smile. Holly looked into his blue eyes and didn't see what she'd expected, but that just went to show...

"Come on, Rob, be a sport and let go. If you end it now, I'll let your girlfriend live," Tom called.

"No need to keep her alive, she's nothing to me,'" Rob said, perhaps mishearing Tom, or perhaps choosing completely the wrong moment to display his usual dark sense of humour. Holly only just resisted kicking him in the ribs.

It would have been a very fatal kick.

"Nice to meet you, Tom. Killing the other detectives so you could be the brightest and best, huh? That's pretty clever!" she said, trying to play for time.

Fortunately, Tom was more than happy to gloat. "I hated these stupid meetings. Every time, it was always: 'Boast about your greatest case, while the others pick holes and point out how they would have done it all a hundred times better'. Who needs that?" He shook his head.

Behind her, Holly heard Rob sigh. "I know you had a bit of a dry year, Tom, but that's no reason to take it out on us. I thought we were buddies?" Rob said, still hanging precariously over the death pit.

"I hate you. I've told you that several times," Tom said.

"Yeah, sure you have! Like... in the friendly way," Rob replied.

Tom ignored him. "Anyway, this was all a great idea. It's Christmas come early for me! Now, if you'll just be helpful and die, that would be lovely. It was all planned so that you would die last, Rob. I always hated you the most with your easy money cases. I bet you creamed cash from every single one, too! Who's going to miss a few million when hundreds of millions of pounds worth of gold is recovered and returned?"

Rob laughed as delicately as possible. "Have you seen the clothes I wear? And if you saw my house, you wouldn't... Hey! You *can* see my house! Let's go there now and have a cup of tea. I guarantee you'll feel far less homicidal after a good brew."

Tom shook his head. "You are a terrible smooth talker. How have you lived this long?" He snorted. "Oh yes, I forgot. You're more of an amateur metal-detector enthusiast than a true detective."

Rob grumbled something about being better at his job than Tom was, but he didn't get to finish. Tom had balled up a snowball and managed to aim it past Holly. It smacked Rob's thigh and caused him to jerk dangerously over the deadly pit.

"What am I saying? You're amazing! You were always the best of us. You can be the leader of every detective meeting we have from now on. How about you let me up?" Rob wheedled.

"Smooth," Holly muttered under her breath, unable to see

any way out of this. She had one final trick up her sleeve, but she was willing to bet that Tom was a quicker draw than she was, and she would only have one chance...

"Where do we go from here?" Holly asked, hoping that the more Tom talked, the more he'd lose his focus.

To her dismay, he raised his gun. "I think I'll shoot you backwards into the pit. You'll make Rob fall to his death and you'll both be impaled. It seems the most efficient way to end this. It's nothing personal. You were never my competition, Holly, but you know who I am, etcetera, etcetera. It would be inconvenient if you lived to tell anyone that I was the one who engineered this series of untimely endings. It would certainly ruin things when I drive up here tomorrow only to discover that - oh no! All of my old friends are dead, leaving me the country's best private detective. I'll clean up," he added with a grin. "I'll clean up business-wise, I mean. Not the corpses." His nose wrinkled.

Holly realised that there was a reason he'd killed everyone remotely. Perhaps, deep down, he lacked the brutal resolve needed to murder with his own hands, or maybe he really despised seeing dead people. Either way, it gave her a chance...

Her hand twitched towards her pocket, but Tom was quicker. The gun came up and the sound of a final, fatal shot, echoed across the snowy landscape.

Holly opened one eye and cautiously looked down at her coat.

It was bright red.

But that was the colour it had been when she'd put it on to leave the house. There were no additional stains seeping through.

"Rob?" she called, her voice thin.

"Also not dead yet," came the reply, which left only one option. Holly looked in front of her at where Tom March lay face down. A pool of crimson was already spreading out through the snow.

"Did the idiot point it the wrong way or something?" Rob asked, sounding as baffled as Holly felt. She knelt and hauled upwards on his coat, giving him enough support to push himself up and away from the pit and its deadly spikes.

"No idea what happened, but how about we don't wait to find out?" Holly suggested and Rob nodded.

"Too bad he didn't happen to divulge any information about where the landmines are hidden during that annoying, evil monologue. Just our luck," Rob commented, brushing the snow off his knees.

Holly blinked as something silver reflected sunlight directly into her eyes.

"Don't move, or I'll shoot!" a familiar voice called across the snow.

Miranda emerged from the French doors and started walking towards them. The assault rifle she carried looked remarkably at home in her hands.

"Hey... wasn't she dead a minute ago?" Rob asked in a stage whisper.

Holly shrugged. She'd been pretty sure, but looking back, none of them had actually checked the woman's pulse. She'd just looked so... dead. The whole 'not moving' act had been very convincing. When you added one more death to the other murders, they'd all just made the assumption.

"I don't suppose you've just rescued us?" Rob asked hopefully.

Miranda laughed and shook her head. Something about the way her eyes glinted let Holly know she was no longer playing the part of sweet, fluffy Miranda - the super-fan who would do anything at all for her heroes. The woman in front of them was undoubtedly the real Miranda - the person she'd hidden from them all.

"No, this is actually the first wobble in the whole shebang. I thought Tom had already pulled the trigger when I shot him in the back. He probably hesitated, so he could talk some more. Blah blah blah, always going on." She looked down at the dead traitor detective with distaste. "He was a pretty poor villain. We don't really harp on about how life is unfair and how it's all everyone else's fault but our own that we're not achieving anything. Real criminals just get on with the job." She raised the gun to prove her point.

"Wait! Just one thing! You've got to tell us why you did it. Please? Last request?" Holly asked, hoping she didn't sound too pitiful.

Miranda rolled her eyes and glanced down at the highly expensive watch she was wearing. *Looking back, I suppose that watch was a bit out of place,* Holly thought, remembering Miranda's otherwise highly-planned eccentric and fluffy style of dress.

"All right. The condensed version only. I contacted all of the detectives and pretended to be Little Miss Super-Fan, who just wanted to help them solve a case. I did it so that I could keep tabs find out if any of them were close to uncovering my operations. I knew about the murder case I helped them to solve because of my underworld connections, and it was a pleasure to tip the detectives off about the killer. He was an operative of mine who'd become quite a thorn in my side. Obviously, I've had to accept a few losses, but knowing about the detectives' individual methods and the jobs they were on helped me to stay ahead - so they never caught the big game. Everything was great... until this year. Rob busted my biggest funding operation. He dug his way into one of my group's tunnels and ruined the whole heist. It was a job that had taken years of planning, and in a single afternoon, this idiot stumbled upon it. You weren't even looking for thieves, were you, Rob?" Miranda said, her voice cold.

Rob blushed a little. "Ah, well… not so much at the start, but after I found them, I was definitely looking for thieves."

Holly raised her eyebrows at him.

"I was hunting for something else, okay?" he told her.

She decided to leave it at that. If they lived through the next five minutes, they could chit-chat later.

"As I was saying… that was not in the plan. I realised that I had unknowingly been engineering the perfect scenario to end the era of private detectives. Now all I needed was a fall guy…" They all looked at Tom. Rob gave a little groan, probably regretting how easily Tom - and all of them - had been manipulated. Or, knowing Rob, perhaps he was just thinking about how that chocolate cake hadn't been poisoned after all.

"Oh no, this makes so much sense now," he said. Both women stared at him. "I should have figured it out sooner. You knew that Lawrence was going to be killed during the main course. That's why you hadn't bothered to bake the warm chocolate fudge cake. You already knew there wasn't going to be a dessert! I can't believe I didn't see it sooner."

Holly stuck her tongue into her cheek realising that (weirdly) Rob was right. Miranda shrugged as if it changed nothing… which it didn't.

"So, Tom turns out to be the murderer while you, Miranda the organiser, manage to escape the bloodbath and shoot Tom with a weapon you just happened to find lying around the house," Holly said, eyeing the assault rifle with skepticism. There was no way anyone was going to believe that one of those things had been easy to come by.

Next to her, Rob cleared his throat. "My rifle was in my bag," he muttered.

Holly felt her heart drop. She opened her mouth to ask why he'd brought it, but then didn't bother. For all she knew, the detectives brought their weapons with them, to show off how big and shiny they were. It wouldn't have surprised her. Why had she ever wanted to join their ranks?

"Rob, you are an idiot," Holly said, turning to stare at him - hopefully distracting Miranda from what her right hand was up to.

"Great last words," Miranda commented dryly, and hefted the gun.

Holly assumed she'd make it look like Tom had shot Rob and her, and then... Holly glanced at the gun in Tom's hand. She'd need to reach for that, if she really wanted this murder to look the part, otherwise it would be all wrong.

The gun she was holding in her hand wasn't the one she'd use for them.

She'd already shot Tom with it 'saving the day'.

She needed to pick the other gun up to kill them.

"Don't move," Miranda growled, probably reading her facial expressions. "I can see you're being Little Miss Smarty Pants, the amateur detective, but if this crime doesn't end up being perfect, so what? All I lose is my role of the tragic hero-ine. I'll just disappear and leave it as an unsolved massacre instead. I think we've chatted enough. Time to die," she said, levelling the gun.

AGATHA RAISIN

For a brief moment, Miranda had to look down to check the location of Tom's gun.

Holly knew it was her only chance.

She pulled the book free from her pocket and opened it up, keeping the spine towards her and the open pages pointed at Miranda. There was a twang when the spring loaded mechanism spat its deadly dart out. Aiming a book is a hard thing to do with any great degree of accuracy, but Holly had beginner's luck on her side.

The dart speared Miranda's temple and embedded itself deep in her brain. The mass murderer's hand squeezed the trigger of her assault rifle in a death spasm, but Holly had already moved out of harm's way.

"Agatha Raisin, you beauty," Holly said, looking down at the amateur sleuth novel in her hand.

A sound like 'nnnngghhh' came from behind her. She turned around and discovered they hadn't escaped unscathed after all.

"I think I'm dying. Not going to make it. You just… go on without me…" Rob said, his voice strained. Holly looked down at his hand, which was the only part of him that showed any sign of damage.

"Bad luck. You've lost a finger. It's hardly fatal though." She pulled him to his feet using the other hand.

"You don't know that! It could go septic. Or perhaps the smell of blood will attract a pack of wolves. They have wolves in Scotland, right?" he said, his eyes fixed on the stump where his middle finger once was.

Holly almost felt sorry for him. That was probably half of all the sign language he knew gone forever.

"Let's get out of here," she said, not wanting to look down at the bodies in the snow, or even think about the events of the weekend. How could anyone take such pleasure from the demise of people who - despite knowing for a deceptive reason - they'd associated with for years? If you were going to do away with a whole group, something like a bomb disguised as a gas leak would have been a far more efficient way to go.

Holly shook her head, wondering if she was starting to go loopy thinking about the best way to kill people. It was just that she couldn't comprehend the amount of hate you needed to have in order to plan each individual death in such a way that mocked their greatest cases.

"Crazy, so crazy," Rob said, trailing along next to her, but sticking to the footprints Tom had made (just in case).

"How could one person be so cruel?" Holly agreed, assuming he was following her thoughts.

"Yeah, that chocolate cake has gone to waste. All because she pretended it was poisoned! That's one less cake I'll be able to eat in my lifetime. It's just tragic," Rob said, and she thought he might even be tearing up a little. Holly decided to put it down to him being slightly delirious from the blood-loss and shock.

They followed Tom's last steps across a couple of fields to

the side of the main road, where he'd parked a surveillance van. Holly thought about trying the backdoor to see if it was open and taking a look inside, but then realised she didn't want to. It was from here that Tom had executed a group of people who'd thought he was their friend, just by pushing a few buttons.

The police could deal with it.

They trudged along the icy roads, trying not to slip over, both keeping their silence. It was a lengthy walk back to civilisation, and Holly somehow knew it would be a long time before they had a moment to themselves again. Also, her phone was out of battery. Rob hadn't even brought his with him on the trip, having presumably not expected any bad weather... or massacres.

She looked around at the winter trees in the gently fading light as the sun started to dip in the sky. They looked just as peaceful and unmoved as when she'd arrived at Horn Hill House. Yet, beneath their branches, the world had changed. Seven had lost their lives, and there would be no future mysteries solved by those six great minds. She'd like to think that there would be no great crimes committed either, but something told her that there would always be someone ready to take Miranda's place.

It was good of Rob to wait until they entered the foyer of the hospital to pass out. Carrying him would have been impossible. It was not as considerate that he stayed unconscious for an hour afterwards, leaving Holly to explain everything to the police.

By the time Rob came round and demanded food, the police had arrived at Horn Hill House and confirmed all that Holly had told them. The only thing she didn't like was the way the two police officers in the hospital room with her and Rob kept reaching down and touching their handcuffs.

Holly chewed her lip, remembering for the first time that she had technically killed someone. The weapon hadn't been hers, but she'd still ended a life. Would she get in trouble for it?

The strange thing was, the more Holly thought about it, the more she realised she didn't feel any remorse. Instead, there was an emptiness inside. The voice inside her head reminded her that Miranda had absolutely deserved it. If she'd done nothing, both she and Rob would be dead. Thinking practically about the matter was the only way to go. Not to mention, she'd probably done the police a big favour by eliminating one of the most successful criminals around. One they hadn't even known existed.

It wasn't long before the investigation uncovered the traps and found the van to be entirely clean of Rob and Holly's fingerprints or DNA. They were in the clear and hailed as heroes. The press arrived and took pictures and statements, and the rest of the night passed in a whirl. Holly didn't even have a moment to think about any repercussions she may be in danger of incurring - having very publicly ended Miranda's vast crime enterprise.

Saying goodbye was harder than expected.

Rob's hand was still wrapped in bandages when he hugged her goodbye. Holly had been going for a handshake, but Rob had surprised her. She'd returned the hug and had discovered that you didn't go through a deadly experience like the serial killings at Horn Hill House without forming a bond. This wasn't like the initial attraction that had existed between them when they'd first met, what now felt like an age ago. This was something deeper. Holly supposed it was the first spark of a real friendship.

"You shouldn't let an experience like this one put you off. I know it was a tough case, but we got the bad guys and got out alive. That's what matters," Rob had offered, just before they'd parted ways. Holly had smiled and nodded. On the inside, she'd been wondering what would have happened to her if she'd been the unlucky one and had lost a finger. That would have been the end of her piano career - and how else was she going to earn her crust? She'd put that to Rob and he'd immediately suggested that she become a professional private detective and forget all about musical tomfoolery.

He'd also pointed out that there was rather a shortage of them at the moment.

Holly smiled as she drove back towards Sussex, marvelling at the way the weather was cold, but much less bitter, the further down the country you went. There was no sign of any snowfall.

She idly wondered what her area of speciality would be if she did take the pathway of being a detective. Looking back at her previous cases, she'd either be looking at lost and found, or solving mass murders. Neither seemed very appealing.

Rob had offered to help her, should she decide that she wanted to go into business. He'd even hinted at partnering up for a few cases. He'd said that her observational skills and quick thinking had impressed him. She suspected that it was just his way of saying thanks for saving his life using a rather dangerous piece of popular literature.

Holly glanced down at a copy of the book she'd used to save her life. It had felt right to find a normal edition and actually read the novel.

She had to say, she was disappointed. The plot had been a perfect combination of twists and turns, but she'd already managed to figure out who the killer was, and she was only halfway through. If only things were that simple in real life. Looking back, there'd been next to no convenient clues to help them figure it out before the clock had gone down to zero. It really wasn't fair.

Another item was also on the front seat, hidden beneath the book. Her copy of one of the big broadsheets had her picture, blown up to a ridiculous size, on page two.

It was typical that her one shot at fame was a terrible one. Her hair was a winter-weather fright, and she had bags beneath her eyes from the lack of sleep the night before at Horn Hill House. It was definitely not one to frame and put on the wall. Somehow, Rob had contrived to look great - despite being in a hospital bed and wearing a usually unflattering hospital gown. Life was definitely not fair.

Holly shook her head as she neared Little Wemley. Things would be back to normal in no time. In a couple of weeks, this story would be forgotten. Holly would have returned to working as a professional pianist, putting her silly detective dreams behind her once and for all.

Deep in the glove compartment her phone began to ring. Holly ignored it and kept driving. The phone went dead, but after a moment's silence, it began to ring again. This time, she pulled over and answered.

"Hello?" she said, wondering if it was the police looking for more answers. She thought she'd finished with all that.

"Hello, Holly Winter? I've got a serious problem I think you may be able to help with. We suspect that my family's most prized heirloom, the Enviable Emerald, is under threat from thieves. We've informed the police, of course, but they say there's nothing they can do if a crime hasn't yet been committed. We desperately need the help of a private detective. I'm hoping you can solve the case before the crime even takes place," the man on the other end of the phone said.

Holly's immediate instinct was that it was all a prank. Her second was to put the phone down. Hadn't she just said that she was absolutely not going to be sucked into the world of private investigating?

"We'll compensate you generously for your time. How does…" He said a number so large it made Holly's mouth drop open a little. "…sound to you?"

It was more than she'd make working for two months as a pianist - and that was with a full performance schedule!

"You could stay in the house while you work on the case. I read all about your work up at Horn Hill House. I'm sure you can help us," the man pressed.

Holly found herself wavering.

What was one little case involving a not-even-stolen emerald? She'd take the money and the case, and then that would be it. She would settle down again to her nice normal life in Little Wemley. No more Nancy Drew or Agatha Raisin delusions.

Deep inside, she could already feel an itch of excitement as she contemplated the case she'd just accepted. Would she be able to find the thieves before they struck? Was there even a real threat to the emerald?

This is your last adventure, she promised herself.

A FATAL FROST

THE ENVIABLE EMERALD

Holly looked out of the window of her rented cottage. A thick frost covered the field that her property backed onto. She felt a little sorry for the smattering of wild deer she could see, whose coats also glistened with frost in the first rays of sunshine.

She stirred her breakfast hot chocolate - while she watched the deer graze on anything that wasn't frozen solid - and thought about everything she had to do.

Christmas was fast approaching. She'd almost entirely filled up her diary with piano bookings. From pantomimes to office parties, she was going to be very busy during the winter evenings.

Unusually for Holly, her days were pretty busy, too.

On her way back from the horrid happenings at Horn Hill House - where six of the country's greatest detectives had been murdered - she'd received a call about a case. After getting home and thinking it through a bit more, she'd officially accepted and had dashed straight off to assist the Uppington-Stanley family with the perceived threat to their Enviable Emerald.

Holly took another sip of her hot chocolate, made with real dark Belgian chocolate. There really was no better way to start the day, and being single, there was no one to judge her for it either.

She sat down at her kitchen table and flipped her laptop open. After the drama at Horn Hill House, she'd decided it was high time she familiarised herself with a little more technology. In order to get to grips with it, she'd started a blog about the smattering of past mysteries she had solved.

She told herself firmly that it was just so she'd have a way of looking back and remembering why it was such a bad and dangerous idea to become a private detective. However, the annoying little voice in her head whispered that having a blog would also be an excellent way for any potential clients to find out about her. Not to mention, it was fun writing the little stories. She only hoped that recounting them in third person wouldn't be considered big-headed. All of her favourite mysteries were written that way, and she also thought there was no harm in pretending she had a very astute assistant - as opposed to being a one-woman band.

"No more mysteries, remember?" Holly chided herself out loud, realising she was making grandiose plans for the future again. She opened up *The Case of the Enviable Emerald* and started to edit the beginning of the tale.

The problem was, even with all of the resolve in the world, mysteries had a habit of finding her. The simple case of the Enviable Emerald had been no exception when an unexpected complication had transformed it into a full-blown mystery.

Holly sighed a little as she stared at the text on the screen documenting her most recent adventure. *Your final adventure,* she reminded herself for the hundredth time. She copied and pasted it into a new post, clicked on 'preview', and began her final read-through.

The Case of the Enviable Emerald
A Holly Winter Mystery

The first mystery to solve in the case of the Enviable Emerald was why did the Uppington-Stanley family believe their priceless heirloom was under threat? It was unusual for a thief to be considerate enough to give their targets a handy heads-up. Uncovering the truth about why the family even suspected an attempt was imminent was the first thing Holly planned to do upon her arrival at Enviable Manor.

Enviable Manor was every bit as grand as it sounded. The walls had been crafted from grey sandstone, and the building had softened and weathered throughout the centuries. It still retained its original magnificence - the sign of a splendid architect.

After parking her car (which had been complaining ever since it had been left out in a Scottish blizzard) she walked up to the manor and rapped on the door, using the curiously elephant-shaped knocker - its trunk the moveable piece. A maid opened the door and she was invited in for afternoon tea with the Uppington-Stanleys. Despite being pleased by her timing and more pleased by the scones, cream, jam, and teas that were served, Holly knew that her burning question couldn't wait. Therefore, she only allowed herself a conservative three scones, piled high with mounds of cream and jam, before she asked why the Uppington-Stanleys thought that a theft was imminent.

It transpired that the wealthy family had visited their local Christmas fair, taking their children - Isabelle and Nick - with them. Both 'children' were in their twenties and had decided to visit the fortuneteller, who'd set up between the church's booze tombola and the Brownies' sweet stall. Holly had privately wondered about the wisdom of this stall placement on the part of the fair organisers.

The junior Uppington-Stanleys had entered the fortuneteller's tent, one after the other, and had both received the same warning: Your family's most prized heirloom is under threat. Defend your inheritance, or all will be lost, and you will suffer from misfortune forever.

"We found this a bit disconcerting," Mr Uppington-Stanley said, his eyebrows twitching up and down as he alternated between dismay and forced politeness at the number of scones the hired detective had managed to put away.

"Yes, it seemed awfully specific. We're sensible folk and don't believe in any claptrap fortune-telling nonsense, but this seemed like a genuine threat. After our children told us what they'd heard, we tried to find the fortuneteller, but she'd already gone, and the fair organisers had no contact details for her." Mrs Uppington-Stanley wrung her hands - most likely because of her fears about the emerald, but also possibly because Holly had started on the fairy cakes, and they were disappearing at an alarming rate.

"But if the fortuneteller was involved with jewel robbers, how does it benefit her to pre-warn her targets?" Holly mused.

The married couple shook their heads and tried not to look at the crumbs, which were all that remained of their afternoon tea.

"We're baffled by it. Either the woman knew something and perhaps wanted to warn us as a way of getting back at a person who had done her wrong, or she could be a complete crank who just happened to know about the family jewels.

They're quite famous," Mr Uppington-Stanley said with a completely straight face.

Holly tried not to choke on her final fairy cake.

"Well, you seem to have thought about the options," Holly observed, wondering what, exactly, they wanted her to do. Her lips twisted as she inwardly wrestled with the large figure the family had agreed to pay her for the job she was supposed to be doing and the simplicity of the task at hand.

"I should probably come up and have a look at the emerald and review your security measures. Then I'll be able to deduce if there could be any risk of theft," she said, not sure what else she was supposed to do.

The wealthy pair nodded agreeably.

Mrs Uppington-Stanley led her upstairs. They walked down a lengthy corridor, luxuriously carpeted with light-cream pile, the dark wood panels on the walls adding to the air of expense. Holly immediately felt guilty for keeping her shoes on.

"Here we are!" her guide announced, knocking on a panelled door that almost looked like part of the wall. Holly noted that it would be difficult for a casual thief to find the location of the emerald. They'd have to be an insider. Her employer pointed to a CCTV camera that had its lens permanently focused on the door - another security measure.

"Hello Mrs Uppington-Stanley," a man said, unlocking the door from the inside and letting the pair in.

"This is our full-time security guard, Nick. He stays in the room all day everyday, until he swaps with Lewis, our night watchman. Nick never leaves this room," Mrs Uppinton-Stanley announced, rather proudly.

Holly looked around the room and nodded vaguely. To her, the idea of employing a full-time security guard just to look after one jewel equated to some serious overkill, but she supposed if you had enough money, and possessed something as valuable and irreplaceable as the Enviable Emerald, it might be worth it.

"I have to admit, it seems as though you have the situation under control," Holly said, looking around the box room, which didn't even have a window. She hoped Nick was being well-compensated for what must be a very boring job.

"Yes, well... we thought it best to check," Mrs Uppington-Stanley said, slightly flushed from Holly's professional approval.

Holly tried not to feel like a complete fraud. She'd only really solved a couple of small cases and had barely managed to escape with her life from the Horn Hill House incident. That didn't really qualify her for professional consulting, but the Uppington-Stanley's offer had been so tempting...

"I'd better show you the emerald while we're up here. Just in case there is something we might have forgotten," Mrs Uppington-Stanley said, opening the drawer by the bed and pulling out a generic looking jewellery box covered in faded, dark-pink suede. The only thing that stood out about it was the rather flimsy lock, which was broken and hanging off at an angle.

Holly was about to ask if it was supposed to look damaged - as a sort of red herring - when Mrs Uppinton-Stanley's hands fumbled with the lid and flipped open the tall case to reveal... nothing at all.

The emerald was gone.

"No... NO! It can't be!" Mrs Uppington-Stanley wailed.

Holly heard the sound of running footsteps and Mr Uppington-Stanley appeared, his face morphing into a mask of horror when he heard the news.

"Tell me quickly, when was the last time you saw the emerald?" Holly asked, hoping the pair wouldn't dissolve into hysteria. It seemed to her that if the crime had only just been committed, there was a chance that the thief could still be apprehended.

"This morning. I took it out to show it to a visiting colonel over breakfast, but I put it straight back in its case and locked it with this key," Mrs Uppington-Stanley held up the dainty key. "You saw me do it, didn't you, Nick?"

The big security guard nodded. His, dark, expressionless face looked untroubled by the news. Holly supposed it was a professional requirement that he stayed calm in a crisis. She herself felt anything but calm. The gears in her head were already spinning as she felt time - and the emerald - slipping away from her.

"Let us assume the jewel was returned safely to the jewellery box. After all, the lock has been smashed, which implies that the emerald was taken from the drawer. Has anyone else but Nick been in this room since this morning? Anyone else at all?" she asked.

The Uppington-Stanleys shook their heads and then stopped and exchanged a glance.

"Only the maid, but she is watched by Nick. Nick himself hasn't left the room. Well, apart from attending to calls of nature. Even that facility is actually still in this room," Mr Uppington-Stanley explained, pointing to a small corner, which had been partitioned off and presumably contained a toilet.

"Is the maid still here at the manor? It's important that we speak to her if she and Nick were the only ones with access to the room."

Mrs Uppington-Stanley flapped her hands uselessly for a few more seconds and then trotted off, hopefully to find the maid.

Holly could have sworn that Mr Uppington-Stanley shot her a grateful look.

"Did you go to the bathroom while the maid was in here?"

she asked the security guard. He nodded, a little mournfully. Holly chewed her lip, looking again at the broken lock. Despite not being a very convincing lock, smashing it violently would have made some noise. She doubted that it could have been done without Nick hearing it.

"I was only in there for a couple of minutes. The maid was still cleaning when I came out. I know she hadn't left the room because I lock the door after everyone who comes in," Nick explained.

Holly looked pointedly at the currently open door. The guard shrugged. "Everyone apart from my employers, of course," he explained, like she was an idiot.

"What about this door?" Holly asked, noticing a rather ordinary looking cream door set in the wall by the sofa.

"It's always kept locked. I'm the only one with the key," Mr Uppington-Stanley patiently explained.

Holly looked it up and down and noticed that the bottom of the door was nearly flush to the bare-wood floor. "How big is the emerald?"

Mr Uppington-Stanley put his first fingertip against the tip of his thumb, forming a circle. Holly dismissed the possibility that it could have been passed under the door.

"Excuse me? What is the matter?" A young, dark-haired woman, with a surprisingly clipped British accent, entered the room, followed by a still-distraught Mrs Uppington-Stanley.

"You're the maid who cleaned this room earlier today?" Holly asked. The young woman nodded to confirm. She still held her basket of cleaning supplies, presumably from the job she had still been doing.

"May I?" Holly asked as a courtesy and quickly glanced through the supply bucket.

Nick shook his head. "It can't be in there. She doesn't bring much into the room. She just hoovers and dusts and listens to her music the whole time. The hoover is a little handheld thing that's entirely see-through. It wasn't even being used while I was in the toilet. Also, I search her when she leaves," he said, still sounding like he was explaining this to a person who was short of brain cells.

Holly tried not to be goaded... but failed. "From the evidence I've been presented with, I think it's obvious that one of you committed - or at least aided in - the theft of the emerald. The question is, which one of you was it, and where is the emerald now? Until I know that, no one must leave this house," she said, putting her foot down.

"Have you got any leads?" Mrs Uppington-Stanley asked, her expression in danger of dissolving into tears at any second. Holly suspected it was only the time it took to apply her artful makeup that was making her think twice about it.

Holly tried to nod more confidently than she felt. "I need to make a call," she said, praying that her hunch turned out to be right.

She'd only just finished the call when she heard a shout and raced back along the hall to the box room. Mr Uppington-Stanley stood with the Enviable Emerald in his hand. A small carry case, that must have belonged to the security guard, was open on the floor. Globs of hair gel splattered the floorboards and the surface of the emerald.

"Mystery solved! I think it's time we called the police. Our security guard is a jewel thief!" Mr Uppington-Stanley announced, his eyebrows knitted together in fury. "The butler and the chef are keeping a close eye on him. That slippery man! He had such good references, too," he added with a sigh, the fury being replaced with disappointment. "I suppose the temptation just got too much."

Holly chewed her lip again, the gears in her head still turning. "It is time to call the police, but I'm not sure that the case has been solved. Will you allow me to continue my investigation until they arrive?"

Mr Uppington-Stanley nodded, his eyes fixed on the emerald. "Feel free. The emerald is back, and that's what matters," he said and then walked out of the room, already shouting to the butler and chef to make sure Nick didn't try anything.

Holly was left in the empty box room with the strong feeling that she was missing something big. The phone call had been enough for her to figure out how the jewel was stolen, but she couldn't work out how it had left the room. Her eyes were drawn once more to the door leading into the spare room and she began to wonder...

"I've got it!" Holly announced, arriving back in the main room, her face flushed with pleasure. Everyone turned to look at her. She realised that Nick was already in handcuffs, the newly-arrived police having made the arrest immediately.

"We'll hear about it later. We have the emerald," Mr Uppington-Stanley said, dismissing her, as he gestured to the police to take Nick away.

Holly felt her temper rise. Why hire her if they didn't want her opinion? "That would be a mistake," she tried again. Mr Uppington-Stanley shot her a look of exasperation, but Holly hadn't finished. "That emerald is a fake," she announced, praying that she was correct. She hadn't had time to test her theory, as she'd heard the police turn up and had known that time had run out.

"If you'll follow me up to the room where the jewel was kept, I think I can solve this mystery. Oh, and everyone should come," she added.

Oh please, please be right about this! Holly thought, as she led the odd group up the stairs, down the corridor, and into the spare room next to the box room where the emerald had been kept.

"We're not in the right room," Mr Uppington-Stanley informed her, sounding deeply unimpressed. Holly ignored her wealthy employer and instead moved to the centre of the room, taking a deep breath.

It was time to *Miss Marple* this mystery.

"The first problem with this case was 'how?' How was it that the lock could be broken on the jewellery case without Nick the security guard hearing it? The obvious answer was that he did it himself when he was in the room unattended. I thought that was the most probable solution, until I noticed something in the maid's bucket. A lot of people listen to music when they clean, and I could see she had a music player of some sort, but there was something off about it. It looked like it had a kind of external speaker - something which MP3 players don't tend to have."

Holly paused and thanked her lucky stars that she'd done some Googling of the latest technology before she'd rushed off to the emerald case. Her lack of knowledge had let her down at Horn Hill House, but her research had paid off this time.

"It just so happens, that I recently read an article about some new technology. It's meant to still be theoretical, but I think it might have been used here. There is a device which can cancel out external noises by mimicking their frequencies and, therefore, eliminating them. The same applies to internal noises. This theoretical device could be used to create a personal bubble of silence, making it impossible for someone - even if they were very close by - to hear something like... a lock being smashed off a jewellery case," Holly finished. She looked up at her listeners and was met with a bunch of frowns.

"What?" one of the police officers asked, looking completely bamboozled.

Holly resisted the temptation to sigh. "I made a call to a friend who then called on a contact who works for the Ministry Of Defence. They confirmed that the silencing technology does actually exist, it's just not widely marketed yet. You'd have to be a specialist to get hold of it." Holly's eyes fell on the dark-haired maid. "How long have you worked here?"

The maid made a noise of derision. "You're really accusing me of this? The emerald was found in his hair gel!" she complained, and various voices around the room seemed to agree with her.

Holly looked at the bucket she was still holding and frowned. "Where's your MP3 player?"

The maid frowned right back. "It's right here," she said, pulling her phone from her pocket. Holly rubbed her temples. *Great.* The girl had managed to hide the device she'd seen, probably whilst waiting downstairs.

"This detective you've hired is crazy," the accused said, shaking her head.

The police began to move towards the door, taking Nick with them. Holly momentarily reflected that this kind of stuff never happened to Miss Marple. She'd better get on with the big reveal.

Well… what she hoped would be the big reveal.

"I realised that it wasn't possible to get the emerald out of the room through the door, as Nick would have found it when he searched the maid. We also know that he hadn't left the room all day, because you have CCTV outside the door. So, how did the emerald leave the room when there were no windows and doors for it to get through?" Holly asked the audience, but none of them was in the mood for joining in. She ignored their mutterings and bent down on one knee, running her hands over the floorboards by the door, trying to ignore the bead of sweat sliding down her spine. Was she about to make a huge fool of herself?

"Ah-ha!" she cried when her hand detected a loose board. She levered it up and discovered it slid completely out from under the door, leaving a handy hidey-hole that went from one room to the next. The removal of the board also revealed the real Enviable Emerald, glimmering in the dim light. Holly picked it up and held the remarkable jewel in the palm of her hand for all to see. She'd half-expected spontaneous applause, but there were only more surprised mutterings.

"Well, how do we know who committed the crime now, and how do we know which emerald is real?" the very annoying DCI said.

Holly tried not to grind her teeth in frustration. "If you go back downstairs and search the living room, I'm sure you'll find the noise blocker that I was talking about. It should have enough fingerprints on it to close the case. Also, maybe you could run a search or two and find out who our maid here really is. That sort of technology and this kind of crime… it's not the first jewel she's stolen, that's for sure."

"Yes, but, the emerald…" Mr Uppington-Stanley cut in, looking anxiously from one identical gem to the other.

Holly had to keep her cool once more. They never wrote about all of this stubborn idiocy in the detective stories she read! Everyone was always suitably in awe of the detective's brilliance.

"Obviously you wouldn't go to all the trouble to hide a fake jewel under the floorboards where no one is going to look! The fake jewel was planted where you'd be most likely to search, in order to frame Nick," she explained.

"But, the maid…" the policeman jumped in again, and Holly only just managed to stop herself from tearing her hair out.

"Do some research! Find out if she's been caught before. You'd better check the emerald as well for prints. Although, I, ah... touched it a bit," she said, realising she'd made what had to be a very amateur error. "When you take the jewels to a jeweller, you'll see," she finished, hoping they'd finished their cross examination.

"That doesn't explain the fortuneteller, though..." Mrs Uppington-Stanley jumped in.

Holly bit her lip. That was one mystery she hadn't solved.

"Who knows, perhaps she got lucky?" she offered.

"Well, I suppose that's that then," Mr Uppington-Stanley concluded.

The End.

Holly's brow creased when she read the last couple of lines of her story. The ending was definitely a bit of a let down, but then, that's what had really happened.

The police had carted off both suspects for questioning because they'd had no faith in Holly's investigation. One of the officers had even had the cheek to imply that she might have planned the whole thing herself! Fortunately, he'd stopped talking when someone had whispered in his ear that she'd been a part of the Horn Hill House massacre. By default, the officer must have assumed she was a great detective - the same way her first proper employers had.

She'd later been informed that the maid did have a criminal record. Further investigation had turned up her involvement in a number of high profile jewel thefts. Nick the security guard was released, and the maid was going be tried and sentenced for her attempted crime, and anything else the police could find and get to stick...

Holly drained the last few dregs of her hot chocolate and

thought about the cheque that had been couriered to her the day after she'd finished her investigation. That was something at least. She wondered what she'd do with the money. It meant she didn't need to accept as many Christmas piano gigs.

She'd started the season with the intention of turning down any booking that didn't sound like it would be a good show, but the more she'd said no, the more people had asked. Ironically, people thinking she was in demand had actually made her far more popular. She smiled a little. She didn't mind in the slightest.

She was one of those lucky few people who thoroughly enjoy what they do to make a living. Playing piano was a true passion. She'd worked for many years to reach a very high standard, and she still longed to be better. There was always room for improvement.

Her fingers spasmed indecisively for a moment, before she reached for her mobile phone, reluctantly searching through her address book. She dialled the number. It was answered after just two rings.

"I knew you'd come around." Rob Frost's voice floated back down the line to her, with more than a hint of a gloat in it.

Holly bit her lip.

"Wait… that is why you called right? You have changed your mind?" Rob tried to clarify, ruining his cool-guy first line.

Holly smirked. "I think so. I was reading back through the Enviable Emerald case and… it wasn't so bad. Nobody died, and the mystery got solved. So, I was thinking, if I could just have a few more cases like that one… it wouldn't be too dangerous. It should just be fun, right?" she said, and could almost hear Rob's smile of triumph.

"You've got the mystery-solving bug. I knew you wouldn't

quit on me! Now, about the profitable enterprise we're poised to enter into..." He started to reel off a long list of things that Holly would need to do in order to set up her very own private detective business, endorsed by Rob Frost - the great private detective.

Amazingly, Rob hadn't wanted any money for his endorsement. He was doing it all as a favour in return for the time that Holly had saved his life using a rather deadly amateur detective novel.

At least... she was pretty sure that was why he was helping her.

Holly shook her head and took some more notes.

Rob was based in Cornwall at the moment, searching for... something. He'd been vague about the details of the case he was supposedly working on. It meant that he wasn't going to be popping by for tea anytime soon. Any romantic notions Holly might have had were quashed.

"Just remember, you're using my name in your business, so don't screw it up!" Rob warned, but Holly knew he was grinning that beautiful smile of his. His dark hair was probably all mussed up as well, and...

She stopped herself right there.

"I'll do my best. You'd better not do anything stupid either. We're tied together now," she said and immediately bit her tongue.

Rob laughed. "Talk to you soon, Holly."

Holly stared at the mobile phone and sighed. Things had been so intense during the short time she'd spent at Horn Hill House, she hadn't really had a chance to figure out how she felt about Rob. After they'd survived the ordeal and had dealt with the press together, there'd been a seed of friendship between them, which had grown into this business venture that Rob had practically pressured her into. Holly bit back a smile. She hadn't needed much persuading.

She'd sworn off mysteries after Horn Hill House, but the recent case of the Enviable Emerald had reminded her that solving mysteries didn't have to be a terrifying pastime - and she was actually really good at it! Her vast knowledge of mystery books and their story-lines meant she was expecting most twists and turns and could always crack the case.

This detective business wasn't going to be serious anyway. She'd just pick up a few little mysteries, perhaps focusing on lost and found type cases, and the kind of thing that came up locally. Definitely no big crime and absolutely no murders.

What could go wrong?

THE NO.1 LADIES' DETECTIVE AGENCY

"I've rented a little office space, put up a sign, and placed adverts in the local paper and around town. I've designed a website and added the blog to it, so people can read all about the cases and find us online. I've even started a social media page," she said into the phone.

Her eyes flicked back to the Facebook page with its seriously unflattering profile picture of her. The only picture she had in any professional capacity was the one that had been taken by the press after the Horn Hill House massacre. Her hair was a horror wig, and walking miles in freezing temperatures - trying not to get blown up by landmines - had done nothing for her skin. She sighed and promised herself she'd solve another case soon - and this time it would be a far more glamorous occasion when the press arrived.

"Cool, I like Facebook! I shall like your page..." Rob said on the other end of the phone.

As Holly watched the screen, her little 'like' counter jumped from two to three. Rob had liked it, she'd liked it, and her sister had liked it, too. Although, knowing her sister, it was probably so she could see if the business failed.

"Well, it's a start," Holly said, trying not to sound as unsure as she felt. "What should I do next?"

There was an awkward pause.

"Good question. I've never actually set up an agency before," Rob admitted.

Holly felt her stomach drop. "What?!"

She'd assumed that Rob had known what he was talking about, having got years of experience and successful cases under his belt.

"Mostly, I don't get given cases. I just... sort of stumble upon them," Rob admitted, and while Holly desperately wanted to ask exactly what he meant by that, now wasn't the time.

"So, I'm just your little experiment, am I?" Holly asked, feeling crosser by the second. This was so typical of Rob.

"Hey, I'm funding this too," he reminded her. "We're both taking a risk." There was a pause. "I don't know... when I look at you, I just think of how perfect you'd be working as a detective in a little town... solving all of the missing cat cases."

"Now you're just being a jerk," she told him.

Rob had the audacity to laugh. "Come on, lost cats make super hard cases! You can never predict what the little psychos will do next, which makes them hard to locate. I swear I wasn't making fun... or even kidding. Most of your cases will probably be lost cats," he said, his apology vanishing.

Holly would have loved to be able to correct him, but the two cases she'd previously worked on in Little Wemley had involved a lost dog and the mayor's chain - which had been stolen by the world's worst thief and recovered almost immediately. Rob's prediction was probably correct.

"What am I supposed to do? Just sit here and wait for the phone to ring?" Holly griped.

Rob was about to answer when the landline started to ring. Holly heard a snicker of amusement right before Rob put the phone down.

The landline continued to ring. She stared at it for a couple more rings, before finally lifting up the receiver.

"Hello, Holly Winter speaking," she said and heard a rather surprised noise on the other end of the phone.

"Oh, good. You're who I wanted to speak to. I found your details online, and I wanted to invite you to an event I'm putting on. It's a murder mystery night re-enactment of what happened at Horn Hill House. It would be just brilliant if you could appear at the end and answer any questions our pretend detectives might have. It's a charity event, so I'm afraid there's no budget available for..."

Holly put the phone down and shook her head in disbelief. How could anyone be dense enough to think that she'd want to be a part of some twisted re-enactment? That misguided organiser was giving the world of mystery-solving a bad name.

She snorted when she recalled the last line about a lack of budget. She'd heard that old chestnut a fair few times. It was always the same with 'charity events'. There was never any budget for the entertainment, but you knew that the bar would still be selling their drinks at a profit, and that pretty much everyone else at the event would still be getting paid.

Holly sighed. She had nothing against charity - she even occasionally agree to take part in genuine charity events - but what had just been proposed to her on the phone was ludicrous and offensive.

She frowned for a second and then decisively opened a Word document. Now that her agency was starting to become more visible, (although how, she wasn't really sure) she would need to hire someone to deal with answering the phone. The only problem was, she didn't have a huge budget herself. Holly ran her hands through her hair, well aware that she was dangerously close to becoming as unreasonable as the charity events organiser. Perhaps she could take on an apprentice and pay them minimum wage, and only as a part-timer. She had a bit of leeway afforded by the cheque she'd received for solving the Enviable Emerald case. All she needed was a few more of those and she'd be in profit and able to pay a secretary. After a moment's further deliberation, she decided it was worth the risk. Someone else could deal with the cranks on the phone.

Ten minutes later, she was out pinning up her adverts around town and had asked the local paper to place a job available ad. Now all there was to do was wait.

And wait.

Holly sat in her office for the entire day and no one came in.

She knew that starting a business was never easy, and business was hard to come by until the word spread, but she'd still been hopeful. Perhaps she should ask Rob how he came by his cases and start doing whatever it was that he did. There had to be a way to make a name for herself! For now though, it was the end of an uneventful first day, and she had her resident gig at the Little Wemley Cocktail Bar to play that evening.

The next morning, Holly received a few phone calls, all asking about the job. She also had two 'business' phone calls that both turned out to be complete junk. One was a prank call and the other caller had wanted to interview her for his next true crime book - *The Massacre of Horn Hill House*. Holly had reiterated that she didn't want to talk about it. After a little more prying, it had also transpired that the 'writer' had never actually written a book before. Holly had put the phone down again and reflected that she really did need a good secretary to screen calls like this one.

Her first real job landed around lunchtime.

She received a call from a village local who suspected that someone had stolen her pearl necklace. Holly had popped around, and after a very brief investigation, she'd realised that the woman's Corgi had dragged the pearls out of the box and under the sofa. Fortunately, the corgi was so ancient it didn't have many teeth left, so the precious necklace was largely un-chewed. Holly hadn't had the heart to charge the woman anything like the minimum amount she and Rob had agreed was fair reimbursement for taking on a case, so she'd taken a nominal fee and left to get back to her little office, just in time for some late afternoon interviews.

She had three candidates lined up, but after looking at the CVs they'd sent through, she wasn't any closer to picking her secretary. With the low wage and hours available, Holly knew she could hardly afford to pick and choose.

The first candidate was still in school, which made her an impossible option, as Holly needed someone to work part-time in the day. The second was a little old lady, who wanted some easy work to make a little extra during her 'retirement'. Holly felt a bit sorry for her, and would have been tempted, as the woman had years of secretarial experience. The only problem was, she was incredibly hard of hearing and Holly knew she couldn't answer the phone. That just left her with the last option… and it wasn't a pleasant one.

Becky Stoney wasn't a secretarial dream come true. She had skin the colour of light coffee, thick, black hair she swept back into a bun, and a scowl that could make milk curdle at fifty-paces. At the start of the interview, Holly had immediately thought that Becky didn't like her. It was only later on that she'd discovered it wasn't anything personal - Becky didn't like anyone. But unfortunately, she wasn't still in school and she could hear perfectly well, which automatically made her the obvious choice for the job.

"Could you start on Monday?" Holly asked, half-hoping that Becky would be awkward about working, while her sensible side sternly reminded her that she needed an assistant - and with her budget, this was apparently as good as it got.

"Okay," Becky said and promptly left the office without a 'thanks' or a 'goodbye'.

I suppose it might show that she's efficient, Holly mused, but couldn't help wondering if she'd live to regret employing this cactus of a woman.

The next day and the weekend passed in a blur of little cases (several mislaid items and - you guessed it - lost cats) and piano performances. Holly was using all of her time when she wasn't solving cases to look through the endless sheets of Christmas piano music she had in her possession, poised to deal with just about any request that her many audiences might throw at her.

She was so engrossed in this practice, she'd forgotten all about Becky starting work on Monday. That was... until the woman herself stomped into the room, threw her ugly, black leather bag down in the middle of the floor, and plonked herself behind the other desk next to Holly.

"Oh! Good morning?" Holly ventured, and then bit her tongue when Becky just stared at her vacantly. Right on cue, the phone began to ring.

Her new secretary immediately seized it. "What do you want?" she demanded.

Holly winced. She could just about hear the caller on the other end of the line.

"Hello, er... is that Holly Winter I'm speaking to?"

Becky stared at the handset for a second before answering. "No," she replied and put the phone down.

Holly wondered if it was too late to call back the little old lady who was deaf as a post...

"I think we should discuss a phone answering protocol. Perhaps you could start by saying 'Hello, *Frost and Winter Detective Agency*. How may I help you?" she suggested.

Becky's eyes glazed over.

The phone began to ring again. This time, Holly made a grab for it. Becky reached at the same time. They were still playing tug-of-war with the handset when their first ever walk-in client entered the office.

"Good morning! I'm Holly Winter, head private detective at *Frost and Winter Detective Agency*," Holly felt compelled to add, in an attempt to hammer home her seniority to Becky.

Becky wasn't even looking her way. She was on the phone again, and from what Holly could overhear, things were heading in a similar direction to that of the last call. She slapped a smile on her face and properly focused on the visitor.

He was in his late twenties and possessed an unusual head of very pale blonde hair. The hair seemed a little out of place with his dark eyebrows, but Holly could tell he was all-natural, and his eyes were similarly dark. He was dressed in a tailored, navy-blue winter jacket, thrown on over suit-trousers and a shirt. All in all, he looked like he might have just stepped off the page of a magazine, rather than off the street in Little Wemley.

Holly tried to un-notice everything she'd just seen, but it was difficult to ignore the man's perfect appearance. Even Becky fluffed up her bun and did her best to sound as efficient at getting rid of people on the phone as she could.

"A private detective? I had no idea those things really existed outside of storybooks. What cases have you worked on?" the stranger asked. Holly felt her heart sink a little. Clearly, he wasn't here with a mystery for her.

"Oh, this and that," she said airily. "I recently recovered the Enviable Emerald when it was briefly stolen from the Uppington-Stanley family," she said.

The stranger's forehead developed a crease, while he studied her intensely. Holly hoped her cheeks weren't as pink as she suspected they were.

"Now I know where I've seen you before! You were in the papers during that Horn Hill disaster."

Holly decided not to correct him on his use of the word 'disaster'. A disaster usually signified an event that was unavoidable, and that no one could have predicted. The murders at Horn Hill House had been planned and executed with full knowledge and intention.

"Yes, I was. How may I help you today?" she asked, finding her smile again and trying to move the conversation away from the newspaper clipping and *that* photo.

Her visitor raised a hand to his head, showing his forgetfulness. "Wow, I haven't even introduced myself. I'm George Strauss, chairman of the Little Wemley Archaeological Society."

Holly raised an eyebrow. "I had no idea that there was a society of amateur archaeologists so close to Little Wemley."

Her visitor nodded, his enthusiasm overcoming any reservations Holly may have had. "Indeed. We generally meet to discuss any finds. We also talk about past events of historical interest and argue about what may, or may not, have occurred. The older the event and the evidence, the harder it is to be sure what really happened during that time - which is why it makes for such a compelling debate." He smiled and Holly found herself hopelessly smiling back at him.

"So, ah, Mr Strauss…"

"George," he corrected.

"What brings you to the agency?" she finally got round to asking.

George ruffled his pleasantly side-parted hair, clearly embarrassed to have been sidetracked. "Yes, of course! I'm looking for a pianist for the annual Christmas dinner of the Archaeological Society, and you were highly recommended. I called at the post office and they told me I could find you here," he said, probably over-explaining a little, so he didn't come across as a wandering weirdo.

"I'll just check my diary," she told him, feeling her heart sink further still. It wasn't that she wasn't happy to accept the piano booking, but an evening playing piano meant she wouldn't get to socialise at all with this handsome stranger. It would be one night of wistful longing, and then it would be over. Holly wished things could be different.

Had she known what was just around the corner, she wouldn't have made that wish.

FROZEN

"**H**olly! You look wonderful," a voice called from the other side of the dark car-park. Holly turned and smiled in the vague direction, hoping she was facing the right way. She'd just got out of the car and her eyes hadn't adjusted to the darkness yet, just like her skin hadn't adjusted to the cold. It was mid-December and the air felt like ice!

"You look..." She trailed off when George stepped into the light of the distant building, which illuminated patches of the gravel. He was dressed in formal black-tie and could have given James Bond a run for his money. "...great. You look great," she finished, her voice a little strangled. She mentally gave herself a good shake. This was just another gig!

"Thanks," he said with an easy smile, gesturing that they should walk up to the rather grand old building that was the Little Wemley Town Hall. Holly had played many a piano concert here but had been a little surprised when George had told her about the venue. It transpired that his society met at the hall every week and had thought it simplest (not to mention cheapest) if they met at the same location and self-catered for their meal. The only expense they were going to was hiring a pianist.

"It looks like we're the first to arrive. Apart from Maria, anyway. I can see her car. She's doing all of the cooking - the saint!"

Holly bit her tongue and couldn't help but feel a slight stab of jealousy over the way he'd called Maria a saint. Holly already had a vision of a beautiful blonde woman just as lovely as George was. It took a lot of effort to rinse it from her mind and remind herself (for what felt like the hundredth time) that she was here in a professional capacity. This was not a date, and she didn't even know George. He could be a psychopath!

Later, she would reflect that there was a fair chance he really might be.

"Come on in. I'll make sure you're all set with the piano and then we'll get you a drink. If it's okay with you, we only want a spot of music during and after dinner. Hopefully, it will encourage the members to keep their discussions a little less… heated… than usual. Hey, seeing as you're interested in the club, why don't I introduce you to the rest of the members when they arrive? You might like to join us in the future."

Holly ignored the fluttering butterflies in her stomach and instead picked up on George's hesitation. When she looked across at her host, he winced a bit.

"Is it a fun club to be in?" she asked, her curiosity piqued. She sat down behind the grand piano and opened the lid, her fingers running easily over the smooth keys.

George smiled a little ruefully. "I think I told you before that we look back at events from ancient history and then discuss what we believe actually happened back then. It makes for a good old debate. Usually, it's not too contentious, but recently we decided to cover famous unsolved deaths or murders and consider the historical evidence for whether a death was accidental or intentional, and so on. You'd be surprised how heated the exchanges can get! People have an opinion in their minds and stick to it, no matter what. Between you and me, I'm actually starting to regret suggesting the idea."

The distant sound of the main doors being pushed open reached our ears.

George stopped talking for a second. "I'd better go and see who's arrived. I'll get you that drink a bit later on, I promise," he said and rushed off to welcome a club member. He soon returned with an older - but very well-kept - gentleman in tow. Unfortunately, it turned out the same could not be said for his manners.

"Holly, this is Bernie," George said, his voice forcefully cheerful. Bernie looked Holly up and down. She resisted the urge to run off and return wearing a bin bag that covered absolutely everything.

"Why is she here?" he asked, not even bothering to address Holly.

George wrung his hands apologetically. "She's the pianist we all agreed to hire at our last meeting. How about you get settled in and perhaps help yourself to a drink?"

Bernie didn't need to be asked twice. He stalked off towards the arrangement of wine that was already set up on a table.

George pulled a face at Holly and shrugged, before walking back towards the door as the next set of visitors arrived. Rather than being left alone with Bernie, Holly followed George, hoping that the other members of the club were more pleasant.

"Holly! I should have guessed you were the pianist our chairman picked. Nothing but the best for the Amateur Archaeological Society," the newest entrant said.

She smiled back at Chrissy Bartholomew, her old friend from school. The other woman was just as pretty as ever, Holly realised, trying not to feel jealous. A man stood just behind her and Holly thought she recognised him from somewhere.

"Wow, you're Aidan Banks, presenter of *Out With The New, In With The Old!*" George said, clearly in awe.

Something clicked in Holly's mind. She realised that it was typical of Chrissy to find herself a man like this. Chrissy was (rather unfairly) beautiful both inside and out. Her only flaw was the way that she always got bored with men. Holly could remember her having several high-flying partners, all of whom she'd eventually traded in. Chrissy wasn't malicious, she just liked a change of scenery every now and then. At least it meant the rest of the town's females occasionally got a look-in with the local eligible bachelors. *You never know, you might be in luck,* she secretly thought when she noticed another new arrival surreptitiously checking out the TV presenter.

George finished talking to Aidan - rather reluctantly - and introduced her to Jayne, another relatively young member of the Amateur Archaeological Society. Holly was starting to wonder if she was missing something. She'd assumed that everyone in the club would be over sixty. Just what did this group of people get up to?

She grabbed Chrissy before she slid past. "I didn't realise you were interested in archaeology," Holly said as innocently as possible. But as well as being pretty, Chrissy was also pretty smart.

She smiled knowingly, before shooting a meaningful look in Aidan's direction. "I decided to do my research this time," she said, shrugging - as if joining a club and swotting up was something everyone did when trying to get their hooks into a man. *Perhaps that's where I'm going wrong!* Holly reflected. "I joined the club a week ago and thought it would be great to invite Aidan along to this dinner. We met when I was doing a news report."

Holly nodded. That figured. Chrissy was the local weather girl, but it seemed she was finally being given the opportunity to spread her wings into reporting. Any news-worthy men had better watch out...

"Hello there, dear. I'm very much looking forward to hearing you play for us later," a kindly voice said. Holly turned to see an older lady with lavender tinted hair and a suspiciously white smile. This was more the kind of person Holly had expected to meet tonight.

"This is Milly," George said, popping back up for the introduction.

The old lady's smile grew even wider. "Have you already told her about the murder we're discussing tonight? It's my turn to do it!" she said, rather unnervingly.

Holly tilted her head at George, who was definitely starting to look a bit stressed.

"Oh, Milly... we've already said we're not discussing the death of the ice man tonight. We'll do it next week when the club is back to normal." George shot an apologetic smile at Holly. Holly was torn between amusement and disappoint-ment that George thought this sort of thing was out of her comfort zone.

"It sounds really interesting," she said, meaning it.

Milly beamed up at her. "You'll have to join and come along when we decide what exactly befell the poor man. If you ask me, all the signs point to murder," she said gleefully, before trotting off towards the wine.

"Ah, there's Louise!" George said, dodging off to talk to another new arrival. That left Holly face to face with the next person to enter the building... and the face she saw wasn't one she'd wanted to remember.

"It's been a while, Holly." Carl Bounty's eyes crinkled up, as he gave her his best shot at a smile. Eye crinkling was about as far as it got.

"Hi Carl. Are you a member of the club?" Holly asked, and then realised it was pretty obvious he was. Why else would her ex-boyfriend be here? That was the problem with living - and occasionally dating - in a small town. If things came to an end, you could never escape the other person.

"Yes, not gatecrashing tonight," he said, his eyes doing the crinkly thing again. Holly opened her mouth to say that she hadn't meant that at all, but Carl waved a hand in her face. "I'm kidding." His mouth twitched up - just a fraction. "You haven't lost your sense of humour, have you? I read all about that nasty business up in Scotland."

Holly quickly cleared her throat and glanced in George's direction. No... he was seeing to yet another arriving couple. How many people living in the vicinity of Little Wemley were secret archaeologists?

"I, ah... heard you're with someone new?" she said, half-remembering overhearing some gossip the last time she'd popped to the shops. She'd merely been hoping to divert the conversation away from anything to do with the murders of the detectives, but Carl's face immediately lit up with a real smile. His hand went to his dangerously thin hair, and he smoothed it back, looking in the direction of Louise Renley - another native of Little Wemley.

Holly's eyebrows shot up. Her detective skills must be on vacation tonight. She'd wrongly assumed the pair had been lift sharing.

Louise was a couple of years older than Carl. She had mousey-brown hair that curled over her shoulders and a very big bust. And that was all of the good things Holly could say about her. Louise had a reputation for being a gossip and had always seemed a little air-headed to Holly. She twitched her nose. Now that she thought about it, the new couple did make sense! She looked back at Carl and found he was still staring at the other woman with puppy-dog eyes. Wow... this was a serious relationship!

"Goodness, will there be wedding bells soon?" she asked, hoping her voice wasn't too cheery. It wasn't as if she'd ever had any real feelings for Carl. They'd dated briefly when she'd been a lot younger (after Chrissy had finished with him). Holly had chased 'bad boys' back then, before she'd realised that 'bad boys' were more trouble than they were worth.

She always felt a little pressured when someone she'd been involved with got hitched, while there she was - still alone. Even her sister, the awful Annabelle, had got married before her - something Annabelle would never let her forget.

Holly inwardly sighed. She still dreamt of the day when Annabelle's husband would announce that their marriage was a sham, before running off with a rent boy... She bit her lip to keep from laughing out loud. *Jealous much?* she thought with a smile and suddenly felt a whole lot better. *Who wants to pick one dish when there's an entire menu to look at?* She cast a longing gaze in George's direction. It was lucky he wasn't looking her way, although... she was less pleased to discover he was talking to Chrissy. She sighed again. At least with Chrissy, you always knew you could have her castoffs.

Holly turned and scanned the room, wondering when dinner would be served and if she should start playing soon. A pair of eyes looked back at hers. She was surprised to find that the handsome TV presenter Chrissy had brought with her was looking her way. He silently raised his glass of wine in her direction. Holly felt a blush rise to her cheeks. *Well!* she thought, wondering what to make of that.

She didn't have too long to think about it either, because he was already walking towards her.

"So, you play the piano?" was Aidan's opening gambit.

Holly found herself smiling and nodding, and then opening her big fat mouth… "Yes, but I am also a private detective," she told him, and then wanted to kick herself for sounding like such a showoff. The problem was, she did want to show off. Aidan was the opposite of ugly and walked around in a haze of star power. He was a little too much like a puppy dog to be Holly's usual type, but that didn't mean she wasn't as pleased as punch that he'd picked her to talk to.

"Solved any mysteries recently?" he asked.

Holly gave him a brief account of the Enviable Emerald case, deliberately leaving out the arguments she'd had with the police and the part where they'd thought she herself was a suspect.

Luckily, he looked suitably impressed. "I've heard that they try to solve ancient mysteries at this club, which sounds like a fantastic idea. You should join and give them all your professional opinion." His dark brown eyes were filled with admiration.

Holly tried to keep an aloof expression on her face, whilst feeling like a complete fraud. She was not exactly a professional yet. "I'm thinking about it," she said, and then decided a complete change of subject was needed. "What do you think of Chrissy?" she asked, before wondering if that was way too personal. The thing was, she'd known Chrissy for years and had learned her ways. Holly's nosy nature wanted to know what the men she dated actually believed they were getting into.

Aidan's wry smile was all the response she needed.

"She's lovely, but I can tell she doesn't want to settle down," he said simply and asked Holly if she wanted a drink.

She was just about to answer when George arrived.

"I'm afraid you just missed Annie and Wilbur. They've already found Milly to talk to. They'll be arguing about that ice man case for the rest of the evening," he said, gesturing to an older couple Holly had briefly seen before she'd come face to face with Carl.

Holly turned back to George faster than he'd expected and caught the end of a look he was giving Aidan. *I wonder if...* Holly started to think, but then Chrissy popped up by the TV presenter's elbow and pulled him away to get her a drink, leaving Holly unsure of what she'd witnessed.

"Our final guest!" George said, beckoning the most recent newcomer forward. Out of everyone Holly had met so far, this man looked the closest to her idea of an archaeologist. He wasn't the muscle-bound, devilishly handsome Hollywood type, but a real, ready-to-shovel-dirt archaeologist. The first thing Holly noticed was the size of his calves, which were nearly bulging out of his beige chinos. Thick, dark hair covered his arms, but only a few wisps formed the worst moustache she'd ever seen. To top it all off, the man wore a floppy beige hat that his oiled black hair hung down from, like fleeing snakes.

"Nice to meet ya," the man said, his eyes searching around the room for something... Holly didn't know what.

"This is Dylan," George said, before letting the man slip away, as he so clearly wanted to.

Holly and George stood in silence for a moment looking at the other people in the room. Holly considered how amazing it was that such an unlikely group had been brought together by their shared love of one thing. She was going to voice this observation to her employer, but he muttered something under his breath and stalked off to where Dylan was talking to Bernie, their gestures becoming more and more aggressive.

Holly looked at the grand piano, feeling a little sad that her chance to socialise with George had already been and gone. Perhaps if she joined the society... She entertained the idea for a moment, before wondering just how transparent her reasons for joining would be.

Holly shook her head and settled into her professional routine. There was just time for a quick bathroom break before kickoff. She walked off towards the corridor in the far corner of the room that led through to the toilets and the kitchen.

When Holly walked past the door of the kitchen, she smelled burning and saw tendrils of smoke creeping out beneath the door. She immediately tested the metal door handle with the back of her hand. Finding it cool, she opened the door a crack and peered into the room. The first thing that caught her eye was the smoke that was escaping out of the oven door. The large turkey inside the oven had turned from a roast into a flambé. The second thing she noticed was the open door of the walk-in freezer and the body slumped inside it.

She took a step into the room towards the woman and got just close enough to realise that she was definitely dead. Her hands, lips, and face were all blue from the cold, and a pool of dark red liquid had spread around her, before freezing solid - like a gruesome ice lolly. Holly could tell her death had been violent, but she didn't want to get any closer to find out the exact cause. There was no need to touch the body to check for signs of life. This woman was long gone.

"Is everything okay, Maria? We can smell burning..."

Holly jumped at the sound of the voice and spun round just as George entered the room. He looked from the smoking turkey to the body in the freezer and turned pale.

"Oh no... Maria," he said quietly.

"We should call the police." Holly had finally snapped out of the initial shock of coming face to face with a body. The last time she'd seen someone dead was at Horn Hill House... and the first victim had not been the last. She was already starting to shiver as nerves took hold of her. *Calm down. You are not snowed in, and the police will come!* she reassured herself, pulling out her phone and dialling 999.

The dinner party conversation, which had started out lively, was reduced to whispers. Small groups sat around the room, talking amongst themselves and eyeing the police nervously. The officers had arrived shortly after Holly's emergency call. Now the crime scene and everyone at the town hall was under investigation.

The detective chief inspector in charge of the case was a bullish man. His height was only equal to that of Holly's, but he made up for that with his broad stature and short temper. There was no mistaking that everyone in the room was a suspect for murder when he walked in and barked out his statement.

"I can confirm that Maria Jennings was murdered…" *Well, duh!* thought Holly. People didn't tend to suffer the wounds she'd seen on Maria in an accidental fashion. Someone had done that to her and left her in the freezer.

A cold thrill ran through Holly's body. The turkey had burned, but Maria had probably been the one to put it in the oven. Could she have been killed whilst she and George were in the building, both completely oblivious to what was happening?

She immediately dismissed the idea.

Maria's body was half-frozen. It was likely that it had been a few hours ago when she'd met her violent end.

"We are going to interview every one of you individually. You will all remain here until the interviews have concluded." The DCI eyeballed them all, daring someone to contradict him. Holly certainly wasn't going to be the one to break the silence.

The emergency services had sent three officers along with the DCI to investigate Holly's call, which meant that the interviews didn't take too long. It was just unfortunate that Holly's interviewer turned out to be the detective himself. When Annie exited the room in floods of tears after fifteen minutes, Holly thought she'd probably drawn the short straw.

THE ICE MAN'S MYSTERY

"In all the ruckus, I don't think I introduced myself. I'm Detective Inspector Stephan Chittenden." Holly almost extended her hand for him to shake, but the moment of insanity passed when he barked out: "Who the devil are you?"

"Holly Winter," she replied, only just managing to stop herself from adding 'Sir, yes Sir!'. She was starting to get the idea that any attempts at humour would be frowned upon.

Inspector Chittenden narrowed his eyes at her, making his face even more bull-like.

"You're a member of this... *club?*" he asked, making it sound like being a member was a comparable crime to being a murderer.

"No, I'm not!" she said, a little hotly, and then bit her tongue when the detective's eyes lit up.

"Two things... why are you here, and what's wrong with the club?"

Holly wished she'd watched her temper. "I'm a pianist. I was hired by George Strauss to play at the annual Amateur Archaeological Society dinner," she explained, being careful to keep her tone of voice devoid of emotion. Not that she needed to worry. She hadn't murdered poor Maria!

"And the next question?" Chittenden prompted.

Holly tried not to get annoyed again. "There's nothing wrong with the club. As far as I can see, it's a group of people who share a hobby. That's the impression I got when I came here and met the society for the first time tonight," she said, wanting to point out that she had nothing to do with the club, and therefore, should definitely not be a suspect.

"If George Strauss hired you, you must have met him before today," the detective countered. Holly felt a strong urge to kick him under the table for being so ridiculously pedantic.

"Yes, I met George once before. I also know Chrissy from school, and I briefly dated Carl. Quite a few of the others I've seen around Little Wemley. That's the thing with small towns, you get to know everyone," she explained, shooting a pointed look at the detective. .

He sniffed and shrugged. "I wouldn't know. I live in London." Holly knew she should have guessed that much. No one with such rude manners would last long in a place like Little Wemley. They'd be shunned by the entire town.

"You said that Maria was murdered. May I ask how?" She wondered if the police would release any details.

Stephan Chittenden just stared at her, his forehead wrinkling into a frown. "Holly Winter? Your name sounds familiar," he said, as if something was just occurring to him. Holly could guess at least half of what was coming next.

"You were up at that Horn Hill place with the *Sherlock Holmes* gang who all died. Shows just how good their 'detecting' skills really were," he said with a self-satisfied smirk. Holly really bit her tongue this time. If the detective had been stuck in that house with her and the others, she was willing to bet that even a deranged serial killer would choose him as their first victim.

"One of the police officers said that you're running around with delusions of being a detective yourself?" He looked at her with deep distaste.

This time Holly didn't hold back. "Sometimes people aren't satisfied with the way that the police handle their investigations, so they seek a second opinion - much like you would with a doctor," she explained, dumbing it down - just for the sake of digging into Stephan Chittenden a bit more.

His nostrils flared. "But you aren't qualified to do anything - except poke your nose into places where it doesn't belong," he told her, sounding eerily like her sister, Annabelle. Holly wondered if she could arrange an introduction. They would be best friends.

"Continuing with the doctor analogy, there are also complementary therapists. That's what I'm like, but for crime rather than illness."

Chittenden snorted. Holly finally accepted that she was barking up the wrong tree, or more likely, was in the wrong forest altogether.

"You should leave it to the professionals," he said, as if Holly would suddenly see the error of her ways and shut down her little business immediately.

Rather than continuing to fan the flames, Holly stayed silent, waiting for the detective to remember she'd asked a question. For a moment, she saw that she'd thrown him, but he quickly recovered.

"I'll be making a further statement once all of the interviews have been concluded." He glared at Holly, like it was all her fault that the murder hadn't already been solved.

"I can't wait," she replied and wondered if she'd regret it.

Chittenden just glared some more. "Get out. I have better things to do."

Holly hoped he didn't see her fists balling up. How could one man be so frustrating? Thinking about it, being frustrating was one thing all men seemed to specialise in.

Fortunately, it was only another five minutes before the detective and his colleagues deemed the interviews finished. Holly noticed that no one was being dragged off in chains. For now, it looked like the case was still wide open.

"While you have all been interviewed tonight, you will also make yourselves available for any further questions that I, or my colleagues, might have," Chittenden began, his natural lack of charm shining through. Holly noticed he wasn't asking. He was telling.

He nodded to one of the officers, who stepped forwards and asked if they could all please hand over their car keys, so that the police could check for any evidence. A few members bristled at that and muttered over warrants and being treated like suspects, but Holly handed hers over without complaint, noticing the extra use of 'please' and 'thank you'. Presumably the other police officers were trying - albeit in vain - to influence their mighty leader.

"Excuse me please, but how did dear Maria die?" Annie, one half of the older couple enquired. Holly was amazed by her courage - given the way she'd looked when Chittenden had finished with her.

He was clearly surprised, too. It possibly worked to her advantage as he actually answered the question. "The official statement will be that Maria Jennings died from trauma to the head, caused by a blunt instrument. There are some other details that we'll be keeping to ourselves, of course." He straightened his tie. Holly almost rolled her eyes. He couldn't resist adding that, could he?

"You mean she was shot with an arrow as well as being frozen?" Milly piped up, her mouth a perfect 'o' of horror.

The detective nearly jumped out of his skin in surprise

and gestured frantically at the remaining police officer. "Arrest her!" he shouted. There was a ripple of alarm when the man started forward. Milly stuck her hands up, like she was in an American gangster film.

"But... I was just saying," she tried to say, but the officer was already sliding the handcuffs over her wrists.

George stepped towards Milly, too.

"Come on, DCI Chittenden... you can't really think she did it? Milly's 85 years old! You said Maria died from blunt trauma. If there were arrows involved, which I'm not saying there were," he quickly amended, "I doubt she could shoot a bow. It just seems a little far-fetched, don't you think?" George fell silent, probably realising that the entire murder case was far-fetched. Why would anyone bludgeon someone to death while they were cooking Christmas dinner, and perhaps shoot them with a few arrows, too? If anything, it was usually the chef whose mood was murderous after enduring stuffing the turkey, and then stuffing it into the oven, only to later be told by diners that it was too dry.

"She knew information we hadn't released," Chittenden accused.

Milly's eyes sparkled. "So, she *was* shot with an arrow. Poor, poor Maria," Milly said, sounding sorry and morbidly curious at the same time. Holly wasn't sure if it had even registered that she'd just been arrested.

"It's just like the Otzi case," Dylan muttered.

Chittenden turned his furious gaze on him.

Dylan looked around the room at all of the sealed lips and groaned. "Come on, we all know what this looks like!" He turned back to face DCI Chittenden, who was only moments away from making his second arrest. "Next week, we were going to be talking about the death of Otzi the ice man. He lived 5,000 years ago but was discovered in the Alps in 1991. At first, the experts thought he'd died of old age. 45 years old was pretty senior back in the Bronze Age," Dylan explained, becoming more animated as he went. "In 2005, his mummified remains were examined using a high resolution CT scanner. It then became apparent that he had an arrowhead in him and had also suffered massive bleeding at the base of his brain, which indicated a serious head injury at the time of death." Dylan sucked air in between his teeth. "You can probably see the parallels."

"Usually, we meet to discuss whether or not we think it was murder and argue our cases, but poor old Otzi's death is pretty cut and dried. The real mystery is who did it, how they did it, and why?" Milly jumped in, looking as cheerful as ever despite the cuffs.

The detective shook his head in disbelief. "We interviewed you all and none of you thought to mention that you meet up to discuss murders?" he said incredulously.

An unhappy muttering spread around the room.

"We're an archeological society! We don't simply talk about murders. That's just been the theme of the past couple of meetings. Anyway, you only asked questions about how we knew Maria and if we could think of any reason why someone would want her dead, and the answer is still no. I don't know why anyone would," Carl said, facing down the detective in an unusual display of confidence - that was only ruined when he looked at Louise as if to say: 'How did I do?'. Holly tried not to smirk. It was amazing what people would do for love.

DCI Chittenden raked a hand down his face.

"Fine! Un-arrest her," he said, pointing at Milly. The officer obliged. "We'll need to speak to you all again, but we'll do it tomorrow." Chittenden was admitting defeat for tonight.

Holly opened her mouth to remind him that she wasn't

actually in the society, so would be of little to no help at all, but then decided it would be better not to.

It was at that moment that the two car searchers returned, and they weren't empty-handed. A clear, plastic evidence bag held what looked to Holly like a large rock. The inside of the bag was smeared with red clots. There was no doubt at all that this was the weapon which had been used to stave in Maria's head - and had probably resulted in her death.

"This was in the light blue Fiat," the female police officer said.

"But that's my car!" Louise burst out and then bit her tongue. It didn't escape Holly's notice that Carl took a step away from her. Chittenden nodded and the officer moved over and placed the cuffs - that had been around Milly's wrists a moment before - onto Louise.

"But... but... I didn't do it! I've been out all day. I barely made it here on time," she protested.

Carl nodded. "It's true! We shared a lift and she was late. I think I'd have noticed if there was a blood-stained rock in the car." Carl's voice was starting to get heated.

Chittenden's lips narrowed into a thin line. "If you have an alibi this can all be sorted out... down at the station," he finished, and Louise was led away. Carl was left staring after her.

"How can I get back? I can't drive her car, and they've taken the keys," he complained loudly, until George stepped forward and offered to drop him back home. *Rather you than me*, Holly thought. She could sense that George wasn't thrilled to be lumbered with Carl. He shot a sorry look her way. Holly gave him a little smile back. She was sure he could handle Carl.

One thing was clear, the Amateur Archaeological Society's annual Christmas dinner was over before it had even started.

Holly was still musing over the events of the past couple of hours and trying to recall anything she'd noticed at the scene before the police had arrived, when George touched her arm. She jumped but recovered and smiled at him as brightly as she could.

"I'm sorry about tonight. You'll still be paid, of course," George said sincerely.

"It's fine. Don't worry about it at all. I have plenty of work at this time of year, and I couldn't possibly charge you for work I haven't done. I only hope that they find whoever killed Maria," Holly said, hoping that would make George feel a little better.

He looked at her for a long moment, his dark eyes lost deep in thoughts that even Holly couldn't read. "You're a detective. What do you think? Will you help the police to work it out?" he asked - rather naively in Holly's opinion. She didn't comment on that. George didn't share her own experience of the police...

"Something like this should be left to the professionals. No one is going to hire a private detective to solve a murder. Anyway, they already have quite a good lead." She said the last part in a lower voice, knowing that Carl was still nearby.

"I think you should look into it anyway, just in case you see something that the police missed. I bet you'd be great," George said, surprising Holly with his enthusiasm. "I'll help you out with any details. I know all about the society. I even have the minutes from our last few meetings, so I can fill you in on everything. You could come round to see me soon."

Holly nodded distractedly, her mind still on Maria's murder. What exactly had she seen today? Were there any details she'd missed? Somehow, she suspected that all of the answers lay in the very distant past.

"I'll see you soon," she said to George and walked off towards her car, already wondering what her investigation would turn up. At the moment, it looked pretty likely that Louise had done it. The presence of the murder weapon in a car that only she had the keys to was pretty damning evidence. Holly didn't know how she'd manage to wriggle out of that one.

She was so engrossed in her thoughts that she didn't notice the way George looked after her when she walked out into the darkness of the car park.

MISS MURDER

Sometimes in life, you find that the same people keep popping up for no apparent reason whatsoever. Holly had just discovered that this was definitely true in the case of the Amateur Archaeological Society. Before attending their annual Christmas dinner (although the dinner had never appeared) she'd rarely bumped into any of the members. The exceptions were perhaps seeing them in the distance at the front of the queue in the grocery store, or in the local paper when something out of the ordinary happened - such as an overly large marrow being grown - but now it was as if she couldn't avoid them.

Holly was out on a mid-morning run - enjoying how crisp and cold the winter air was against her face - when she nearly collided with Carl, who had stepped out from behind his car without looking. In all fairness, you usually didn't have to look both ways before stepping onto the pavement, but Holly had picked up quite a bit of speed - mostly due to the bag of chocolate drops she had left sitting on her kitchen table. She planned to indulge in a hot chocolate so sinful it would cancel out the next ten mornings' jogs.

"Morning Holly," Carl said briefly, hoisting a bag of golf clubs out of the boot of his car. "Did you hear that they released Louise? Isn't that great news?"

Holly tried not to look surprised. She'd thought that the evidence had been airtight, but if they'd let her go...

"I knew it all along. She wasn't lying when she said she had an alibi. She'd been at a baby shower all afternoon with a whole group of friends, and it had run on longer than expected. That was why she picked me up so late. The police agreed that there was no way she could have done it." His lips twitched a little. Holly could tell he was pleased.

"That's great news," she said to Carl, privately thinking that it meant the murderer was still at large. She hoped the police had some more leads up their sleeves. She nodded at Carl, motioning that she should really be going, and ran off again, pleased to be away from one of the poorer past decisions she'd made.

She rounded another corner and nearly bowled over Annie and Wilbur - the old couple who'd been at last night's meeting.

"Hello Holly," they greeted her, clearly pleased to have remembered her name. Given the traumatic events of last night, Holly thought it likely that none of them would be forgetting any details of the event in a hurry.

"Hi Annie. Hi Wilbur," she said, running on the spot.

"Did you hear they let Louise go? I'm not sure if that was wise." Wilbur stroked his chin thoughtfully.

Annie swatted him with her bag. "The police know what they're doing, dear! Also, Louise is such a lovely girl. I don't see her lumping someone on the head with a big rock. She always got on so well with Maria. *She's* not the archery fanatic either," Annie said, and then pursed her lips. Holly opened her mouth to ask a question, but the couple had dissolved into further bickering - this time about what was, or wasn't, for dinner that night. Holly wished them goodbye and left them to their discussion.

Her next encounter was when she popped to the shops after finishing her run. She had known that Bernie looked familiar, but it wasn't until she went to pay and saw him standing there in the supermarket manager's uniform that she realised why.

"Good to see you," he began, his smile false and his eyes already roving.

Holly swallowed down her revulsion and butted in before he could get any further. "I heard the news about Louise."

Bernie nodded, his gaze unable to meet hers because it never seemed to rise above chest level.

"I'm sure we'll all be dragged in for questioning now. The police will think that one of us did it!" His tone of voice made it clear that he thought the idea he could be implicated was ludicrous.

Holly tried her very best to look understanding. "I'm sure it will all be over soon," she offered, but Bernie didn't seem to be listening anymore.

"You should come round my house and make it easier for the police to ask their questions," he said abruptly.

Holly blinked. Had he just...? Was he really...? She blinked a bit more and then decided to make a small allowance, just in case his rudeness was some sort of affliction.

"I'm sure you like older men. All girls do," he added.

Both of Holly's eyebrows shot straight up. How had this man lived for so many years, presumably using the same deluded tactics, and yet no one had called him out on it? *Allow me to be the first!* she thought, mentally rolling her sleeves up before getting stuck into a lengthy ear bashing.

"... you're nothing more than a misogynistic, chauvinist, who's stuck in the caveman era!" she concluded her rant, and then wondered if she'd been too liberal with the word 'misogynist'. She tried not to count back.

Heads had turned all around the supermarket, and people were eyeing the showdown between her and the manager. Holly was just wondering if she might have taken things a tad too far, when he flicked a hand up into the air and made a noise of derision.

"Should have known you're one of those man-haters," he said, completely missing the point of everything that Holly had just said. "I wouldn't waste my time." He raised his voice before walking away, presumably so the watchers would think that she was the one bothering him - rather than the opposite being true.

Holly sighed and pushed her brown fringe back from her face. She'd probably used too many long words during her admonishing speech. The truth of the matter was simple: men like Bernie never changed - no matter what was said to them.

It wouldn't be long before Holly would sorely regret trying to re-educate the cantankerous man.

Having managed to get home without bumping into any more members of the Amateur Archaeological Society, Holly was ready for a night of rest and relaxation - starting with the relaxation bit. She walked up to the bathroom, which was one of the best bits of her little cottage, and the main reason she'd been renting here for so long. The room had a beautiful wooden floor (well-treated to avoid damp) and a very generous bathtub. Holly took her time browsing through her collection of bath bombs, before picking the one that smelt right for the night.

She'd just popped it into the water and was watching it

fizz and bubble when the landline rang. Normally, she'd have been tempted to leave it, but some intuition pushed her out of the room and onto the landing to answer the phone.

"Did you have an altercation today with Bernie Bolton?"

Holly frowned at the handset, quickly figuring out who it was that was calling her. It was typical that DCI Chittenden thought he could forgo any greeting sequence.

"Not an altercation, no. I just put him right when he tried to persuade me to go home with him. He was rude, and I told him so," she said flatly, wondering who would have bothered to tell the detective that. "Why do you ask?"

A nasty suspicion was forming in her mind.

"He's dead," came the reply.

THE PHARAOH'S ADVISOR

"I'm sorry to hear that," Holly said and let a beat pass before she added: "How did he die?"

Chittenden drew in a deep rattling breath that Holly heard all the way down the other end of the line. She privately thought it was probably high-time the detective considered quitting smoking.

"He was poisoned. It may have been part of the reason why he acted out of sorts earlier in the day with you," he allowed.

"What was the poison?" she asked and then bit her tongue. The police weren't going to give away all of the details.

She heard another sigh. "Digitalis, foxglove - which, according to the Archeological Society, is reminiscent of another murder mystery of the past. Some officer, or some-thing, may or may not have been poisoned by it... Somebody thought it was a fun idea to play copycat. It's bad news," he said and trailed off.

Holly knew exactly what he was saying. Maria's death

wasn't a one off. There was a serial killer loose in Little Wemley.

"I'm going to need you to account for your whereabouts at various times," the detective told her matter-of-factly.

Holly tried not to splutter. He really suspected her? Then she remembered that the late Bernie had felt much the same about being considered a possible candidate for the culprit. No one was above suspicion in this case.

"But Detective... I'd never even heard of Otzi the ice man before I went to play piano for the society! When Milly brought it up, it was the first I knew of it. Surely it's far more likely that it's one of the members?" she reasoned.

"Are you going to tell me that it's obvious who committed the murders? Because if you don't have anything useful to say, stop wasting my time. You're expected at the station in half an hour," he said and hung up. Saying goodbye was also apparently beneath him.

Holly thought of her bath - filled with warm, fragrant bubbles - and went back into the bathroom to pull the plug. She knew feeling annoyed because of a wasted bath was ridiculous when you considered that a man had died, but at the same time, why did she have to be dragged in so promptly? They didn't really think she'd killed him, did they? She chewed her lip, wondering what a professional private detective like her friend, Rob Frost, would do in this situation. *Probably dig a hole,* she thought and shook her head. She needed to get herself out of a hole... not make it even deeper.

"Let's get this straight... Bernie Bolton turned you down and then you got angry and started yelling long words at him," the DCI said.

Holly tried not to grind her teeth together. *Long words?!*

"Who said that?" she queried. The doughy man immediately clammed up. "Let me guess... it was a male witness," she said and sighed. Why was it that the people words like 'chauvinist' and 'misogynist' best described never knew their definitions? "That's not what happened," she added to be clear, and then launched into her own explanation. She was just getting to the part where she'd walked back to her house, and definitely hadn't killed Bernie, when the phone on the wall of the room rang.

"What? Oh, fine." DCI Chittenden glared at her. "You can go. Your alibi checks out for the time that Maria was murdered. Although, there is still a possibility you killed Bernie in a copycat killing - just to settle your personal grudge."

Holly tried to not let her mouth hang open too much. "The first time we ever spoke was at the Christmas dinner before Maria was found!" she complained, but the police detective just crossed his arms.

"So you say," he said and showed Holly to the door.

It was lucky, she reflected, that she'd hired barmy Becky. Where would she have been without an alibi?

She shook her head as she walked back down the street. The police were definitely clutching at straws if they were trying those tactics on her. Their evidence must be next to nothing.

She turned the corner and started down Duke Road, just one street away from her little cottage. Chrissy was arriving home with a bag of groceries. Holly waved at her, resigning herself to bumping into everyone that was involved with the case. This town was starting to feel a bit too small.

She'd only walked another twenty paces when she heard a scream.

Chrissy ran straight back out of her house. "Help!" she shrieked.

Holly dashed over, sensing her deep distress.

The other woman shut her front door and slid down the wall next to it, ending up sitting on the edge of her driveway. Her eyes stared at nothing and her jaw was slack.

"Chrissy, are you okay? What's wrong?" Holly asked, fearing that she'd been poisoned, too. It was then that she looked down and her sharp eyes picked out the flash of red that streaked Chrissy's left hand, crimson and bright.

"Aidan's in there... I... I think he's dead."

Holly knelt down next to her old acquaintance. She reached out and steadied her arm.

"I'm going to go in there and check. Do you think you can go to a next door neighbour, or use your mobile phone to call the police?" she asked, keeping her voice level. She'd heard that giving people who were panicking or in shock something to focus on could help. Chrissy nodded mutely. Holly hoped the instructions had got through.

With a sense of growing dread, she walked into Chrissy Bartholomew's house.

Groceries were strewn all over the hall floor where Chrissy had presumably dropped her bag when she'd seen the state of her living room... and of her boyfriend.

Holly raised her gaze and looked through the open door. Her stomach tied itself into a knot. There was no need to double-check if Aidan Banks was dead, his head had been so bashed in, it was misshapen. Holly tried to breathe through her mouth, so she wouldn't choke on the stench of death that hung in the air.

There was something odd about Aidan's face, something she hadn't noticed before...

She leaned through the doorway, careful not to disturb any of the blood that was liberally splashed around the room. Whoever had murdered Aidan Banks hadn't stopped hitting him as soon as he'd died. Holly felt her stomach twist around some more. She closed her eyes for a second, before focusing her attention on Aidan's left cheek. There was a raised, red area that hadn't been there when she'd met the TV presenter at the club dinner.

It looked like an infected mosquito bite.

Holly swallowed nervously. She got herself out of the room and back outside into the icy air. Chrissy was just ending a phone call.

"The police will be here in one minute," she confirmed.

They both sat on the step at the entrance to the house, looking up at the last fading rays of sunlight in silence. All Holly could think about was that bite mark and what it meant.

Unlike the members of the Amateur Archaeological Society, she wasn't an expert on ancient mysteries, but even she could recognise the similarities between Aidan Banks' murder and the death of the pharaoh, Tutankhamen.

"What about the bite? The police won't talk about it, but it could be a big part of this case," Holly said, taking a sip of her chai latte and looking up at George.

It was two days since Aidan had been murdered. They were sitting in the best (and the only) coffee shop in town, a small cafe called Auntie Something-Or-Others. (No, that really was the name).

George frowned and sat back in his chair. His own drink - a double espresso - was practically untouched.

"They're probably keeping quiet about it. They might be hoping it's a detail that only the murderer would know. What makes you think it's important?"

Holly wrinkled her nose and shook her head, as she mentally re-entered the murder scene. "It wasn't what I expected - the bite, I mean. There aren't any biting insects around at this time of year. It was either caused by something else, or... it was fake," she finished, feeling a little thrill of elation as she suspected she'd hit on the right answer.

George shrugged his slim shoulders, which were currently clothed in a lovely blue and dark grey striped sweater. "You could be right. After all, the killer clearly wants the deaths to mimic ancient murders and the mysteries that surround them." He sighed. "I know I said I thought it would be a good idea for us to talk and bounce some ideas around, but all I keep thinking is why? Why would any member of our little club want to start murdering the other members in such sick ways? It makes no sense at all! There isn't a clear motive for any of it. Perhaps it's someone on the outside who found our group offensive in some way and is now punishing us all." His eyes met Holly's and there was an awkward moment.

"Don't worry, I'm still a suspect," she told him, her tone dry. George had the good grace to blush.

Holly tilted her head and looked at the man sat across the small table from her. "Have you been okay? I know what it's like, wondering if..."

"...If you're next," George finished for her.

She nodded.

He ran a hand through his blonde hair and sighed. "It's on my mind, of course. I can't help looking through the history books and trying to figure out which murder from the past I'd be matched up with." He shuddered. "But you've got to get on with life. There's still work to do, and things still blow up all over the place. Just the other day, I had to get Carl out to fix a sink that had decided to flood for no reason that I could find. Then Chrissy came over wanting to borrow a book on a Roman site." Holly tried not to bristle at the mention of the other woman being so close to George. She had no right to be jealous.

"It was only after the news of Bernie's death came through that I wondered about the wisdom of being alone with another member…" He frowned and shook his head. "I'm still not sure it's one of us."

Another silence fell. They both looked out of the window at the street outside. Few people were walking around in the cold weather. The sky was a depressing slate grey, although nothing fell from it yet.

Holly sighed. The weather was only exacerbating her current mood. This spate of killings had also killed off her business - from local sources, anyway. People had noticed her trips to the police station… and people had gossiped. Holly supposed there were some who thought she'd picked up a few pointers during her stay at Horn Hill House, or had perhaps even been involved in the mass killings herself. The fingers on her right hand itched when she remembered she technically was a killer. Although - killing someone with a book wasn't one of the most bloodthirsty methods of dispatch.

"Weapons…" she mused, as something snapped into place in her brain. "Where are the weapons?" she said a little louder, her eyes focusing on George.

He looked mildly interested again. "Yes, there's the rock… but they haven't found what was used on Aidan. I suppose with Bernie, they'll probably never know. Half the town has foxgloves in their gardens. They're a regular plague!"

Holly finished her latte, reflecting for a moment that it was a shame that this was definitely not a date. When she'd first met George, she'd had her hopes. Now she could see his mind was far from thinking about any of that. She couldn't blame him. He thought he was on the murderer's kill list, and she knew exactly how that felt.

"I have a feeling the weapons will turn up," she said.

George looked at her in surprise. She pushed her fringe out of her eyes for a second. "Look... that rock wasn't in Louise's car by accident. Someone wanted to make her appear suspicious. The killer is playing with us."

"But why? And why make the deaths mirror history?" George's hands shook a little as he downed his coffee. Holly privately thought a double espresso may not have been the wisest choice. She impulsively reached out and steadied him, before withdrawing as quickly as she'd done it, her cheeks already colouring.

"If we knew that, I think we could probably solve the mystery."

CUPID'S ARROW

A day later, Holly was no closer to cracking the case, and she had a nasty feeling that it wouldn't be long before the killer struck again. The first three deaths had been pretty close in time to each other, and she didn't see why they'd slow down now that they had a taste for it. It wasn't as if there was a shortage of historical deaths for them to choose from. Everyone from history was dead.

She'd invited George along on a research mission to keep his mind on other things. As they walked down the little side-street that led away from the main high-street, Holly wondered if this was a good idea. Most people thought the narrow cobbled streets of the town were quaint. She just thought they made it much more likely that you'd twist an ankle.

The other reason she'd never normally have come down the side street is because of the shop that existed at the end of the narrow road. In a town as small as Little Wemley, it was unusual for there to be a specialist costume shop, but they had one. Even more remarkably, it had been in business ever since Holly could remember.

The reason she wasn't fond of this particular cobbled road was because of the clown the shop kept in its window. It was a life-size monstrosity that contained some sort of sensor, which meant it shrieked with laughter and flashed its LED eyes at you whenever you walked by. She was a rational adult and knew that clowns were nothing to worry about, but that didn't stop this particular clown from giving her the heebie-jeebies.

Unfortunately, the creepy costume shop was their final destination.

The man behind the counter of the costume shop didn't fit with his slightly creepy surroundings. His face was round and jovial and you'd struggle to get the smile to fall off his face. Holly immediately decided she hated him.

"Excuse me please, do you sell any costume makeup - for example, to make fake scars?" George asked.

The counter man nodded, far too happily.

Holly stared at the rear of the window clown and wondered if perhaps the noise of its maniacal laughter had finally driven this poor shopkeeper loopy, and he was now stuck with that smile on his face for good.

"What sort of kit were you looking for? We have lots," he said, gesturing to a wall of brightly coloured makeup. Holly's eyes alighted on a couple of very likely possibilities. The costume shop's makeup was surprisingly good quality. She thought that her theory was looking more promising by the second.

"Have you sold any kits recently?" she inquired.

The man rubbed his bald head.

"They're pretty good sellers. I've sold a few in the past week. Two women wanted some for a birthday party their children were going to. A young man wanted to prank his girlfriend, and then another man bought a kit but didn't hang around to chat." The shopkeeper looked disappointed about that last man, but Holly's ears pricked up.

"What did the last man look like? If you don't mind," she hastily added.

She needn't have worried. The shopkeeper loved to talk.

"There's not much to say about him really. I told you he wasn't the friendly sort. He was an odd kind of fellow, dressed in a beige waistcoat with pockets and a floppy hat."

Holly looked at George, who had already turned several shades paler.

"That sounds like Dylan," they both said together. They thanked the man and left the shop, where they stood outside the clown window wondering what to do next.

"But it can't be him! He wouldn't hurt a fly," George was saying, while Holly chewed her lip, remembering the way he'd argued with Bernie at the Christmas dinner.

She wondered what they should do with the information. It should be a matter for the police, but after the way they'd treated her lately, she wasn't feeling inclined to be helpful. She also wasn't sure if they'd even be interested.

She sighed and frowned at the ground, realising that this information could be the difference between life or death for whomever was unfortunate enough to be the next intended victim. She'd just have to suck up her prejudices.

Holly's eye was caught by something on the ground. Her frown deepened.

"George..." she said, staring at the dark red spot just in front of her foot, and the trail of dried droplets... which she could now see led down the tiny alley by the side of the costume shop.

"That looks an awful lot like blood," he commented, his face turning even whiter.

They started to follow the trail that led to nothing good at all.

"George, don't!" she said when her companion reached out and lifted the flap of the stained cardboard box, which had been balanced on the bin. It was from this box that the red liquid had been leaking.

George had already touched the flap and the open box now displayed its grisly contents. A crude flint axe was inside, its sharpened edge clogged with gore. Holly swallowed and took a step back, but George's eyes were fixed on the deadly weapon.

"Don't touch it," she warned, having learned that lesson the hard way during the Enviable Emerald case.

"I'm not going to," George reassured her, his voice strangely calm.

Holly pulled out her phone and started dialling. "We've got to call the police. This weapon doesn't fit any of the other murders, which means someone else is either dead, or seriously wounded..." She paused when the phone started ringing.

"There's just one problem," George said, still staring at the axe. "That's mine."

Holly hung up just as the operator started speaking.

"What?" she asked, suddenly feeling nervous.

"It's my axe. I'm not the one who used it, but it was on display in my living room. I collect ancient weapons, you see," he said.

Holly struggled to draw in her next breath. "You know how bad this looks, right?" was all she could think to say.

George nodded. "It must have been stolen by someone. Make the call. The police have to know. I just hope they'll believe it wasn't me," he said, turning his eyes on Holly, who felt her heart jump in her chest. They both knew he was really asking for her to believe it wasn't him.

At this moment, she wasn't certain of anything.

"I don't like this George guy," Rob immediately said after she called him and recited the whole sorry story. She'd been hoping for an outsider's opinion, thinking that it might turn up something she'd missed due to being too involved. She probably shouldn't have chosen Rob.

"I know it looks bad right now, but I'm telling you… he's nice! He doesn't seem like a murderer to me. Anyway, if he was, he's had plenty of opportunities to kill me, and he hasn't," she finished, her voice sober.

She heard Rob hiss on the other end of the line. "Plenty of opportunities? I hope you're not dating a psychopath?!"

Holly spluttered and protested. "We aren't dating!"

"Jeez, but you want to! He's bad news. It sounds to me like he's the leader of the club. It could be he feels like he owns everyone who joins, and that's why he thinks he has a right to kill them." He paused. "Look, I'm coming up for a visit. Could you try to not get yourself killed before then?"

"Rob, I'm perfectly capable. Becky and I have everything under control here," she said, shooting Becky a big smile across the room.

Becky pretended not to have seen.

"Becky? Who's Becky?" Rob asked.

"My secretary," Holly said, a light frown creasing her forehead.

"What does she look like, I mean what is she like… at her job?"

Holly's frown deepened.

"Terrible, if you must know," she said, smiling even more brightly at Becky.

"Do I detect a hint of jealousy?" Rob teased.

Holly rolled her eyes. She'd forgotten that talking to Rob

had that effect on her eyeballs. "I'm afraid it's the truth. I didn't have many options."

"Sure... sure," Rob said, his voice telling her he didn't believe a word.

"What are you working on right now? I wouldn't want to drag you away from a case," she said, hoping he'd take the hint.

"Nah, it's fine. I've been, you know... digging holes. The usual. So far, nothing really interesting has turned up. Just a few unexpected archaeological finds while on the trail of some bullion thieves from the 1920s. Good for the coffers, but not what I'm looking for." Rob sighed.

Holly tilted her head thoughtfully. When she'd first met Rob at Horn Hill House the other detectives had hinted - quite heavily - that Rob's cases weren't always intentionally solved. His greatest strength was his ability to dig up the truth. Literally. Whether it was buried treasure, stolen money, or even collapsing the tunnel of would-be bank robbers, Rob was a menace with a spade. But Holly had a feeling his mind wasn't always on the case. It was almost as if there was something he was forever searching for and hadn't yet found. She wondered if he'd ever tell her what it was.

"Didn't we agree to share all income fifty-fifty?" she joked.

Rob coughed out a laugh. "Funnily enough, no!"

"Worth a try," Holly said with a smile.

That was another thing about Rob. He claimed to not have a lot of money. She believed him when he said that he never took any of the stolen goods he uncovered home with him, but she knew as well as anyone that there were such things as finder's fees... and Rob was one hell of a finder. *It's none of your business!* Holly reminded herself.

"I'll leave as soon as I can," Rob announced.

Holly grudgingly gave him her address before hanging

up. On one hand, it would be great to see Rob - especially as she wasn't exactly sure how she felt about him - but she objected to him butting in on her case and saying that George was the bad guy. She chewed her lip, thinking of the time she'd spent with George. They hadn't known each other for long, but she just couldn't picture it.

She sighed and rested her head on the table. Was it terrible that she was just a little bit excited to see George and Rob together? She frowned and shook her head. Now was really not the time for picking an eligible bachelor, especially when the body count of this case was steadily rising.

She jerked back to life when her house phone rang.

"You're coming in for questioning," the voice on the other end announced. Holly deduced it was Stephan Chittenden, just from his unique phone manner. She'd expected a call. George had gone in earlier that day, but the police had needed time to look at the weapon, talk to George, and then (theoretically) figure out who was dead.

"Did you find anyone?" she asked.

The long silence on the other end of the phone told her all she needed to know.

"Just get here," Chittenden growled and hung up.

PSYCHO KILLER, QU'EST-CE QUE C'EST?

Jayne was dead.

The police had phoned all of the society members. When she hadn't answered, they'd paid the young woman a visit and had discovered a scene even bloodier than Aidan's.

A sergeant who was doing his best to model himself on DCI Chittenden sat on the opposite side of the table. His smile remained non-existent. It was as if everyone in the local police department had decided to play 'bad cop'.

"How well do you know George Strauss?" the officer began. Holly felt a shiver run down her spine. There was something about the way he said it that made her suspect it wasn't just the stolen weapon that had made them suspect George.

"We only met a couple of weeks ago. He made a really last minute booking for the club's dinner, and I agreed to play. We've since met for coffee, and another time to visit the costume shop to check a theory I had." She looked at the police officer, hoping he'd give her something in return for her honesty.

All she got was a frown.

"You shouldn't be investigating anything. This is a police matter. Anything you find should be passed on to us."

"It was passed on to you! As soon as we found the axe we called," she said, but all she got in return was a withering glare.

"You should have told us before you found it," he complained - so ridiculously Holly didn't even bother to argue.

"Back to your question. The answer is: not very well at all," she admitted and then clammed up. Now the officer would have to contribute something.

Fortunately, he liked the sound of his own voice.

"We think we've found our killer," he said, transparently thrilled to have one over the 'private detective'.

"You really think it's George?" she said, still unwilling to entertain the idea.

"It looks that way. He's a historian whose hobbies include archery, and the weapon you both 'just happened' to stumble upon belonged to him." The officer shook his head. "Maybe it was his way of impressing you. Why he'd want to do that, I don't know..."

Holly ignored the last part. She was thinking back to the way George had looked when he'd seen the weapon. He'd been pale and scared. Unless he was a brilliant actor, she'd have staked a lot that he hadn't known the axe was in the box.

"But the guy in the costume shop described a customer who looked like Dylan. He came in to buy the scar kit."

"Criminals wear disguises," the officer said, as if that solved everything. She knew she couldn't be sure, but disguised or not, wouldn't the shopkeeper have recognised George? He'd seemed more observant than most.

"We'll know for sure any second now," the man said, his eyes fixed on the phone on the wall.

Holly crossed her arms. "Why am I here if you're so sure it's George?" she asked, already suspecting the answer.

"You two seem pretty friendly. Chittenden thinks there may have been an accomplice for some of the murders."

Holly snorted. She couldn't help herself. It was just beyond ridiculous.

"Actually, I think he's just doing it to waste my time," she muttered, finally starting to understand why all of the private detectives she'd met at Horn Hill House had not been the police's number one fans.

The phone rang just as Holly said 'Well, if you're not arresting me...'

"They found it? I knew it! Chittenden is always right," the sergeant said excitedly. He even smiled before he hung up. "The golf club that was used to batter Aidan to death was just found in George's house. Case closed."

The silence stretched out before Holly meekly asked: "Can I go?" and was released.

She walked along the streets on her way back home, wishing she'd brought a thicker coat with her. She also wished this case made more sense. The police were sure they'd got their man, but something was tickling in the back of Holly's mind. There was something that she was missing...

"Hello Holly!" Wilbur called from his front garden. Holly nodded politely to him, unwilling to be the first to share the news. She walked a little faster and wondered whether she should call Rob.

No.

He was already convinced that George had done it.

She sighed. What if she was wrong? Perhaps she'd got too involved with the case and couldn't see what was right in front of her. She twisted her fingers around her keys, using the motion to calm her mind so she could think.

She almost had it…

"Evening," a voice said. Holly looked up to see Carl standing right in front of her, before something hit her on the head from behind and she blacked out.

Holly woke up with one hell of a headache, but at least she woke up.

She looked around and found she was tied to a chair in a cold, dark room. She was in someone's cellar. It looked like the house had been built on a natural cave, she observed, as she looked around and dreamily wondered if they'd reported it. She'd heard that buildings of this nature were quite rare. She tried to stand and quickly remembered she was tied up. Then her last memory of Carl saying 'Evening' came flooding back, and she realised how much trouble she was in.

It was a lot.

Right now, she was sitting in the cellar of a murderer. *No… two murderers!* she realised.

And she had no way out.

"So… you're the world's worst private detective," Carl said, walking down the stone stairs that led into Holly's prison.

"You and Louise…" Holly said.

There was an excited giggle from behind Carl. "Ooh, she has worked it out," Louise said. Holly wished her voice wasn't so shrill. It was hurting her head.

"You've been working together. Carl… you killed Maria and must have planted the weapon in Louise's car and made it look like someone could plausibly have broken in to plant it. You did it before you even got to the Christmas dinner.

That meant she had an alibi. The police assumed you did, too, because you were waiting around for her to pick you up. That in turn meant you needed a lift and couldn't possibly have walked all the way out to the town hall, only to walk back again..." Holly paused, her head felt like it had an axe embedded in it. With these two around, it might not be long before that actually happened.

"Let her go on, this is interesting," Louise said, holding Carl's arm and looking up at him adoringly.

He grumbled and picked up the modern-looking bow that was leaning against the cave wall. "We've got time. But get on with it," he said.

Holly chewed her lip as she quickly put everything together and wished she'd managed to figure out what had been bugging her before.

"The golf clubs... I saw you with the golf clubs the other day before you killed Aidan. I assume you stole them from George when you went to fix his sink?" she asked and found herself starting to loathe this awful pair - who were looking more proud by the second.

"That's right. I took the axe, too. The problem was with the drain... I was the one who caused it by blocking it on the outside of the property, so it would all back up," Carl announced.

"George is so scatterbrained, we thought he wouldn't notice a few things going missing. Golf was one of his past hobbies. He always flits from one to another," Louise explained. Holly gave her a questioning look. The other woman beamed. "He's only lived near Little Wemley for a few months, that's why no one knows him, but I used to work in London at the same office," Louise told her.

Several things suddenly made sense to Holly. Louise's prior knowledge of George's habits and the town's view of him as an outsider made him the perfect person to frame for their crimes.

"You murdered Aidan and made it look like Tutankhamen. Carl - I suppose at that murder you were playing the role of the jealous, older advisor to the pharaoh - who was most likely the killer in the original murder? The advisor then married the murdered king's wife against her wishes. I know you never got over Chrissy, but to kill Aidan like that…" Holly trailed off, feeling sick when she remembered the scene of Aidan's murder and realised her own scene of death wasn't far away.

"What?!" Louise said, whirling on Carl.

He shook his head. "It's one of the theories about the original death. She's just trying to divide us," he told her - rather cleverly for Carl.

"I still think we should have killed Chrissy," Louise pouted, but Carl ignored her sulkiness.

"You wore a disguise to the costume shop, so the owner would describe someone who looked like Dylan," Holly added. She noticed Carl was looking at her with more predatory intent. His grip on the bow was tightening.

She didn't have much time left.

"How about Bernie? How did he die?" she asked.

This time it was Louise who spoke up. "That old fool? He was easy. He tried it on with anything that moved. I got myself invited over to his house and spiked his coffee."

"Why did Jayne have to die?" Holly questioned, and then realised the answer as soon as she said it. Jayne's eyes had wandered to Aidan at the Christmas party. She was probably used to picking up Chrissy's leftovers, which meant that she and Carl had probably had a dalliance or two themselves.

Louise's stony face confirmed it, but Carl looked a bit awkward. "Louise did that one," he said and raised the bow.

"Wait a second… how does killing me fit in?" Holly

desperately played for time and wondered if there was a way she could talk them out of this. She didn't have any hope of rescue. No one would even notice she was missing until Rob arrived in town.

"The police are going to be bailing George, probably sometime later tonight, or even tomorrow. There's a lot of evidence against him, but annoyingly, I know he has an alibi for Maria's death. That was part of the reason why Carl put her in the freezer. We hoped it might make people question her time of death. You know... like they do in films and stuff," Louise said and then sighed. "But we forgot about the turkey."

Holly's mind was racing now. "What happens now? You kill me, and somehow that will prove George did it once and for all because he'll have been released by the police?"

Carl and Louise exchanged a glance.

"Actually, it'll probably only be another inconvenience for George. There's evidence, but they'll figure out he didn't do it in the end. We don't really care. We're going away. We've had our fun. Louise and I just don't like you," Carl said, and Holly wanted to scream.

"This town is too small for us now. We can go anywhere we want and do it all over again," Louise whispered lovingly to Carl.

Now Holly felt sick. "Sounds great, guys. Here's the thing, how about you let me go? You said it yourselves... George probably won't go down for this, so is there really any reason to kill me? You could just let me go..."

The pair laughed.

It had been worth a shot.

"You also know too much. The police will probably put two and two together when we suddenly move away, but by then, it will be too late. We'll be gone, and they'll never find us," Carl said, and Holly realised it was her time to die.

"Just one more thing…" she said weakly, staring down the shaft of an arrow. "How is shooting me in the face with an arrow historically accurate?"

"It's the Battle of Hastings. King Harold was shot through the eye. No one knows who shot him, although there were numerous claims. That's why it's so appropriate for you. You're the owner of the most successful new business in town, which can symbolise kingship. And all because you survived at Horn Hill House." Carl shook his head to show how disgusted he was by the other mass murderer's failings. "An arrow through the eye will be your end and your death will have fingers pointing in the wrong direction, before they realise it was us all along. We'll be long gone by then."

"Why make it all about history in the first place?" Holly asked, trying to make it sound casual whilst she tested her bonds. It was no use. She was really stuck.

"It was the society that brought us together. When we began looking at ancient murder mysteries, Carl and I really enjoyed it. That was when we started dating. I finally let slip my little fantasy, only to find out that Carl shared it," Louise simpered.

Holly felt the bile rise in her throat. She'd been living in the same town as two genuine psychopaths and hadn't known anything about it until now.

"It's been so much fun," Carl confirmed. "We get to see what it must have looked like when those people died, so long ago. We recreate their deaths and we get to watch. It's the best thing I've ever done in my life. In fact, I wasn't really living until now," he said, raising the bow. "Try not to move or you'll ruin my aim," he warned, which was Holly's cue to thrash around wildly.

THE EXPLOSIVE ENDING

There was a muffled boom.

Holly dazedly wondered if Carl had shot her with a gun instead of an arrow, but no - she was still in one piece.

She opened an eye and saw that her would-be killers were both staring at the cellar door that had just been blasted off its hinges.

"Holly!" a voice called. She recognised George when he staggered down into the room. He slipped on the steps, having misjudged his footing in all the smoke and dust. It was lucky that he slipped, or the arrow Carl had already had notched and drawn on his bow would have got him right between the eyes. Fortunately, it sailed over his head and out through the doorway - where it harmed no one.

"ARRGH!"

Holly heard a scream of pain from outside the door.

"An arrow? Are you serious?!"

Holly was elated to hear the familiar voice of Rob Frost.

"Looks like there'll be three bodies instead of two," Carl said. He fired blindly out of the door, before re-notching and drawing with the bow fixed on George - who only stood a foot away from him.

"There's something you should know about archery," George said, calmly standing there until Carl released the string. George nimbly stepped to the side. "It only works well long range," he informed the killer and booted the other man in the crotch.

It wasn't the most heroic of takedowns, but it had the desired effect. Carl dropped the bow and crumpled on the ground. While all this was going on, Rob had staggered in with an arrow sprouting from his thigh, before promptly falling off the steps and landing on Louise. Holly wouldn't like to say whether it had been intentional or not.

A minute later, both villains were tied up.

Holly leaned against the wall at the entrance of the cellar, standing between Rob and George. "Thanks for saving me, but how did you know?" The two men exchanged a look over Holly's head that she didn't see.

"I arrived in town earlier than expected. Your secretary girl told me you'd been taken in for questioning," Rob said and frowned. "She was very nice to me, by the way. I think you're being too hard on her."

Holly ground her teeth and didn't bother trying to explain to Rob that it was because he was male and good looking.

"I'd been released by the police - although, they said they were going to have an officer check up on me every couple of hours. They let me know you'd also been let go. I have alibis for a couple of the deaths. The police couldn't figure out how I could have done it - despite the weaponry evidence," George said... and not without some bitterness.

Holly could empathise.

"I was on my way to the station and George was on his way back home. We bumped into each other and realised you'd gone missing. We walked back towards the station and that's when we saw your keys on the ground, halfway under a parked car," Rob informed her.

Holly's eyebrows shot up. She suddenly remembered she'd been playing with them before the villainous pair had knocked her out.

"Then, I just figured out the rest," Rob said, none too modestly.

George glared at him. "I was the one who realised that whoever had framed me must have got into my house. That left me with Chrissy or Carl. You'd already told me how Chrissy reacted to Aidan's death. That didn't sound much like a coldblooded killer to me. I've also called on her since, and she's not the same person she was before what happened to Aidan. I knew she was innocent."

"That and the keys were right outside Carl's house," Rob said. George just shrugged.

"It's lucky I always carry a few army regulation explosives with me," Rob continued.

Holly squinted at him. "Army regulation?"

Rob shuffled his feet. "I'd already sneaked into Jack's room and stolen them as a joke before he was, you know... disintegrated. I'm sure he'd have wanted me to have them," Rob said, wiping an imaginary tear from his eye.

Holly sighed but didn't bother contradicting him. Rob seemed to have the luck of the devil, but this time, that luck had been extended to her - and for that she was grateful. Stolen grenades and all.

"I don't even think the door was locked. The front door was open, but he didn't let me try the cellar door," George said.

Holly glared at Rob, who smiled back at her.

"You've got to make a proper entrance!"

She resisted the temptation to ask just how long it had

taken him to set up the explosives and also resisted the urge to tell him just how close she'd been to getting an arrow through her eye.

"At least we're all fine," she said, deciding to make the best of it.

"Yeah, apart from the arrow in my leg," Rob said.

Holly looked down at it. "Oh."

Rather a lot of blood was leaking from the wound. She suspected that the tip may have pierced a vein.

"We should probably get you to a hospital."

A day later, nearly dying felt like a surreal bad dream. The police had arrived and taken away the crazed killers, and Rob had been carted off to hospital. There was no acknowledgement of anyone's help by the police force, but Holly would always remember that she owed her life to Rob and George.

She hummed a tune as she added the chocolate drops to her hot chocolate. She supposed that made her and Rob even again. A thought flashed across her mind as she wondered if he would withdraw his support of the agency now he didn't owe her a life debt, but she shook her head. Bridges like that could be crossed when everything was back to normal again. Anyway, the agency had started to turn a small profit - despite Becky's brusque handling of calls. Holly thought it may turn out to be a success after all - especially now that the townspeople would hopefully revise their opinions of her potentially being involved in the recent spate of murders.

There was a knock at the door. Holly got up to answer it, knowing that the chocolate would be perfectly melted by the time she returned.

She'd been expecting the postman, but when she opened

the door, Rob stood there with a bunch of flowers and an envelope.

"For me?" she asked, a little startled.

"No, for me. You didn't send any, so I got them for myself," he said, walking straight past her into the kitchen. "Thanks by the way. They're my favourites! How did you know?" He plonked himself down on a chair and took a slurp of her hot chocolate.

"You're an idiot," she said. "I heard it only took them an hour to fix you up. You spent the rest of the night at the local pub telling your sob story to anyone who'd listen. Don't try and fish for sympathy from me."

Rob grinned and lowered the bouquet and envelope onto the table. He was about to say something else when there was another knock at the door.

"George!" Holly said when she answered it, surprised, but pleased, to see the other man. She invited him in. The two men sat on opposite sides of the table, one dark and one blonde, both attractive in their own ways.

"I just wanted to check on you," George said, sitting down and eyeing how settled Rob looked drinking his stolen hot chocolate.

"Would you like a hot chocolate, George?" she offered, already regretting having to share her special drink. If it was in the name of teaching Rob a lesson, she could deal with it.

"Shouldn't you be at work, or something?" Rob asked - quite rudely.

"Ah... well, I'm one of the company directors, so I can decide when I go in," George casually dropped in.

Rob's expression grew even darker.

Holly placed the new hot chocolate down in front of George and wondered if there was a way to diffuse this situation.

"You're the digging detective, right? Shouldn't you be

working on a case?" George inquired, just as innocently as Rob had.

Holly raised her eyebrows at Rob's nickname. She hadn't known he had one, but it made sense.

"I've got to rest up before returning to work. The arrow wound makes it hard to dig. I'm sure you know all about that though, being an archery expert. I bet you can judge trajectories too..." Rob said. He left it hanging that he thought George's slip on the steps had been deliberate.

Holly decided to make herself a new hot chocolate and to double the chocolate bit. She was going to need it.

"There was a lot of smoke around. I'm sure no one really knew what was going on," she said fairly.

Both men looked annoyed.

"Oh, Holly, I wanted to let you know that we're having a club meeting... what's left of the society anyway," George admitted, looking sad. "It's the last ever one. We're just meeting to talk through everything that has happened and lay it all to rest, as best we can."

Holly noticed he sounded emotionally shattered. Sometimes the true depth of a tragedy took time to sink in. It was only a while after everything had happened that you might do something ordinary and realise the true extent of what had been lost. For George, that was the Amateur Archaeological Society.

"I was just wondering..." he carried on, his voice hesitant.

"I'll come," she said and smiled encouragingly.

He nodded, his eyes fixed on the table.

Rob had folded his arms and was looking between them. "I've just remembered. I do have a case I should be working on. See you around, Holly," Rob said, draining his drink and getting to his feet. He walked towards the door, clearly trying to disguise his limp.

Holly shot an apologetic glance in George's direction and

hurried after the retreating man. "You don't have to go. What is up with you?"

The detective turned in the doorway. "I get it. You like him," Rob said simply.

Holly frowned, but then nodded. "Sure, he's nice. But I like you, too," she added.

Rob sighed. "I'll see you around. I actually do have a case I should be getting back to. There's something I need to find," he said, his eyes growing misty. Holly was reminded that she really needed to ask Rob about what it was he was looking for. She knew that today wasn't the day.

"Okay, well... could we talk soon? There's lots to discuss about the agency. That is... if you still want to do it?"

Rob's mouth twitched up. "Of course I do! I like the business cards. They're great for chatting up girls," he said and waved goodbye, before stiffly walking back to his pickup truck.

Holly was left standing on the doorstep wondering if she'd made a mistake.

"Everything okay?" George asked, coming up behind her.

Holly nodded, finally turning away from the outside world.

"Hey, I was wondering if... uh, as well as the meeting, my office is having a Christmas party, the day before Christmas Eve. I know that's only a couple of days away, but I was wondering..."

"You want me to play piano?" Holly asked, feeling her heart sink inexplicably.

George pulled a face. "No! We've already got entertainment... that is, I mean - I'm sure you'd be better. Although, I haven't actually heard you play yet." He fell over his words and shook his head furiously. "That's not what I meant. I was wondering if you wanted to go with me?"

Holly felt herself being pulled in two directions as she

thought of Rob's departure and George's invitation. George pulled an envelope out of his pocket and handed it to her.

"You can let me know?" he said kindly and walked up her garden path, pausing to wave to her at the top.

Holly closed the door and went back inside to sit at her kitchen table, placing the envelope beside the one that Rob had left her. She looked at the bouquet of flowers and the two sealed envelopes and wondered what on earth she should do with this new mystery.

Unfortunately, the mystery of men was something she doubted she'd ever be able to solve.

MURDER BENEATH THE MISTLETOE

THE SANTA CLAUS CONUNDRUM

Holly Winter sat at her kitchen table looking at the two envelopes in front of her. She'd opened both and had read the contents of each, but was no closer to a solution.

One envelope contained an invitation to George Strauss's Christmas work party in just a couple of days' time. The other envelope held a handwritten note from Holly's private detective friend, Rob Frost. The note simply read: 'We need to have a serious talk.'

In Holly's experience, serious talks were never about anything good. You didn't have a serious talk about the plausibility of unicorns having once existed, or what a tyrannosaurus rex would look like trying to put on a duvet cover with its tiny arms. Serious talks were always about relationships going wrong, or finding yourself deep in debt with no way out. The main thing that bothered her was that she didn't even know what he wanted to have a serious talk about. He'd written the note before inviting himself into her house. It had also been before George had turned up and made things awkward.

Holly couldn't remember committing any grievous offence against Rob prior to that time, or even during the visit. She wondered what was on Rob's mind while also not really wanting to call and find out. It was nearly Christmas, and having narrowly avoided being murdered for the second time in less than a month, the last thing she wanted to think about was anything serious.

After a brief period of indecision, she picked up the phone and dialled.

"Hi… I'd like to accept your invitation to the Christmas party," Holly said when George picked up the phone. After a few further pleasantries were exchanged, she hung up and got herself ready for another day's work at her private detective agency, *Frost and Winter*.

When she arrived, she wasn't surprised to find that her secretary, Becky, was nowhere to be seen. Having only just begun her business, Holly was still discovering whether or not it could truly be profitable, which meant she'd been unable to take the financial risk of employing a full-time secretary. She'd been reduced to employing a part-timer. Unfortunately, she was getting exactly what she paid for - which was, admittedly, not a lot.

Holly opened up the little office, her breath clouding in the morning's chill. She couldn't believe that Christmas was suddenly so close and that she was unexpectedly the owner of her very own detective agency. One month ago, she'd never have predicted it.

The agency had come about after Holly had won the chance to attend the annual meeting of the seven greatest detectives in the UK. However, what was supposed to have been a weekend of good food and thrilling stories had soon turned to murder and mayhem, as an unknown killer had picked the detectives off one by one. Holly and Rob Frost (one of the great detectives) were the only survivors. It had been Rob who had given her the little push she needed to start the business.

Unusually for a brand new business, she'd had a good start and had solved many small local mysteries. However, after a woman was murdered at the local Amateur Archaeological Society Christmas dinner - where Holly had just so happened to be playing piano that night - her name had been dragged through the mud when the police had tried to pin the crime on her.

Holly pushed her dark fringe out of her eyes as she straightened her desk and even turned on the string of LED lights she'd strung around the place, just to look a bit more festive. It was lucky that George and Rob had managed to stop the real Amateur Archeological Society psychopaths and save her life. It also meant that business was back to normal. The townspeople seemed to have collectively decided that she wasn't a deranged killer after all. Once again, they trusted her to find their lost cats and adulterous husbands.

Holly flipped through a few case files, staring at a whole collection of furry faces and a few lost items (most likely mislaid, rather than stolen).

She sat back and sighed, before putting the files to one side and mentally sorting through the few nice dresses she owned. Which one would be right for George's work do? The invitation hadn't been very specific. It could be full black tie, or it could be smart casual. She could call and ask George, but she wanted to show some initiative. She chewed on her lip for a moment, mentally dithering over a short cocktail-type dress in black satin and tulle. It would do, no matter the dress code. It was smart enough for black tie and would only look a little too dressy if it was smart casual, as so many events were these days. She smiled. Every girl had to have *that* little black dress. It was all you needed to get yourself out of a fashion crisis.

She was still day-dreaming about a night of dancing and witty conversation with George when her first customer walked into the office. Despite her brilliant powers of deduction, Holly didn't immediately realise that this rather small person *was* a customer.

"Hi, are you okay? Are your parents around?" she asked the small girl, immediately worried that she was in some sort of trouble. She had ginger pigtails and a chubby, rosy face. Her teeth were at that awkward stage of falling out, so her smile was more gap-toothed than a sixty-year-old with a boiled sweet addiction.

"My parents don't know I'm here," the little girl whispered, setting alarm bells ringing in Holly's head. Holly estimated that she was about six years old. That was hardly an age to be wandering the streets on your own. Little Wemley may once have considered itself a sleepy, safe town, but recent local events showed that danger lurked where you least expected it.

"Where are your parents?" Holly asked again, wondering what the best thing to do with a runaway child was. She didn't think she had any pet carriers large enough…

"They're outside, but they don't know I'm here. They said they'd cover their eyes," the girl told her.

Holly inwardly breathed a sigh of relief. She was willing to bet the girl's parents had peeked.

"I've got a tough case for you," the little girl said.

Now Holly wanted to find her parents to ask them not to treat her agency as a play thing…

"It's Santa Claus. I want to know if he's real or not. A horrible older boy at school said it was all made up, but I think it's true. I want you to prove it, so I can show him."

Holly opened her mouth and then shut it again. She knew she didn't possess a maternal bone in her body, so her immediate knee-jerk reaction was to tell the girl the harsh truth. It was only the pair of eyes that glared at her through the office window that made her hesitate. She knew who those eyes belonged to.

"Sure, I'll use all of my resources looking into it," she told her youngest client yet.

The girl frowned at her.

"You'd better come up with the goods! I want to know before Christmas Eve. It has got to be infallible evidence," she said the words carefully, "or Max Dyer won't believe me."

Holly glanced at her calendar.

Great. She had two days.

She was about to open her mouth again when something else caught her eye. She looked up to see a wad of cash waving up and down in the window.

"Yes, I'll definitely have something for you by then," Holly said, a little grudgingly. She waved goodbye to the girl and waited another couple of minutes for her old flame to sneak in through the door.

"Hi Scott," she said, staying sat behind her desk when the big man entered the office. Scott had the build of a rugby player but the brain of a sheep. Holly had ended things between them years ago when she'd found out about Scott's family plans and his easy attitude to finding someone - anyone - to settle down with. She understood the need to be with someone, but she was still waiting for that special person before she even thought about settling. Judging by the small, ginger Santa-stalker, Scott had got what he wanted.

"Hi Holly. How are you doing? This is great, isn't it?" he said, gesturing around at the little office.

Holly pasted a smile on her face and nodded. "It is nice to finally have my own business. I still play the piano," she added, for no reason other than she didn't expect people to take her seriously when she said she was a private detective who made a living from the job. The crazy thing was, she actually was starting to make enough money to scrape by.

"I bet you do. You were always great at that," Scott said. This time, Holly's smile was genuine. She'd forgotten how complimentary Scott was. He may not be book smart, but someone had taught him somewhere along the line that politeness went a long way, and he'd stuck with it.

"Was that your little one?" Holly asked, trying to inject some enthusiasm into her voice.

"Yeah, that's Sally. She's just turned seven," Scott told her. Holly was pleased that her guess had been close, especially considering she didn't exactly spend a lot of time around kids.

In fact, she actively avoided them.

"How lovely," she said, hoping that covered all of the bases. "Sally wanted me to find her proof that Santa Claus exists." She hesitated and looked Scott in the eye. "We both know that's going to be difficult."

Scott was already counting out bank notes onto the table, but Holly hadn't been asking for more cash.

"No, I'm serious, because you know... he doesn't really..." She pulled a face at him. Scott gave her a surprisingly withering look back. *Ah, good. He does know Santa doesn't exist,* Holly thought. She'd had to check.

"Can't you make something up? Sprinkle some snowy footprints around and take some photos? Or get a sample of reindeer poop?" Scott asked. Holly was tempted for a moment to say she'd take the poop option and get some from the big man himself...

"It has to be infallible evidence, apparently," Holly said and raised her eyes to Scott's again. "Look, if she's even asking the question, isn't it time to tell her? She'll only be more disappointed in a few years if she finds out you lied to her now."

Scott rubbed his thick thatch of golden brown hair and then shook his head. "No. I know this stupid kid Max wants to ruin it for her, but I think she deserves a few more magical Christmases. I know you'll be able to find some proof that will convince her," he said and flashed her a smile. His smiles used to do something funny to her insides. Now, Holly just felt worn out.

"But as we've just covered, there is no proof because he's not..." She bit her tongue. "I mean, it could ruin my integrity as a private detective!"

"It will just make you look like the good guy," Scott replied.

Holly tried not to visibly sulk. Sometimes the easily observed truth was the best way to cut someone down. Scott was great at saying things the way they were.

"I suppose I'll figure something out," she said, feeling completely uninspired.

Scott went back to smiling. "Great, I'll bring Sally back on Christmas Eve. See you then," he said and walked out of the office, leaving a stack of cash on the table. Holly looked at it and shook her head. She was a private detective who was great at unravelling complex cases, but when you already knew the answer to a mystery - but had to make it look like the real conclusion was the wrong one - she had zero clue. For this Santa Claus case, she'd essentially be playing the role of the villain who knew the answer to the mystery all along, but did their very best to mislead the investigator - in this case, the little girl, Sally. Holly slumped down on her desk and wondered just what she could do about the Santa Claus conundrum. She just hoped she'd figure something out in a day or so, because that was all the time she had.

An idea suddenly popped into her head. She impulsively picked up her phone and dialled a number. The phone rang and rang, but for the first time ever, Rob Frost didn't pick up.

Holly frowned at the handset, wondering if he was avoiding her. He was the one who'd written a note saying he wanted to talk, but perhaps he hadn't meant over the phone. She sighed and slumped even lower. She'd been hoping that someone as slippery as Rob would have had a few ideas about how to solve her Santa situation. *He's not the only friend you have who could help*, the voice in her head whispered.

It was with a smile that Holly dialled a different number.

CHAMPAGNE AND SECRETS

"We'll figure something out. I'll see if there's anything in my collection that I can modify," George said and then took a deep breath.

Holly sensed similar thoughts to the ones she'd had when the Santa Claus conundrum had been brought to her. "It seems wrong, doesn't it?" she commented. "We're fabricating and even falsifying history."

"But it's for a good cause," George argued.

Holly tilted her head. *Was lying ever for a good cause?* she wondered, but then discarded the thought. Santa Claus was as white a lie as it got. Did she really want to be responsible for ruining that illusion before its time of magic was over?

"Okay, I'll do it," George said, both of them apparently reaching the same conclusion.

It was nearly Christmas. Behaving like Ebenezer Scrooge was not an option. Holly did not want to find herself face to face with any ghosts from her past. She shook her head, trying to erase the image of Kermit and his froggy family. Why was it that *The Muppets* made great literature stick in her head like nothing else?

"We can work all of this out tomorrow. I'll pick you up at eight?" George suggested. Holly replied with the affirmative.

A ripple of excitement shot through her when she remembered that this would be her first proper date with George. She smiled, privately thinking that no matter what happened, it couldn't be as eventful as the first Christmas dinner they'd attended together.

She was dead wrong.

Holly looked in the mirror and tilted her head from side to side, checking that there were no tide marks from her bronzer. She was admittedly a bit out of practice when it came to makeup. She tended to wear a little concealer and a spot of mascara and call it a day, but tonight she had someone to impress. The eyeshadow, eyeliner, highlighter, foundation, and bronzer had all come out of hiding, but she was having a hard time getting to grips with it all again. It would appear that makeup was a skill you had to use or lose. She felt like a kid who'd broken into her older sister's makeup palette and had made a beeline for the blue eyeshadow.

It wasn't really that bad. But it had taken her three attempts to get her face looking presentable. Holly flashed herself a nervous smile in the mirror and tried not to think about how good George looked in a suit. She only hoped that her black satin cocktail dress - which cinched in at her waist and puffed out a little in the skirt - would measure up to the occasion.

The doorbell rang causing Holly to nearly jump out of her skin. She'd known she was running late, but she'd only just finished getting ready in time! She rushed downstairs and had a natural blush to complement the pale pink blusher on her cheeks by the time she pulled open the door to her cottage.

"Hi George. Come in for a second. I'll just grab my jacket," she said, immediately feeling her stomach attempt to do cartwheels when she briefly took in the beautiful dark navy suit he was wearing and his smooth, white blonde hair.

His dark eyes twinkled with amusement. He pulled a package out from behind his back before she could rush back inside. "This is for you. It's the best I could do on short notice. I hope it will pass muster." He handed over the brown paper-wrapped parcel. Holly opened it a trifle nervously. The last time she'd opened a mysterious package with George, it had contained a murder weapon.

"Oh! It's a..." She shook the round item and it tinkled a little when something inside moved around. "It's a bell?" she asked.

George nodded. "You guessed it! It's from around the time when St. Nick was actually alive, so I thought it appropriate. They're quite common, actually, but I thought that this one seemed special. It is in fact my professional opinion that this bell fell from the harness of a reindeer on Christmas Eve, a long, long time ago. I've written that, too... see?" he said, pointing to a little certificate beneath the bell. It was signed 'George Strauss, Chairman of the Little Wemley Amateur Archaeological Society'. Holly looked up at George and grinned.

"That's amazing. I only hope I can come up with something this good. I've been thinking all day, but nothing. Hopefully inspiration will strike tomorrow morning," she said, and was about to run a nervous hand through her hair before she remembered she'd practically glued it into place with hair spray.

"Jacket," she said and ran off, only to return a moment later.

George's eyes slid up and down her dress and Holly blushed again. "You look lovely by the way," he said, helping her on with her jacket.

She breathed in the scent of verbena and grapefruit that he carried around with him and tried to calm herself down. She was a professional pianist and a private detective. She was a very capable and intelligent woman. She could definitely handle being the date of one of the company directors at George's work do.

"Um, George… what exactly does your company do?" she asked, realising - with horror - that she had no idea. To be fair, there hadn't been time to ask. They'd both been busy trying to work out who was killing off members of the Amateur Archeological Society and convince the police that they personally weren't guilty. That had been the last time they'd spent any 'quality' time together.

To her relief, George laughed.

"Oh, don't think I've been holding out on you. It's deadly boring. We're an indie graphic design agency. It's all pretty mundane, which is why I have my hobbies," he said.

Holly gave him a small smile. She was lucky enough to get to do exactly what she wanted to do full-time. She wondered if she could figure out a way to ask George if he'd ever thought about taking his hobbies further. She hated to see people stuck doing something they didn't love - even if it was for good money. Holly got into the car and shook the thoughts from her head. Unfortunately, life decisions like that could only be made by the person themselves. To her, it seemed that some people even actively avoided pursuing their dreams.

They pulled up outside the Carson Hotel in Orton Hills, twenty or so miles away from Little Wemley. Holly got out of the car and instantly felt the nerves build in her stomach again. She could see couples walking up the steps. It was definitely a black tie occasion. Should she have worn something longer than her cocktail dress?

"I can't wait to introduce you to everyone," George said, taking her hand and pulling her after him.

Holly fought against the worries that popped into her head. Why was he so eager to introduce her to people? Was there some ulterior motive here? She racked her brains, wondering if the company had a use for a pianist or a private detective. She'd been in newspapers. Was that it? Was George treating her as a celebrity guest? *Maybe he just likes you and is proud to say he's on a date with you*, Holly thought, surprising herself with a sudden lack of skepticism.

George's company was a lot bigger than he'd let on.

Holly had assumed that his graphic design agency consisted of maybe ten people, tops, but there were at least 100 in the room. She supposed if they'd all brought partners that meant George's company employed around 50 people - probably more. It wasn't bad at all for someone who was clearly only in their late twenties.

"Holly, this is Janet, Marlene, and Cleo. They're our admin and HR department. Basically, they run the company," George said, suave as ever.

The three woman laughed politely and one jabbed George in the waist. She quipped back; "If that was the truth, you'd pay us more!" Now it was George's turn to laugh, but Holly detected it was all in good fun. Even so, she couldn't help wondering how much George himself made from his business. By the size of the company, and its obvious success, she'd wager it was quite a bit. *Not that money is a good reason to like someone more!* she chided herself. Some people dreamed of landing themselves a wealthy other half, so that they could never work another day in their lives, but Holly knew she would never retire. She'd keep playing piano until her fingers stopped working, and she'd keep working as a detective until Miss Marple appeared to be a young whipper-snapper by comparison.

George gently slipped an arm around her waist as they moved to the next group. Holly felt a jolt of excitement run through her. She immediately noticed a couple of women that they were approaching throw her appraising looks. She wondered if she'd measure up and then remembered that she wasn't meant to care about other people's opinions.

"This is Holly. She's a very talented pianist and a very great friend," George said, his eyes warm. It was a lovely introduction, but Holly couldn't help but feel disappointed by being introduced as a 'friend'.

"A pianist? That must be an interesting job. You're a professional?" A man with rose-gold hair and a charming smile asked.

Holly knew better than to bite his head off. People often found it hard to believe you could make an okay living just by playing the piano.

She knew singers had it worse. Most people thought they could sing, so why should someone be getting paid to do something they could surely do as well themselves? She tried not to think about the number of times she'd seen people demand that a singer let them do a song, or even grab the microphone out of a singer's hands. All Holly had to put up with was young piano learners, and if she played at a family event, she always let them have a go. As far as she was concerned, whoever paid her the money to play was the boss.

Holly smiled back at him. "Yes, I'm a professional, but that used to leave me with quite a lot of free time, so I set up my own private detective agency." She couldn't help boasting after the man's natural skepticism. Eyes around the group widened, and Holly realised she was the centre of attention.

"Hey, we've got a pianist playing tonight! I'm sure you'd

be better. Why don't you get up and play one?" another man in his thirties asked.

Holly couldn't let this one slide as easily as the first man's remark. "That pianist is here tonight to do their job. I'm afraid it's not polite to step in. It's also my profession. Maybe think of it this way," she said, realising her words were coming across all wrong. "Let's say you're a graphic designer and you're at an event that used graphic design work done by another designer. Only, when you're there, people notice you are also a designer and ask you to do some designs of your own - even though they've employed another designer for the event. That would be weird, wouldn't it?" she said as lightly as possible.

Fortunately, George was there to save her. "Don't mind Liam… he probably would whip out some of his own designs if that situation ever occurred," George said in her ear, using a carrying whisper. People around the group chuckled. Liam grinned a little shamefacedly.

"I don't know about the rest of you, but why are we asking about piano playing when being a private detective is way more exciting? No offence," a woman with mid-length black hair quickly added.

"I'm a bit of a detective myself," a redhead cut in. "Just the other week, my neighbour's cat disappeared without a trace. I was able to figure out where it went. Of course, I didn't get paid for it, but what's a good deed amongst friends?" she said, deliberately self-deprecatingly.

"That's wonderful, Lizzie! How did you know where it was?" Yet another lady said while the woman next to her, who was wearing a shimmering light blue dress, tried to hide her smile. Holly immediately got the impression that Lizzie had a habit of drawing attention back to herself and everyone there knew it.

"Hey, I think I heard about one of your cases," a man with

a ridiculously posh voice piped up. Holly prepared her fixed smile, knowing it was Horn Hill House that he was thinking of. "You found that emerald, didn't you? I'm friends with the Uppington-Stanley family. They said the way you handled the case was… unique," he finished politely.

Holly tried not to sink into the ground with shame. The case of the Enviable Emerald had resulted in her finding the gem, which had been apparently impossibly stolen from a locked and guarded room. However, along the way, the police had suspected her of being a fraud and hadn't taken her seriously - until they'd uncovered the criminal history of the maid.

All in all, it was a case that Holly would rather no one knew about. She was actually glad this time when Lizzie piped up, only to be shut down by one of the two watching women. Holly picked up that they were called Lauren and Lana. She hoped none of the office women possessed initialed mugs, or they'd be forever fighting over them, and it looked like they had enough to fight over already.

Holly was still smiling politely as the battle raged over who was the best detective, while Lauren and Lana picked holes in everything. She'd started to daydream about what might happen between her and George later (if anything) and didn't notice anyone sidling closer to her until someone took her hand. She glanced down when she felt the stranger's palm against her own, and the crumpled piece of paper that he'd just transferred to her. By the time she looked up at his face, he had already turned and walked back through the crowd, his dark hair the only distinctive feature Holly could pick out.

With George and the others still engrossed in the banter, she un-crumpled the piece of paper and read the neat and curling script.

. . .

I must speak to you urgently about a case. Meet me beneath the mistletoe in five minutes. I need your help.

Holly re-read the note a couple of times, wondering if she should be worried. Was it some kind of joke that the whole office was playing on her? Or was it a transparent attempt to get her alone beneath the mistletoe? She considered the secretive way the note had been passed and her inability to identify the man who'd passed the note, but could get no closer to a conclusion. Was he in danger? And was she about to walk straight into it?

She turned to George, who was still happily arguing with the man with red-gold hair.

"...George," she said, hoping to gain his attention, but he was mid-conversation and unwilling to stop. Holly gave up and wondered what to do. A couple of minutes had already passed. She looked above the room and located the sprig of mistletoe, which had been suspended from a chandelier. She thought it was next to the drinks table, but couldn't see through the crowd to know for sure.

"I'm just getting a drink," she said in George's general direction and didn't wait to see if he'd heard her.

She started moving through the crowd, politely nodding and excusing herself as she slowly made progress. Before she could reach her destination, someone else got there first.

A scream cut through the tinkling piano and gentle hum of conversation. The crowd in front of Holly parted, and she saw a woman drop a champagne glass. The glass and liquid mingled with the champagne and shards that were already on the floor, lying beneath the body of a dark-haired man.

ON THE NAUGHTY LIST

Holly's hands fiddled with the crumpled note. She and the other guests stood in hushed silence. The company's first aider had tried to attend the man, but anyone could see that there wasn't a flicker of life left in his body. Foam bubbled at the corners of his mouth. Holly already had her suspicions as to what may have killed him. She was willing to bet that there was poison in the shattered glass of champagne.

Were you the man who passed me the note? Holly wondered and concluded it was almost certainly the same man. All she had to go on was the dark hair, but surely it could be no coincidence that a man who had handed her a mysterious note talking about a case and claiming he needed help had ended up dead beneath the mistletoe a few minutes later? *Murdered,* she mentally corrected herself. He'd been murdered beneath the mistletoe.

"Listen up! The deceased is Timothy Marsden. You will all be interviewed and give statements. This death is being treated as suspicious. You will also make yourselves available for further questioning in the future. That means no

Christmas Caribbean holidays. No exceptions," a familiar voice barked.

Holly winced and tried to keep her head down. She supposed she should have seen it coming. They were still quite close to Little Wemley, and a probable murder case would be handed over to someone who had the relevant experience.

Someone like Detective Chief Inspector Stephan Chittenden.

"I can't believe anyone would kill Tim. I know you don't know him, but he was a good guy. Christian and I were literally just talking about him," George whispered in her ear. Holly nodded when he continued to say how he had no clue why someone would want to kill Tim, and might it have been an accident instead? Perhaps it was a freak aneurysm, or a heart attack? Holly just kept nodding and chewing on her lip.

She was going to have to show the police the note.

She really didn't want to.

Even in a room filled with other people, you can't hide forever. Holly's decision was taken from her.

"Holly Winter - I suppose I should have known you'd be here," Stephan Chittenden said, giving her a withering look.

Holly bristled, tempted to remind the impolite detective that she was the one who'd helped him solve the last murder case he'd worked on. She'd even nearly died in the process.

"Let me guess... you're not a part of this. You don't know any of these people. You didn't do it. But you'll be sure to stick your nose in anyway," Chittenden continued.

"She is a private detective!" a male voice piped up from the crowd. Holly wished he hadn't spoken. Chittenden's face was turning redder by the second.

"I'm here with George. This is his office Christmas party," she explained, and George sheepishly joined her.

The detective rubbed his face with his hand.

George tried not to wilt. He'd been the prime suspect when someone had started killing off members of the local Amateur Archaeological Society. Being present at another suspicious death, well... it wasn't ideal for proving innocence.

"I don't believe it," was fortunately all Chittenden had to say, before turning back to his assisting officers and motioning that they should divide up and start taking statements.

Holly took a deep breath and walked closer to Chittenden, nervously tapping him on the shoulder. "I, uh, was handed a note by a man a few minutes before Timothy died. I think it might have been from him," she said, thrusting out a hand containing the crumpled paper.

Chittenden looked at it disdainfully, took it, and then glared at Holly. "This note makes it sound like whoever gave it to you was in deep trouble. The sort of trouble that you should go to the police about."

Holly raised her hands defensively. "I thought it might be some twisted joke! I was going to meet him to find out."

Chittenden rolled his eyes. "Of course you were." He pointed towards one of his colleagues. "Go give your statement to Rivers. I don't want to see either of your faces again tonight. It's almost Christmas, dash it all," he added in an undertone. Holly found it was a sentiment she could empathise with. She'd been looking forward to the party with George, and it had turned into yet another crime scene.

She glanced at the body, lying on the glass shards in a pool of spilled champagne. A man in a white plastic-looking suit was bending over him.

"Suspected cyanide," Holly overheard him say to another officer.

Holly and George gave their statements and then headed home. George dropped her off without a word, even when

Holly asked him if she could do anything for him. She knew he was in some kind of shock, but he'd just raised a hand and driven off, leaving her with an empty house and an even emptier feeling inside.

It's got to be someone else at the office, Holly thought.

It was approximately four in the morning on Christmas Eve, and she'd been lying in bed with her eyes wide open for hours. She knew she should be leaving the case to the police, but the case wasn't willing to leave her alone. After all, if Timothy had been the one to give her the note (and she assumed that was the case) he'd wanted her to be involved.

She was thinking back to the way the note had been passed prior to the poisoning. Timothy must have got himself a glass of champagne, and his drink had to have been poisoned - just moments before he'd drunk it. No one else at the party had died, and they'd all been drinking the same champagne, so it stood to reason that her theory was correct. It was even more likely that he'd been passed a drink by someone he'd thought he trusted. Someone who he worked with.

Holly racked her brains, trying to position everyone, but she found it was impossible. There were too many people and she didn't know them all. Anyone could have killed Timothy Marsden.

Holly nearly jumped out of her skin when her mobile phone started to ring. "Hello?" she said, her eyes not adjusting enough to read the name on the screen.

"I think Timothy was blackmailing someone," George's unmistakable voice said. Holly breathed in and held it. "It's definitely murder, isn't it?" George carried on, sounding depressed.

"I'm starting to think so," Holly confirmed. "The note he passed me suggested he needed help, so perhaps whoever he was blackmailing decided that enough was enough."

She frowned for a moment. "How did you find out he was blackmailing someone?"

Now it was George's turn to pause. "I, er, might have remotely accessed his office email account. As company director, I can do that…"

Holly was torn between horror and respect. With the police investigating, hacking into a colleague's account was asking for trouble, but on the other hand - they had a lead.

"Did you see who he was blackmailing?" she asked, eager to know more.

George sighed. "That's the problem. I think he was black-mailing several people, and their names are masked. I don't believe he was using his office account to send the emails, he just sent himself a file called 'graphic designs for Gorgon'. I was suspicious enough to open it. We don't have any clients with that company name. Lo and behold, it was a file containing screenshots of emails. I'm no expert, but it looks real, and if it is, I'm sure it will be financially traceable," he said, but Holly wasn't so sure. Professional blackmailers probably didn't leave clues. She suspected that Timothy had assumed the file with its misnomer was safe. It was likely to be the only personal record of his crimes.

"We should tell the police," she said, not without a grudge in her voice.

George made a similarly unimpressed noise. "I suppose so. I'll do it in a bit. Sorry if I woke you up. I just had to tell you."

Holly smiled a little. "I was awake anyway. I couldn't stop thinking about it all."

"Well, maybe you'll be able to rest now. Or maybe not," George added with a light chuckle that sounded like the normal George she liked so much. "I'd better be going. Good luck with the faux Father Christmas case tomorrow!" He hung up and Holly was left staring at the dark wall opposite her bed.

She had completely forgotten about the Santa situation!

I hope this will do it, she thought, looking down at the pieces she'd put together on her desk and wondering if it would count as infallible evidence. In front of her was the old harness bell and the certificate George had supplied. Then there was her own contribution - a theoretical guide to quantum physics that explained how Father Christmas could plausibly deliver all of the presents in one night (rather dry, but if the girl wanted evidence...). Finally, there was her personal favourite - news reports of various items that Santa had lost around the world, including his boots and hat. There was even a report of a real elf being caught. Holly herself was a little unsure on that one, as it seemed spookily real, but if it was enough to give her doubts about the unknown, she hoped it would thoroughly convince Sally.

She had no more time to wonder because at precisely ten o'clock in the morning, Sally and Scott walked into the office, and Holly gave her presentation. There was a pregnant pause at the end. Both adults held their breath, before Sally clapped her small hands and danced with delight.

"I knew it! I knew it! I can't wait to show this evidence to everyone," she said, carefully gathering up the files and taking special care over the old reindeer harness bell. She strode back out of the office leaving a grinning Scott behind.

"Thanks, Holly. I think you just made our Christmas," he said and passed over a little wrapped box. "The Mrs cooked this up for you. We both knew you'd pull it off." He wished her a Merry Christmas before walking back out into the cold.

Holly unwrapped the box to find a miniature iced fruit-cake with Father Christmas made from icing sat on the top. She wasted no time in bisecting Father Christmas and the cake. It was a good thing Sally wasn't around to see icing Santa's sticky end.

DEATH BY CHOCOLATE

Holly woke up the next morning to a thick coating of frost and that serene feeling you have when it is Christmas Day, and there is nothing at all to worry about. For just one day, she was going to shunt all thoughts of the case from her mind and just enjoy herself. She was due around her parents for lunch, but until then, she had some time to kill. A morning jog followed by a hot chocolate would be just the ticket.

She reached the front door and discovered that a small wrapped box was sitting on her doormat. Holly opened the door to look around and discovered that a further package had been left on the step. Feeling mystified, she brought the packages indoors and put them on the kitchen table, wondering if she dared open them. The package on the doorstep had a label that let her know it was from George, but while it looked just like his writing had on the invitation to the Christmas party, she knew it may still be a forgery. The other present - a small box - had no label and was wrapped in purple paper and tied with a purple bow. Any other time, it might have been exciting to receive a mystery present, but Holly was feeling cautious after the suspected cyanide poisoning.

Feeling very glad that no one could see her, she pulled on a pair of plastic gloves and the balaclava she wore when it was really cold, hoping that her face would be protected. She gingerly unwrapped the present from George, figuring that it would be the safer option.

A beautiful light blue and white scarf, hat, and glove set, was what she found inside. They were all lined with fluffy fleece and she sensed it was an expensive present to have bought. A note fell from the scarf when she picked it up.

Meant to give this to you yesterday when I dropped you off. Have a Merry Christmas.

Love,

George

P.S. Lizzie asked if we wanted to go round her house for a Boxing Day dinner? I think Christian, Lauren, Damien, and a few other couples are going. Give me a ring if you fancy it!

Holly felt her heart leap in her chest when she read the note. It looked like George might not have given up on her after all if he wanted her to attend a couples' dinner with him. She was tempted to pick up the phone there and then, but decided to text instead - as it was Christmas and she had no wish to intrude on his day.

That just left the other box.

Keeping her gloves and balaclava on, she gingerly pulled on the ribbon and then unfolded the purple paper wrapping. Inside was a dark blue jewellery box. She flipped off the lid and stepped back in case there was some sort of spray mechanism. Nothing jumped out and bit her, so she moved closer and looked in the box at the stunning amethyst and silver necklace that lay there. She gasped and resisted the temptation to touch it - just in case.

A note was pinned to the lid of the box.

From your secret admirer. I can't stop thinking about you! Merry Christmas. xXx

Holly frowned and wondered again if this was some sort of trap. If she took the gift at face value, it was probably from a man who had some cash to splash. She couldn't think of anyone (except for George and Rob) she knew who would A - have the money, and B - secretly admire her. George had written his name on his present, and Rob was the kind of guy who came out and said exactly how he was feeling. None of this secret stuff. That was actually why she was dreading their 'talk' whenever it was to happen...

She lightly touched the necklace and nothing sprang out or burnt through her gloves. It seemed to be safe, but who had it come from? She had a feeling that she would find out soon. No one sent an expensive present like this one and then didn't follow it up.

She considered whether or not to wear it, knowing it would act as a symbol of acceptance to whoever had sent it. She really shouldn't, but it was pretty - and purple and silver *were* her colours...

She sighed and shut the box. She'd decide later. She definitely wasn't going to be wearing it to the Boxing Day dinner with George. She smiled when her phone made a sound and she saw that George had sent back a smiley face and a time he'd pick her up.

Holly sat down at her kitchen table, forgoing the jog in

favour of hot chocolate. After all, it was Christmas. Although she'd promised herself otherwise, she started thinking about the case. Holly wondered about the people Timothy had been blackmailing. Which one of them had finally snapped?

The next morning, Holly dressed in a dark blue dress with a print of white flowers and wrapped herself up in a faux fur gilet. Then, she added a coat and the scarf and gloves George had bought her. She would wear the hat to a less social occasion, as it would mess up her hair if she put it on now - and her hair didn't need much encouragement to look like a mess.

"Happy Boxing Day! You liked the present?" George asked, walking up her narrow path and nearly slipping on the ice. She suppressed a giggle.

"Yes, they're so warm! I'm just sorry I didn't think to get you anything. Christmas sort of jumped up and bit me this year," she explained, and then felt even more guilty when she remembered that it must have been the same - if not worse - for George.

"Your present is coming with me to this awful couples' dinner that I'd have to go to alone otherwise," he said and pulled a face.

Holly felt deflated again but tried to not let it show. Did George really only see her as a friend? He turned to look when a dog barked somewhere down the street, and Holly drank in his white blonde hair, dark eyebrows, and stunning jawline. If only he felt the same way that she did.

"I'm happy to help. Let's hope that everyone lives to see dessert," she joked, but it fell flat. They both knew there was a chance that they'd be dining with a killer. All they could hope was that Timothy's death was to do with his blackmail business, and they didn't have another psychopath on their hands.

After a brief drive, they pulled up outside Lizzie's house. It was an idyllic property that must have once been a farmhouse. Set in the middle of nowhere and surrounded by a heathland, the views over the still-frosted fields were stunning. Judging by the number of cars grouped around the house, they weren't the first to arrive.

The door sprung open and Lizzie practically dragged them inside. "Come in, come in! Did you have a good Christmas? Come and see the duck that Christian has cooked for us! Doesn't it all look lovely?" she said, never pausing to hear an answer.

Holly and George entered the large living room with a crackling fire in the hearth and several tartan upholstered arm chairs. Three men were standing by the drinks cabinet. Holly looked down the corridor to find Christian walking towards them all. He winked at her.

Lizzie practically jumped on Christian the moment he entered the room and smothered his face with kisses. Everyone in the room looked away. Holly noticed Lauren and Lana exchange a grossed-out look.

"Thank you so much for helping me to cook the dinner," Lizzie said to Christian. "You're my angel."

Holly saw Lana mime sticking her fingers down her throat, her face hidden from Lizzie's view by the armchair.

"What are we eating? I'm super hungry," a new woman said entering the room. The man with the posh voice who'd asked about Holly's piano playing moved next to her. She vaguely remembered the woman being called Vanessa. She'd learned a lot of names two nights ago when they'd been waiting to get interviewed. There'd been nothing to do but chat.

"Yes, let's all sit down!" Lizzie said, ushering them into the dining room.

Holly held back and tilted her head at George. "Is Lizzie a company director?"

He shook his head. "No, she's head of PR. You can probably tell," he added dryly. "She's dating a company director, though. Christian is my business partner. As is Damien, who is here with Vanessa," he explained.

Holly raised an eyebrow. "So, everyone dates each other in the office? Doesn't that lead to trouble?"

George shrugged but his facial expression hinted at what he really felt. "You can't stop it from happening," was all he said.

Lizzie rushed back into the room and seized George's arm, a smile ever present on her face. "Come on, George, I've saved the best seat for you," she said, and it didn't escape Holly's notice that she didn't refer to Holly at all. She wondered if there was some history between the two.

"See you in there," Christian said to her, walking past when George had been dragged away. His hand rested on her arm for a second and she felt his thumb stroke her skin, before he walked away in the direction of the kitchen, leaving Holly to wonder if she'd imagined it.

"George… George!" she hissed when she'd managed to sit down beside him at the table. "This isn't a swingers' party or anything, is it?" she asked, feeling horrified by the thought.

George gave her an odd look. "No, why would you think that?"

Holly opened her mouth to answer and then shut it again. Perhaps she was just imagining the strange way Christian was behaving - and the tension between George and Lizzie was almost certainly ancient history. She didn't want to know.

"I was just kidding," she said weakly. Fortunately, the

prawn and avocado starters were served and Holly didn't have to talk to George again for the next several minutes.

The conversation focused on the company and what the New Year would bring for them. Holly found her attention drifting. She looked around the room at the photo frames. Quite a few photos showed pictures of a very young Lizzie and a boy, close to her age. The boy had light-brown hair and a deep tan that made him look like he might have some hispanic blood, in stark contrast to Lizzie's pale face and red hair. She didn't know why, but there was something about the boy's facial expression that hinted there might be something wrong with him.

There was a lapse in conversation and Holly thought it would be a great idea to do some bonding with Lizzie over the old photos. People loved to talk about that stuff!

"I was just admiring your photos, Lizzie. Who's the boy in the pictures with you?"

A hush descended in the room. Holly looked around at all of the blank faces. "...Sorry?" she said, wondering what she'd done wrong.

"It's okay. That's Jason. He's my brother, but he died when we were teenagers. There was an accident. We were out walking close to this house. He fell into the river and drowned," Lizzie explained. There was a long pause before she pushed herself upright, the smile only slipping from her face for a second. "Now, who wants dessert?"

Holly pulled an apologetic face at George and tried to ignore the amused looks Christian was giving her across the table. What was his deal?

Something creaked above them. Holly glanced up.

George shrugged. "I guess Lizzie's either got a ghost up there, or rats," he said, and they shared a smile. Holly's smile was a little wider as she felt a wave of relief that George had forgiven her for her unknowing faux pas.

"George, I made this dessert with you in mind because I know you love chocolate. It's my almost famous, death by chocolate pudding," Lizzie practically oozed over George when she put the plate down on the table. Holly accidentally caught the eye of Lana and Lauren. They both looked sympathetic.

Holly bit her tongue and ate some dessert. George would have to make his own decision.

She just hoped he picked her.

THE RUNNING MAN

Holly slumped onto her desk and stared at the desktop calendar. It was the 27th of December - that awkward date where you had to work between Christmas and New Year. Being the owner of her own detective agency, she could have given herself the time off, but she hadn't wanted to. She loved her job. The only part she didn't love was early mornings spent in the agency, waiting for the phone to ring and a case to arrive, or - like this morning - waiting for Becky to turn up, so Holly could abandon the phone and leave to solve a mystery.

A quarter of an hour later, Becky walked into the office. This morning, she wasn't alone.

A little bundle of black and tan fur bounced into the office after her and immediately latched onto the leg of a desk and started chewing.

"What is that?" Holly asked, looking at the puppy distrustfully. It looked like an odd mix between a Rottweiler, German Shepherd, and a Collie.

"It's a dog," Becky said, stating the obvious. She sat down

behind her desk and dumped her bag on top of the surface. Usually, she dumped it on the floor. This concerning alteration of behaviour did not escape Holly's notice.

"I can see that. What is it doing here?" she asked.

Becky let out a sigh, like Holly's question was totally unreasonable.

"I thought we could have an office dog. This one seemed perfect," she said and started to turn on her computer, doing her best to look busy.

Holly wasn't finished. "Did you buy a dog, without asking me, just so it could live in the office?" She bit her tongue to keep from shouting. Puppies were cute, but they were also a handful. She couldn't believe Becky would do something so stupid and thoughtless!

"Actually, I found him by the side of the road in a cardboard box. He looked lonely."

Holly immediately felt terrible. Someone had abandoned this poor puppy and now she was going to turn him away, too.

She narrowed her eyes. "Show me the box," she said, not wanting to have the wool pulled over her eyes. Her part-time apprentice secretary looked surprised but got up and walked to the door, the makeshift lead still in her hand. She gathered the young dog up, as he wasn't old enough to walk any distance on the lead.

Ten minutes later, they were standing on the small road that led in and out of Little Wemley. Holly inspected a cardboard box that definitely looked like it had been inhabited by a playful puppy.

"Okay, but that does not mean we are keeping him." She paused, feeling unfair again. "You'll take him home at the end of the day, right?"

The other girl's pained expression gave away the truth.

"Oh… you want me to take him," Holly said, looking at the bundle of fluff, who was eagerly jumping up and down in front of her.

She rubbed a hand through her hair, trying not to think about just what she would be committing to, and the sheer size this dog might turn out to be - given her initial estimate of its breeding.

"Fine. It can have a two week trial. We shall see how it behaves," she said, already accepting she'd just gained a pet dog.

Becky smiled for the first time since the pair had met. "I named him Watson," the secretary said.

Holly's lips twitched up. Perhaps Becky did have a sense of humour after all.

The rest of the day passed without incident, if you didn't count the number of accidents Watson had and the laptop charger he completely destroyed. At least it made an otherwise uneventful day more interesting. It was only in the afternoon that things looked up when George walked into the office.

"Hi Holly, are you busy? I was wondering if…" He stopped as Watson tore across the room and jumped up and down in front of him, before running off to hide behind the desk where Holly was. "I didn't know you had a dog?!" He bent down and tried to persuade Watson to return to him, but the puppy was now being shy.

Holly looked down at the big brown eyes that looked back at her with such joy. She knew she didn't stand a chance now.

"I didn't either until this morning." She shot a pointed look at Becky. "But he's grown on me already," she admitted.

George was smiling at her and she could immediately see he was a dog person. Holly had always been more into cats, but with Watson being abandoned just after Christmas, it would be heartless to get rid of him. Who knew? Perhaps he'd be a great detective dog, like *Scooby Doo*.

"Well in that case, you'll need to take him on walks. I know he's a bit young to walk very far on the lead, but maybe I could show you this great walk I know? It's cold outside, but a lovely day." George hesitated. "Unless you're busy. I've given my whole office time off until after New Year's Day. No one commissions graphic design work over the Christmas period."

Holly looked down at Watson, who had collapsed on the floor in one of his brief puppy sleep moments. "I think I can spare some time. Things have been pretty quiet here, too."

Becky had been playing some awful game on her phone all day and Holly had been reading a book after the morning's mystery (a missing cat) had been resolved before she'd managed to leave the office. A walk with George didn't seem too much like skiving.

Becky nodded that she'd keep an eye on Watson, and off they went. Holly only wished she'd had a chance to freshen up and had put on better makeup that morning. What if this trip was all planned and George was going to ask her to be his girlfriend?

"It's a short drive away, but it's one of the best walks around here. It's on the heathland... quite near to Lizzie's house, actually." He pulled a face, remembering the dinner party.

Holly looked sideways at him, sensing an opportunity. "I hope you don't mind my asking, but is there any history between you and Lizzie?"

George winced. "No, but she hasn't stopped trying to get together with me since she joined the company a year ago. I've told her no, but she hasn't got the message." He quietly grumbled to himself for a couple of moments. "I don't like being pushed into things, and I'd definitely never date someone like Lizzie." Holly felt a little warm glow of hope start in her chest and wondered if *she* was the sort of girl George would be inclined to date. She still had a chance!

"Isn't she with Christian?" she asked, knowing she was being nosy.

George's lips twitched up, forgiving her curiosity. "In theory, but I think they've just paired off because it's convenient. Did it look like love to you?" He threw her a knowing glance.

Holly felt her cheeks turn pink as she remembered Christian's not so subtle contact with her. They definitely weren't much of a couple.

Frost was still sparkling on the tall, wiry grasses when George parked up on the edge of the heathland. It was a testament to just how cold it was outside, and how cold it was going to get again that night. Holly thought about lying in her bed all alone with a hot water bottle, before remembering she wouldn't be alone anymore. She'd have a very unhousetrained and generally naughty puppy staying with her.

"Come on," George said, walking ahead.

Holly had worn her gloves, scarf, and hat to the office that morning. She was already feeling the benefit of their warmth when she took her first steps across the heathland. She only wished that George would have taken her hand, or given her any sign of his interest. The more she thought about it, the more he'd been giving off 'just friends' vibes recently.

"It's a beautiful day," she remarked as they walked along, talking about nothing of any consequence. George asked how the Santa Claus case had ended, and then she asked him what his plans were for New Year's Eve. Holly got the impression he was attending a party but wasn't about to extend an invitation. She couldn't say she blamed him for that. The past two events they'd attended together had both ended in murder.

Their thoughts must have both turned to the most recent death.

"I forgot to say, the police confirmed it was cyanide. I turned over the blackmail file to them. Got a bit of an ear bashing for looking at the emails, but they were okay in the end. Now they're investigating the whole office. They've asked anyone who was blackmailed to come forward, but - surprise surprise - no one has. Chittenden is furious. That's why you haven't been dragged in for questioning. They're all but certain it's to do with the blackmail." He turned to face Holly. "Do you think you could work on the case?"

Holly looked up at the blue sky with its scattering of white clouds - perfect, but so cold.

"I don't think I should. I'm sure the police will find the answer using some techno magic, if that's how he was doing it. But, if Timothy was using good old-fashioned methods, I don't know. Hopefully they'll work it out. It must be whoever handed him the drink before he drank it, right? Maybe someone saw."

They carried on walking in thoughtful silence for a bit, both wondering what kind of secrets people at the office were keeping that made them targets for blackmail. Holly had a feeling that before the case was finished, they'd know the answer.

"Hey... what's that?" George's voice changed and he pointed in the distance. Holly squinted and saw someone running flat-out. And they were coming closer.

The runner changed direction, probably when they saw Holly and George, and ran through the heather instead. Now the runner was closer, Holly could see his brown hair flying in the wind. He was dressed in rags and his tanned feet were bare, bloodied, and covered in freezing mud.

She drew a quick breath. "He must be in trouble!" She looked at George helplessly. What could they do to help a man who was already running away from them?

"Maybe we should call the police?" George said. They both considered it as they carried on walking up the hill. They were still deciding when they nearly collided with Lizzie, who was power-walking in the opposite direction.

"Oh! Hello," George said, forcing a smile to his face.

"Sorry, no time to chat! Got a PB time to beat," she announced, showing them both an equally forced smile, before striding onwards.

Holly pulled a face at George. "That's different. I thought she'd be all over you."

George nodded vacantly, looking after the receding figure of Lizzie. "I wonder if she has any secrets," he said, and then shook his head. "I'm wondering that about everyone on my staff at the moment. Even Christian has been acting a little off." He sighed. "I think he was being blackmailed, but I don't know what it was over. What if he did it? I could lose my business partner and the company's reputation…" He bit his tongue, realising the callousness of his final remark.

"Maybe I could look into that. Just that little part of the case," Holly offered.

George gave her a real smile. "We'd better get back before it gets dark and we turn into icicles," he said, and they turned around and walked back to the car.

Holly took a sip of her coffee (she was being good today) and raised an eyebrow at the email she'd just received. After

George had asked her to look into Christian's affairs, she'd headed straight for the internet and had discovered that there were people you could pay to sleuth online for you. She'd paid the very reasonable fee and had waited, wondering if Timothy Marsden had used the same strategy, or if there'd been another way he'd gathered his secrets.

She wasn't disappointed with the results. The email she received back was a list of online casinos that Christian's IP address had visited. They even showed that some websites were blocking him. It looked like Christian had a gambling problem... and Timothy had probably known about it.

She was disturbed from her inner thoughts by someone biting her hand. She looked down at Watson - who was a bundle of energy this morning. "Look, I know you aren't really meant to be out too much, but you have so much energy, and learning to wear a harness would be a step in the right direction. How about we go out for a walk?" Watson yapped happily in response and didn't mind a bit when she put on his new harness - a purchase she'd made the previous evening along with a whole bunch of doggy goodies. Watson had also been dragged off to the vets for some shots. That was another good reason not to take him out, as he wasn't fully inoculated yet, but Holly's garden wasn't big enough for any kind of proper walk, and she knew the puppy needed exercise. She'd just have to make sure that they didn't meet any other dogs.

"Oh, Watson, why is it now you decide to sleep?" she moaned as she carried the comatose dog down the High Street, drawing many curious looks.

For a puppy, he was big. She worried that other people

might think there was something wrong, rather than it being a case of sleepy-puppy-itis. She glanced at the board outside the newsagents when she walked by, just as Watson started to wriggle and decided he could walk after all.

She nearly dropped him when she read the headline.

Unknown man found dead in Wimble River

Holly's breath caught as she reread the headline and felt her brain stitching the possibilities together.

The man they'd seen running across the heathland yesterday... he'd looked like he was heading in the direction of Wimble River - the small, but fast-flowing body of water that passed just outside Little Wemley. Had the man they'd seen ended up in the river? She thought back and remembered Lizzie had been walking that way, too. *A murderer is on the loose,* she thought and started to wonder if...

"Morning Holly!" Sergeant Pinkington called to her.

She smiled and returned the greeting. After her recent time spent with the local police department, Sergeant Pinkington had been the only one who had always been polite and helpful.

"Did you hear? They've arrested someone over that Timothy Marsden business!" the police officer said in a hushed voice. Holly inwardly smiled. The other reason she had become so fond of Sergeant Pinkington was because she was a dreadful gossip.

"Who did they arrest?" she asked, wondering if the other woman could be persuaded to part with more information.

"Lana Gently," Pinkington carried on, not needing any encouragement.

Watson sniffed at the police officer's shoes. Holly prayed he wasn't thinking about relieving himself.

"But why would she do it?" she asked, wondering if she'd been blackmailed.

The other woman shook her head. "An anonymous witness came forward and said they'd seen her passing him the poisoned drink, and it turned out that she had been sending him some rather suggestive text messages."

"But she's seeing one of the other men at the office - Liam!" Holly protested, and then shut her mouth. People would always surprise her.

"Tell me about it. Anyway, we confronted her with the witness' statement, and she broke down and confessed to giving him the drink. She still won't admit that she poisoned him. I think it's obvious it was a spurned lover's revenge." Pinkington ran a hand through her thick, chestnut hair. "We asked her who had given her the drink, if she wasn't the poisoner, but she wouldn't say. She seemed almost scared. It was probably because Chittenden was in the room," she finished, rolling her eyes.

Holly smirked. "I hope you get to the bottom of it," she said, careful to heavily imply that she herself wasn't getting involved. But that wasn't true, was it? She'd already snooped enough to know that Christian had gambling debts, and if Lana was scared of something, Holly was willing to bet she had secrets of her own - perhaps a secret worth killing for. It was one way to ensure the matter was silenced.

She pulled out her phone and tried to call George but got no answer. Instead, she wrote out a lengthy text including the info about the man who'd died and Lana's arrest. She listened for her phone on the walk home, but no new message appeared - despite George telling her he wasn't working again until the New Year.

She'd just begun to worry when her phone buzzed a

couple of hours later. A message from George popped up on the screen.

Sorry. Busy.

That was all the reply George had to her new information. Holly had no idea what she'd done wrong.

THE WRONG HORSE

Holly popped into work but then decided to give herself the day off. Becky wasn't in, but the lack of calls meant it really wasn't worth hanging around. The answer machine could deal with any new enquiries. She wouldn't admit to it, but she was in a mood. She'd just sent George all of that juicy information and he was too busy to react? It was so rude!

She ruffled Watson's head and let him out of the back-door, so he would hopefully go to the loo in the right place. Why did she never seem to get it right when it came to men? The opposite gender was one mystery she wasn't sure she'd ever solve.

Her phone buzzed on the table. She looked at the screen and discovered Rob Frost was calling her. Holly sighed and pressed the button to cut him off. Whatever he wanted to say to her, now really wasn't the time for a heart-to-heart. She knew she'd only snap at him right now and potentially ruin their friendship. It was better to leave the call unanswered.

The doorbell rang. Holly felt her mood leap, as she suspected George had come to his senses and was popping in to discuss the case. She pulled open the front door and found a completely different man was standing on her doorstep.

"Christian!" she said and then took a step back. "How do you know where I live?" she asked, hoping she sounded curious - not accusatory.

Christian smiled a bright, white smile back at her. "I did a little snooping." His eyes slipped downwards - something which Holly did not fail to notice.

"Can I help you with anything?" She didn't have a good feeling about this social call. All she could think about was Christian's gambling debts and the way Sergeant Pinkington had described Lana as 'scared'. Christian was definitely big enough to be scary. What if he knew Lana's secret and was using it against her, just as Timothy had with his colleagues? Holly knew something was wrong with all of this, but she couldn't quite put her finger on it.

"I'm actually looking for George. We're not meant to be working, but we're all workaholics. I wanted to run a concept by him, but I can't get hold of him. He's not answering his phone and isn't at his house either. I just assumed..."

Holly blushed and then tried to recover herself. "He isn't here, I'm afraid. I haven't been able to contact him either," she said, deciding to leave out the rude text message.

Christian ran a hand through his rose-gold hair. "I wonder what he's up to! Anyway, are you busy? Seeing as I'm here, we could go for a drink," he said, far too casually to have just come up with the idea. Holly hesitated as she tried to think of a way to politely turn the offer down. She had far too much to worry about if George really was missing. The man on her doorstep might even be the one responsible!

"You could even wear that necklace," Christian continued when Holly didn't speak.

She felt her stomach drop. So, it was Christian who had

given her the mystery gift! She'd suspected that the sender wouldn't stay anonymous forever.

She had to come up with something fast. Sometimes the truth, or at least some of it, was the best option. "I'd love to go for a drink with you sometime, but I'm really worried about George. I haven't known him for as long as you have, but it seems unusual for him to be out of contact. With the recent murder and everything, I'd really like to know if he's okay," she explained. Christian nodded understandingly, and Holly was glad he couldn't hear her heartbeat racing. If Christian was the killer, now was the time he'd probably act, thinking she'd figured him out.

"Oh man, I knew I shouldn't have come on so fast. I just thought you looked amazing at the Christmas party and didn't want to let the opportunity pass me by," he said.

Holly really looked at him for the first time, with relief flooding through her veins. Christian was almost as good-looking as George. He possessed more of a careless appearance to him that Holly quite liked and that smile really was to die for, but Holly already knew his little secret, and she also knew just how hard a habit it was to kick. She was almost tempted to return the necklace, knowing that the man in front of her surely couldn't afford it, but it would only embarrass him.

"I really mean it, Christian. We will go out for a drink. I'm just concerned at the moment," she said, giving him what she hoped would pass for a decent smile. He smiled back and waved goodbye before walking back down the garden path. Something about the last thing he'd said bothered her, but her thoughts were all at sea.

A sudden idea occurred to her. With the recent success of her internet sleuthing, what if the same people she'd employed could trace phone numbers to locations? She eagerly typed out an email and a few minutes later her request was answered. The company had managed to trace George's location via his GPS (she didn't ask just how illegal it was to do). She put in the co-ordinates and held her breath. Her forehead furrowed into a frown when she figured out exactly where he was.

George was round Lizzie's house.

Holly rested her head in her hands, staring at the laptop screen. Why would he be round there? He'd said he'd never consider Lizzie, despite her obvious interest in him. Had he been lying? After all, Christian was hardly being the faithful boyfriend he was supposed to be if he was sending Holly necklaces. Perhaps the same was true of George and Lizzie.

Then again, he might be there because of work, and his text about being busy was completely honest.

She chewed her lip, deliberating. Her instincts were telling her that there was something wrong.

What if Lizzie had something to do with Timothy Marsden's murder?

She had to find out. Without thinking too much more about what she was going to say when she got there, she stepped out of the house and walked to her car.

She was so wrapped up in what might have befallen George, she completely forgot that she'd left Watson out in the garden - and had no idea that he was currently amusing himself by digging a great big hole under the hedge.

STASH IN THE ATTIC

Holly immediately spotted George's car parked in the lane near Lizzie's house. He was definitely here, but why? She decided to creep up and do a little spying. Hopefully no one would spot her, or she'd end up with a restraining order. That would definitely be bad for business.

She peered through the hedge that bordered Lizzie's house and could just see movement through the kitchen window. It looked like Lizzie was washing something up. There was no sign of George, not even after several minutes had passed. Holly took a deep breath and decided to listen to her instincts. The man running across the heathland had come from the direction of this house and now George was possibly missing, or at the very least - acting exceedingly oddly. Holly was starting to suspect that Lizzie might be keeping a secret. And Timothy Marsden had known what it was...

Her fingers itched on her phone as she wondered whether now would be a good time to call for reinforcements. If she was correct, it would be the sensible thing to do, but all she had was a feeling - a feeling that something wasn't right. If Holly was being completely honest with herself, it could just be jealousy talking. She didn't want George to be all loved up with Lizzie.

You've got to know either way. He could be in trouble! the little voice in her head said and she steeled herself, thinking of an excuse.

She marched up to the door and saw Lizzie look up from her washing up when she approached the house. There was no need to ring and the door was soon answered.

"Hi Holly, can I help you?" Lizzie asked, sounding rather putout.

Holly pasted on her best PR smile. "Yes! George's sister contacted me to say there's a family emergency and they need to speak to George. I haven't been able to find or contact him. I thought I'd come here on the off chance he was around. I know you two are close," Holly said, hoping to flatter the other woman.

"You probably saw his car on the way in," Lizzie said with a small smile that said it all to Holly. It was an 'I win' smile.

Holly nodded.

"He's just upstairs. I think he'll be down in a few minutes. In the meantime, why don't you have a drink? I was just about to put the kettle on. I know it's an emergency, but a few minutes more probably won't make a difference."

Holly half-nodded along. She hoped the other woman wouldn't start probing too far, and then what would she do when George came down and asked her what exactly she was doing there? The truth would have to come out, and the sooner the better. She should start talking now and hope the pair would forgive her for being so suspicious and sticking her nose in where it didn't belong. Something creaked up in the eaves of the house, as if Lizzie's attic ghost agreed with her.

Holly walked into the kitchen after Lizzie. "Lizzie, I haven't been completely straight with you…" she started. The other woman tilted her head questioningly and passed over a mug of tea. Holly held the warm mug in her hands and tried to think of the best way to come clean. "I came here because I was worried about George. There wasn't really a family emergency. I just thought…" She trailed off. "I don't know." Lizzie could read between the lines there. "Anyway, I'm happy that you're happy together," she finished weakly, not wanting to make eye contact any longer. Instead, her eyes fell on the overstuffed rubbish bin and the packet of brown hair dye and empty spray tan bottle that had fallen onto the kitchen floor.

"Anyway, I've bothered you too much. I'll be off now," she said, carefully putting the mug on the kitchen unit, the tea untouched. The cogs in her mind were turning quickly and every sense was screaming at her to run.

Something clunked upstairs. The two women's eyes made contact when they both heard the low moan.

"Old houses are so weird, right?" Holly said, the smile straining at her lips as she turned to walk out of the kitchen.

"No you don't," Lizzie told her.

Holly felt something cold press into her back. "What have you done to him?" Holly asked, her voice barely louder than a whisper. She turned slowly.

Lizzie stepped back, and now Holly could see there was definitely a gun in her hand. It looked so wrong seeing something like a gun so near to Little Wemley. It was the sort of thing you only thought people had in the movies, but there it was…

"He's fine. You should be more worried about yourself. I'm afraid your ending isn't so happy." She looked down at the tea on the table and sighed. "If only you'd drunk that."

Holly felt the hairs on the back of her neck prickle.

"It was you who killed Timothy. I'm guessing you poisoned the champagne and then somehow persuaded Lana to give it to him."

Lizzie nodded. "Poor Lana. Much like me, she was stuck with the wrong man. Timothy was the one she wanted, only, he never showed any interest. I gave her the drink and told her it had a little something in it that would give her a helping hand in persuading Timothy to return her feelings." She laughed. "She thought she was drugging him, not killing him. Of course, she won't admit that I was the one who gave her the drink because I know her little secret." Her smile turned predatory. "Timothy isn't the only one who had puppets dancing on strings. I found out that Lana's been creaming off the tax returns she files for the company. It was quite clever really, but she left some evidence lying around, and I found it. I suppose she'll take the blame for Timothy's death. It makes sense, doesn't it? She loved him and he didn't love her back, so she kills him."

"What about me? What about George? Your plan doesn't work with us gone, too," Holly said, but Lizzie's smile never faded.

"Oh, I planned for this. I was going to persuade George to stay with me, but... things changed."

Something clicked in Holly's brain. "The man on the heathland... he looked like your brother. You said your brother drowned in the river?" Holly said, wondering just where this was leading. She glanced at the fake tan and brown hair dye again and started to feel sick.

"He didn't die. He just got hurt one time. He had a lot wrong with him from the start. He was a unique child, but I was always there for him. I always looked after him. One day we'd climbed a tree and had a fight. I was angry and pushed him, just a little, but he lost his balance. He was injured..." she said, blinking her eyes furiously. "My parents said it was my fault. I was the one who was supposed to look after him. The injury was bad but time healed that. It was his mind that was worse. One night, he left his room and murdered my parents before disappearing from the house. The police never found him, but I did. I took him home and hid him and looked after him. I've been looking after him for years."

Holly felt the chill start to crawl up her spine. Lizzie sounded like she was telling the truth, but there was something off about it. Who was the man who'd run across the heathland and died in the river?

"I'm sorry about your family," Holly started, hoping it was what Lizzie wanted to hear. She looked at the rubbish some more and drew a deep breath. "Where is George?" she asked, already knowing the answer.

"In the attic. He's not George anymore," Lizzie said, matter of factly. "Come and see." She jerked the gun to show Holly she should move.

The climb up the stairs into the roof of the house was the longest of Holly's life. All the time, she was supremely aware of the gun at her back and the lack of options she had for escaping this situation. She was aware that Lizzie was unhinged and wasn't sure if there was a way she could be talked down. Logic was almost certainly beyond her.

"Holly, meet Jason - my brother," Lizzie said, opening the door of the attic to show George sprawled on a bed. A cuff that linked to a chain was around his wrist. His skin was stained dark and his white blonde hair was now a faded shade of brown. Holly finally knew her suspicions were correct.

"I think your real brother died a long time ago," she said and heard Lizzie's fingers drumming on the barrel of the gun. It wasn't a comforting sound.

"I killed them for him. Our parents were going to send him away, but I couldn't let them. He saw what I'd done and ran. But it's okay, I have him back," she said, smiling at George. George's eyes opened a little and then closed again. Holly assumed he'd been drugged.

"Your brother died a long time ago, Lizzie," Holly repeated. "The man we saw running across the heathland... you were pretending he was your brother, too, weren't you?" she said, already knowing it was true. While she spoke, her eyes searched the room for a weapon. There was nothing. This place was a prison that had been stripped of all possible weapons.

Lizzie scowled.

"He ran away, but I have him back now, see?" She pointed to George.

Holly realised there would be no arguing with Lizzie. Instead, she changed the subject. "Timothy knew about this, didn't he?"

Lizzie's expression darkened even further. "There was a man who wanted a job with the firm. He came all the way from Germany just for the interview. I interviewed him and invited him back home. I knew then I'd found him. I'd finally found my brother." She frowned again. "Until he broke his hand and ran from me."

Holly winced, imagining the man who had been held captive getting desperate enough to break his hand to slip the bonds. He'd have had to practically sever his thumb. Holly tried not to let the horror of it show on her face when she remembered the poor man's awful end.

"No one came looking for him, so I knew he was definitely my brother. He belonged to me. But Timothy didn't think so. He went through old emails and saw the exchange I'd had with the applicant. He made enquiries and found out the man had eventually been reported missing. That was when he got suspicious." Her face developed red blotches. "He spied on me! Then he confronted me and told me what he thought he knew. He didn't understand that it was the right thing. He didn't understand that it was my brother I'd lost and had finally found. He made me pay him to keep quiet, but I knew I wouldn't do it forever. He thought he was safe, but I confronted him just before the Christmas party and pretended that the evidence was all gone. I told him that I'd let the man go and that he'd forgiven the mistake. He had nothing over me anymore." She paused and Holly remembered the note that Timothy had passed her. He'd been scared that night.

Lizzie played with the gun, her finger twitching on the trigger. Holly tried not to jump like a scared rabbit.

"He was expecting trouble from me, not Lana, which is why he happily downed the champagne." She smiled. "And all of my problems went away." She raised the gun.

Holly comprehended that time was up, and this time around, there was no Rob to save her. She was on her own - unarmed against a gun.

"Now all there is to do is get rid of you and pin it on Christian, whose gun this is…" Lizzie shared a smile. "I stole it when we were sleeping together," she confided. "I know he likes you. He even asked me what to do about it, and I was the one who encouraged him to send the necklace. I'm sure the police will find it and realise you rejected him." Lizzie shook her head. "What are the chances? Two violent rejected lovers at one party!"

"But what about George? People will notice he's disappeared." Holly glanced at the bed where George was lying. His eyes were half-open and unfocused. She wished he'd wake up so he could help her - even if it was just by giving her a distraction.

"The man previously known as 'George' is going to be moving house with me. We're both distressed by the murders and need time on our own to develop our newfound romance. He doesn't have any family that I know of…" Lizzie tutted. "You really should have come up with a better excuse for barging in on other people's affairs. That was so sloppy. Anyway, we'll be gone from town. I'll handle the company remotely and answer any contact via text or email. Poor George has seen so much death recently, I'm sure people will understand that he needs some time out of the rat race in order to recuperate." She smiled nastily, and Holly had a bad feeling that Lizzie's word would be taken as the truth. George had been through a lot, and she had noticed he'd become far more stressed during the time she'd known him. People would probably believe the story.

"So, there you go. I'm going to live happily ever after with my brother, and you're not," Lizzie said, bringing the gun up.

THE CURIOUS INCIDENT OF
THE DOG

Holly thought about diving to the floor just before the gun went off, but she had a feeling Lizzie's finger would be faster. There was nowhere for her to run to and no one coming to save her. This time she'd run out of luck.

Holly closed her eyes and wondered when it would all be over.

She heard the click of the gun when the safety came off, and at the same time, the sound of scrabbling on the front door outside and a loud yapping. Holly shook off her surprise more quickly than Lizzie and threw herself forwards onto the other woman, knowing this was her only chance.

The gun went off and Holly felt a blinding, white hot pain in her shoulder. She ignored it and kept trying to wrestle the deadly firearm away from Lizzie. Unfortunately, Lizzie had spent a great deal of time dealing with full grown men and winning. Holly didn't even regularly go to the gym and felt outmatched in every single way. All she could do was fight as dirtily as possible and hope for a miracle.

The pair were still rolling around the floor together when George groaned and rolled off the bed. It was only blind luck that Holly had been pushed clear of Lizzie - and was probably just about to get her ass kicked - when it happened. George fell as dead weight and landed on Lizzie, crushing her to the floor. Lizzie struggled beneath George, trying to push him off, but George was so drugged up it was like pushing a corpse.

Holly seized the opportunity and grabbed the gun. "Where's the key?" she yelled at the struggling woman, who stopped wriggling for a moment and glared at Holly.

"Go to hell," she said.

Holly felt her finger tighten on the trigger, and despite George's proximity to the target, she wondered if she should just pull the trigger. It would be so easy, and after everything this woman had done... She shook the feeling away. That wasn't who she was. She wasn't a killer. She wasn't like *them.*

"The key... or I start shooting bits of you," Holly said, figuring that maiming wasn't the same as murder.

Lizzie's eyes flickered to the opposite eave of the attic and Holly could see the silver key dangling on a hook, probably placed there to torment her victims. Forcing down the feeling of disgust, Holly took the key and unchained George's wrist. She opened the manacle and then snapped it shut around Lizzie's wrist, keeping the gun trained on her the whole time. Fortunately, the pinned woman didn't try anything. Instead, she was gently sobbing and talking to her 'brother'. Holly thought about pulling George off her, but she didn't seem likely to harm him and getting close to Lizzie again was just asking for trouble.

She pulled out her phone and dialled 999. It was crazy to think that less than a month ago, she hadn't ever had to dial those three digits.

As the adrenaline faded, Holly again became aware that

she'd been shot. Blood stained her top, and she could feel the sting the bullet had left behind. A quick glance beneath her clothing let her know that the bullet had just creased her collar bone. It hurt a lot, but no major damage had been done. She'd been lucky to escape with her life, and it was all because…

She heard another yapping noise and remembered what had saved her.

Holly rushed downstairs and opened the door, a little cautiously in case Lizzie had some ferocious guard dog. She should have trusted her ears. Watson looked up at her like butter wouldn't melt in his mouth.

"Huh! So you get too tired to walk on a lead, but you can somehow follow me cross-country to a house?" she complained but bent down and ruffled the dog's wonky, floppy ears. He was only a baby but some instinct had already helped him save her life. There was no way she would be turning him out of her home. She and Watson were going to be a team like, well… Sherlock and Watson.

DIGGING UP THE TRUTH

It was New Year's Eve when George was released from hospital and came round to see her. Holly didn't comment on his orange face and the way his blonde hair was still several shades too dark. He probably didn't need to hear that right now.

"Thank you for saving me," he started, his eyes meeting hers when they both sat down at her kitchen table.

"You were the key to saving us both in the end. If you hadn't fallen on Lizzie like that, I'd have been done for," Holly said and smiled a little weakly. George echoed it.

"I'm just glad I didn't end up locked in that attic for years and years, until everyone forgot about me," he said. Holly opened her mouth to tell him that she would never have forgotten, but then remembered if all had gone to plan, she would be dead.

"I heard that the police have released Lana," she said, not knowing if George was up to date with the news, having been in hospital while the tranquillisers left his body.

"Yes, Lizzie has admitted everything. They told me that."

"It doesn't surprise me. The way she was talking was

crazy. She really believed that the people she made look like her brother were her real brother." Holly sighed. "I wonder what happened to the actual Jason. I suppose he really did die."

George rubbed his chin. "I'm not convinced it happened the way she tells it. I think she killed her parents and her brother ran. Maybe she found him and got him, too. Then the poor absent kid took the rap for it just because of his mental illnesses," George finished.

"When really Lizzie was the mentally ill one. It just didn't show on the outside," Holly finished.

They both sat in silence, looking at the tinsel that decorated Holly's house. All Christmas spirit had fled during the last couple of days. She couldn't believe it was the New Year tomorrow.

"Look... I need to talk to you," George finally said. Holly could already read in his tone that it was nothing good that he wanted to talk about. She reached down and stroked Watson's furry head, steeling herself for what was coming.

"I'm moving away. Too much has happened during the past few weeks, and I need to get away from it all. I don't actually need to be at the office to do my work, so I thought I'd do it remotely for a bit," he said. Holly tried not to think of Lizzie saying she would make George do the same thing.

"I... I wish things could have been different," George said, filling Holly's heart and then breaking it in a single moment.

"I understand," she said, patting his hand. "You should start somewhere new. It will be the best thing for you."

George nodded and gave her one last sad look, before he pushed himself to his feet.

"I hope we see each other again one day. I'll call you and we can catch up," he promised, but they both knew he was just saying it to be polite. George would be cutting as many ties as he could and trying to forget about the darkest December he'd ever experienced.

Holly completely understood where he was coming from, but the way she saw it, there was nothing wrong with the town. A few screws had come loose in some local people, but the same could be true anywhere. Little Wemley was her home, and the more crime she could uncover and solve, the less of it there would be. That was her view.

She waved goodbye to George when he walked back down her garden path. She shut the door a little sadly. Watson was already there waiting for her to stroke him. She went into the living room and curled up on the sofa with her puppy.

"Looks like it's going to be a quiet New Year's Eve, boy. Just you and me, okay?" she said. The dog yipped happily before burrowing under the blanket. Holly silently thanked Becky for finding him by the road and for bringing them both together. She needed a reliable sidekick.

Her phone buzzed in her pocket and she pulled it out, reading Rob's name on the screen. She shrugged at Watson and answered the phone.

"Finally! What have you been up to?" Rob said as soon as Holly answered. She allowed herself a small smile, pleased that Rob sounded just the same as ever. She'd been dreading this call, but somehow, she had a feeling it might just be okay after all. Perhaps it was the spirit of the New Year. Fresh starts all round!

She gave Rob a brief synopsis of the happenings of the past week.

He was silent for a few moments after. "You do know how to walk into trouble, don't you? Ever thought of solving the mystery before you barrel in and find out the truth the hard way?" he teased.

Holly grinned. He did have a point. It also didn't escape

her notice that his voice had brightened up considerably when she'd finished her tale by letting slip that George was skipping town for good.

"How have your cases been?" she asked, equally curious. Rob was always digging for the truth - literally. He used a spade. He uncovered archaeological finds and tons of stolen cash. She hadn't seen his name in the newspaper recently, which was quite unusual.

"I've been looking for something for a long time. I think I'm finally getting close, but it's dangerous, really dangerous. That's what I need to talk to you about. I think I need a partner on this one, and as we are business partners…"

"I'd love to work on a case with you," Holly jumped in.

"Thank you! I think it's best if you come and meet me here. I don't want to say too much over the phone. This is incredibly important to me. It's what I've been looking for my whole life, and I think I've finally found it…"

"I'm with you all the way," Holly reassured him, insanely curious about what it could be that Rob was after. When she'd first met him, the other detectives had hinted that he was searching for something he'd never found. Was she about to find out the truth about Rob Frost's dearest ambition?

"Before you make your mind up, you should know this…" Rob carried on and Holly's ears pricked up. "At least one other person is also looking. And they've already tried to kill me."

WINTER'S LAST VICTIM

PROLOGUE

For once in his life, Rob Frost was glad of the British weather. It was the night before New Year's Eve and the world was dark. Clouds covered the full moon. Rob liked the darkness. It reminded him of the depths of dug holes, and it was especially useful if you were planning to do something illegal.

Rob shouldered his spade and cast a final look around the field he was standing in, before he risked turning on the torch light on his phone to safely navigate the barbed-wire fence. A few seconds later, he was on the other side and turned the light back off, allowing his eyes to adjust to the black night before walking on.

His footsteps crunched on the grass. The frost had begun to take hold. He tried not to think about just how hard the ground would be and instead walked a little faster. At least staying warm was one thing he wouldn't need to worry about. Once he started digging, he'd be glad of the winter's chill.

He used his spade to swipe a path through the thicket of weeds that blocked his way into the scrubby woodland. The woods were part of the South Downs National Park. Rob knew from past experience that you definitely weren't supposed to dig holes in national parks. He didn't usually go out of his way to destroy national heritage, but he was finally on the trail of something he'd searched for his whole life. Tonight might be the night he found the treasure he'd dreamed he'd find ever since he was a kid.

He breathed out. His breath misted and froze in the air as he walked around the small clearing until he felt a familiar tug in his gut and began to dig.

At first, the ground hardly yielded to his spade. It had been cold for a whole month. Rob knew it would be hard going, but then the earth broke and gave way and Rob made his first impression. A smile lifted his lips. He forced the spade in deeper and began to dig a hole. All the time he dug, he thought about the truth he was going to unearth and felt the piece of metal that hung from a string around his neck warm against his skin. He knew it was around here somewhere, and he wouldn't give up until he found it.

Rob only paused for breath when his head was all that was poking out above the deep hole. So far, he hadn't found anything, but he would dig a little deeper down and then try again. He'd waited his whole life for this dig. He could wait a little longer. He'd listen to his gut some more and one of these times it would be right. He'd find it.

He frowned when the woods suddenly became silent. The sounds of the nocturnal creatures stopped. Hairs rose on the back of Rob's neck. All of his instincts screamed that something wasn't right.

Someone - or something - was coming.

The buzzing sound was out of place in the woods. If it had been the summer, his thoughts might have gone to a hornet, but it was the wrong season. When the sound got closer, he realised it was far louder than any insect. Curious,

Rob lifted his head a little over the lip of the hole and then instinctively ducked, as something swooped down on him. He blinked and turned his head, trying to see where the thing had gone, but he was unable to see much at all in the darkness. Rob felt strands of something fall on his face and dusted them off using a hand. He'd thought a leaf or a cobweb had landed on him, but he immediately realised he was wrong.

It was his hair that he was brushing off his face.

Rob nervously reached a hand up and discovered that his perfectly styled 'do was an inch shorter than it had been. The buzzing intensified again. Rob threw himself flat in the hole just as the drone swooped down again. He'd figured out that a drone was what this thing was when he'd seen the little pilot light. Going by the circular saws that were attached to the otherwise innocuous piece of technology, he'd say that this one had been somewhat modified. He stayed still in his hole as another fly-past was made. He was willing to bet that whoever was flying the thing was using night vision. He just hoped he'd vanished from their radar. He thanked his lucky stars that he was so quick at digging holes. A few inches more shallow, and he'd have lost his head.

The buzzing drone flew away, the noise fading into the distance. The nighttime sounds of the woods returned. Rob scrambled out of his hole and moved across the clearing until he collided, rather painfully, with a holly bush.

"Perfect," he muttered and slid behind it, just as the moon broke free from the clouds and illuminated the clearing where he'd dug his hole.

He didn't have to wait for long.

A minute later, two men walked into the clearing. They were both dressed in black - the universal fashion choice of people up to no good. The first thing they did was to go over to Rob's freshly dug hole and peer inside. One of the men shrugged. Rob detected some disappointment.

They'd been hoping to find a body - his body.

A chill ran up his spine as he watched the men raise their spades and start to dig their own holes. He could take no joy from the way their spades clanged against the frozen earth and the diggers swore when they made little to no progress. He didn't know who these men were, or how they'd managed to find him, but he was certain about one thing:

Someone else was looking for the same buried treasure... and they were willing to kill their competition.

STORY OF MY LIFE

Holly had a lot to think about when she started the drive down from Surrey to Sussex. She hadn't even known that Rob was so close geographically until he'd texted her, just moments before she'd told him she was going to leave. Something about all of the secrecy was making her skin prickle. She sensed that whatever Rob was caught up in, it wasn't good. He'd told her that someone had already tried to kill him, although he hadn't filled her in on how. All he'd said was that he needed her help, and like the good friend and business partner she was, she'd jumped straight in the car.

The other reason she'd been so happy to go on a road trip and ditch the sleepy town of Little Wemley was because of George. The company boss she'd thought she'd had some real feelings for had told her he was moving away for good. She couldn't blame him. Since she'd met George, he'd been accused of being a serial killer and then kidnapped by a crazy woman who'd imprisoned him in her attic. Holly acknowledged that there hadn't been a whole lot of time for romance to blossom between them.

For George, it had been too much. He'd decided to take a break from the weirdness around Little Wemley - and presumably around Holly - and had left. She'd be lying if she said she wasn't feeling a bit sorry for herself right now, but this case of Rob's was the perfect distraction. If she were being truly honest, Rob himself was distraction enough.

She smiled when she drove down the main road, her thoughts already drifting to Rob's dark hair, and his eyes that always glinted with trouble. She sighed. The first time she'd met Rob, she'd been immediately attracted to him, especially that dark wit of his, but before she could blink, they'd been caught up in a string of murders and had barely escaped with their lives. The situation had pushed them together and brought about the founding of their detective agency, Frost and Winter. But fortune had not favoured any romance.

She glanced in the mirror and tried to blow her fringe out of her eyes, so she could see Watson (her dog) properly. As usual, she'd let her fringe get too long but wasn't daring enough to take a pair of scissors to it herself. She'd lost count of the times she'd wetted her dark brown hair and hovered in front of the mirror with the scissors, never finding the courage to cut. Something inside her always warned it would be a mistake, and Holly had learned to listen to that instinct. The fact that she was still breathing proved it hadn't failed her yet.

Watson yapped from his place on the back seat and she thanked her lucky stars that the puppy wasn't travel sick. It was also fortunate that the boisterous crossbreed (who was looking more like a Collie mixed with an Alsatian everyday) was having a rare sleepy session. Otherwise, her upholstery would be in pieces. She only hoped that Rob wouldn't mind the addition of a puppy to their team, but she couldn't leave Watson behind - especially when he'd so recently saved her life.

An hour or so later, Holly pulled into the car park of a rather rundown hotel. Despite the January chill, they still had their faded, striped awnings out. Holly noted it was an attempt to cover the slew of mould that was crawling up the walls. She chewed her lip as she took in the awful establishment. What was Rob doing here?

She got out of the car and thought about leaving Watson behind but decided against it. He was too young for that. Hopefully, she'd be able to smuggle him in. It wasn't as if one little dog was going to contribute much deterioration to the general heap of a building.

A window on the second floor opened and she looked up.

"Room 28!" a voice said. She was almost tempted to tell Rob to stop being such a drama queen. This wasn't a spy movie. She held her tongue and walked inside, past the unmanned reception desk and up the stairs. Until she knew the full story, she wouldn't make any judgements.

Holly wound her way up the uneven steps (that had no right to be uneven, given that the building wasn't old, just in poor repair). The smell of old plastic and disinfectant drifted up from the floor, and if she'd closed her eyes, she might have imagined she was in a rather dirty hospital. The difference was, the guests were presumably paying to stay here. Watson whined at the steep steps and she picked him up, even though she knew he was just being lazy.

"Did anyone follow you?" Rob asked, sticking his head around the door when Holly approached.

She glanced behind her. "I wasn't really looking, to be honest. Seeing as I didn't even know where I was going, I doubt anyone would have followed me?" she said, wondering if that was a silly assumption to make.

Rob grabbed her arm and pulled her and Watson into his room before slamming the door. He stared at the dog for a moment and then seemed to dismiss him.

"You'd better tell me everything," Holly said, wondering if Rob had gone completely nuts, or more worryingly, if there was a good reason for his paranoia.

Rob nodded, pacing the room. Holly noted that his usually deliberately dishevelled dark hair was now simply messy, and there were dark shadows beneath his eyes she'd never noticed before. Holly was starting to have a really bad feeling about all of this.

"You'd better sit down. It's a long story. In fact, it's my story- the story of my life and what I've been looking for since I was a kid," he said. Holly seated herself on the threadbare armchair by the side of the bed.

"Oh, do you want some tea or coffee, or something? I wouldn't recommend it. The kettle is so covered in limescale I think it's just as likely to combust as it is to boil water," Rob said, returning to his usual snarky self for just a second. Holly managed an encouraging smile but shook her head, politely. Watson walked over to Rob and bit his bare foot, as affectionately as he knew how.

Rob stared at the lanky puppy. "I'm not even going to ask," he said and gently shook Watson free, although not without sacrificing his sock.

"So… someone tried to kill you?" Holly prompted.

Rob sighed and sat down on an incredibly ancient leather stool. "Yeah, but I'd better start at the beginning. Although, it would be cool to kind of jump around, you know - like films and authors do, just to add to the general confusion?"

Holly gave him a look, and a smile briefly lifted his lips.

"I like digging. I always have done. Even as a kid, that's all I did. I went out in the garden and dug up the lawn when I outgrew the sandpit, and so on. My parents used to go nuts at me, but eventually they gave in and bought a metal detector. I was obsessed with the idea of buried treasure. I guess I still am. Since then, I've got pretty good at finding it. My first ever find was a Roman coin. It wasn't worth much, but it was something. I still have it, you know..." he said, and then shook his head to free himself from the mists of the past. Holly waited patiently, knowing he would return to the present soon. "You know what happened next. I got better at finding things and started getting feelings about places. Pretty soon, I was digging up stolen hoards and accidentally caving in tunnels dug to rob a bank." He shot her a look when he said the last one. Holly nodded. She remembered. "I suppose you could say I was just lucky, but I like to think that the sheer number of holes I've dug makes my odds pretty good and my feel for it even better. But all of that stuff... those finds... they were just perks. I still haven't managed to locate what I've been looking for my whole life."

He took a deep breath. His mouth quirked up when he thought of something. "I know I said I wouldn't jump around, but we need to go back in time again. I was twelve when I first found the book that introduced me to the one piece of buried treasure that I would dedicate my life to finding. I'm not even sure what that book was doing in the local library, but it was great. It was super old. It didn't even have a publisher's mark, but it had so much stuff on archaeological curiosities." He paused for a moment, shooting Holly a surreptitious look. "I sort of... permanently borrowed it," he admitted. "The book talked about all things Roman, Iron Age, Bronze Age... you name it. Any legend of treasure in Britain from the past, it was in this book, but so was something else. There was one legend that talked about Midastophians. They were described as being the so-called golden race because they'd managed to accrue so much wealth - namely, gold. There was no mention of whether they mined it, or stole it, but I was intrigued. I'd never heard of the Midastophians before and the more I read, the more I wanted to know. The book I'd found said that their society was only legendary, much like Atlantis. And, just like Atlantis, they'd disappeared without a trace, leaving no proof of their existence." He looked at Holly with the light of adventure shining in his eyes. "If anyone ever managed to find the missing proof, they would turn the history of the world upside down. The Midastophians were said to be an incredibly advanced society, perhaps even more advanced than we are now. Yet they were theoretically wiped out without a trace. That's the biggest mystery of all, and the one I've always dreamed of solving. Right after finding proof of their existence, of course."

Holly tilted her head and ruffled Watson's floppy ears.

"What makes you so sure they existed?" she asked, as carefully as she could. Rob smirked and she sensed he'd been asked that question many times before.

"I did do further research and found mention of the Midastophians in journals and so on. Just to double-check that the book I had wasn't some spectacular work of fiction. Aside from that, I think I just know in my heart and in my gut." He turned his dark eyes on Holly. "You know the feeling, don't you?"

She slowly nodded. She'd always thought that gut feelings were one of the most reliable ways of making the right decision.

"So, various publications speculated as to where the society might have once existed. Some even speculated that, much like Atlantis, the society was a floating one. My feeling has always been that if they lived on the land and somewhere in this country, I would find them." He paused for a second. "I think I finally might have done it. Two days ago, there was an article in *The Daily Mail*..." He took a second to shake his head at that. "The article claimed that a man had dug up a piece of alien technology near the South Downs. The writer was basically mocking the poor man, and I'm sure no one took it seriously. I contacted the archaeologist and asked to look at his find, the way I have done for years with cases like that - just on the off chance that it's a lead. This one was different." He pulled the string around his neck and a tiny piece of gold swung out on top of his shirt.

Holly stood up and moved closer to look.

At first, it looked like the interior of a watch with many cogs and pieces miraculously melded together, but the closer she looked, the stranger it got. She could see tiny, clear vials of unrecognisable substances and realised that the design was more complex than she'd ever seen before. She couldn't even fathom what this odd piece of technology may have been used for, or even if it was of human design.

"I looked at it under a microscope and some of the workings have been microscopically engineered," Rob said. Holly started to chew her lip as she thought it all through. "Before you ask, I carbon-dated it. It's not modern. In fact, it's at least five thousand years old." He paused again. "The Midastophians really did exist, and I'm so close to finally finding the evidence that will prove it." Rob rubbed a hand through his hair, making it even messier. "Unfortunately, I'm not the only one who read the article in *The Mail,* or perhaps I've been followed. I'm not sure which, but two things I know for sure. I'm not the only one digging, and someone tried to kill me yesterday."

THE DEADLY DIG

"What happened? How did you survive?" Holly asked, feeling as though she'd been dropped straight into the plot of an *Indiana Jones* film. Rob shifted his weight and stood up, walking over to the grimy window to look out across the car park.

"I've been digging at night, so as not to draw attention to myself. The Midastophian artefact was found in a small patch of woods, next to an official dig site. A farmer owns it and lets amateurs do what they like there, but the woods next to it are technically off limits. You're not allowed to dig there, as it's part of the South Downs National Park. Even though it's not as if anyone ever goes to that bit. It's just weeds."

Holly tried not to roll her eyes. It was typical of Rob to disregard anything that wasn't to do with digging. His 'weeds' were probably a patch of incredibly rare orchids.

"So I went out to dig and had just got started on a good hole when I heard something buzzing." He made eye contact with Holly. "It's January and freezing at night, so I was immediately suspicious. No way are there any hornets floating around. So," he continued, "I stuck my head up above the hole and nearly lost it when this drone swooped down. It happened so fast, it took me a few seconds to realise what the stuff falling into my face was. I realised it was hair - my hair. The drone had been equipped with rotating blades - that was what made the buzzing noise. It had got close enough to take a little off the top." He shook his head. "It was lucky I'd dug deep enough, or it would have taken a whole lot more off the top."

Holly's hands had gripped the sides of the armchair when Rob had begun his near-death experience tale, but now she relaxed, patting Watson while she thought about all that Rob had said.

"What are we thinking... are the council trying a more unorthodox approach to weed control, or is some big, bad, unknown trying to stop anyone from digging there?" she said.

Rob frowned at her. "Hey, I'm the only one allowed to make tasteless jokes!" He shook his head in mock disbelief. "It was totally a bad guy. I kept my head down... literally... after that. Once the drone was gone, I decided to do a little reconnaissance. I crawled out of my hole and hid behind a bush. A minute later, a couple of guys dressed in black walked through the woods and started checking out the pit I'd dug. I could tell they were up to no good because they were wearing black. At the time, I was also wearing black... see? It all makes sense," he said, diverting himself. "Anyway, they seemed pretty disappointed that I wasn't headless in the hole I'd dug, after their deadly drone had done its work. It didn't stop them for long, though. They were soon digging their own holes, which is when I left."

"Who do you think they are?" Holly asked, but Rob just shook his head.

"I don't know, and I don't know why they'd want to kill me to stop me from looking. If I were paranoid, I'd say it was a secret government force who are tasked with covering up any evidence from the past which conflicts with our current widely accepted version of history." He raised an eyebrow at Holly to show he wasn't serious. "That, or someone knows more than I do about exactly what it is that's buried somewhere around here." He rubbed his head and sat down on the edge of the bed. "I wish I knew more, but I don't. All I'm good at is digging holes and finding things, but I don't think that's enough this time. I know I'm viewed as a detective, but beyond historical research, I'm fairly useless. The other detectives were annoyingly correct when they hinted that a few times. That's why I need your help." He looked at Holly imploringly.

"What do you want me to do? Should I try to find out who it is that's also looking for the treasure? And what about the treasure itself? If someone has a clue about what it really is, I should find that out, too, right?" she said, speaking her thoughts aloud.

Rob nodded enthusiastically. "Yeah, and while you're at it, if you could find the exact location, too, that would be great," he joked. Holly shot him a sideways look.

He grinned at her. "Come on, Hols, I know we can crack this together! You do all of the detective stuff. I'll figure out where to dig using my super secret, tried and tested method." There was a pause while Holly waited for him to share the method. Rob clammed up.

Holly narrowed her eyes. "You just guess and get lucky, don't you?"

Rob spluttered indignantly. "There's a lot more to it than that, but I wouldn't expect you to understand," he said, airily. Holly tried not to roll her eyes again.

"Sure," she said, deciding to leave it there. "I think we should start by going back to the place where you were attacked by the drone from *Robot Wars*," she said and smirked at her own joke. "Also, Watson needs a walk, so it makes perfect sense to start there."

"Cool, well, I'll see you later then," Rob said, lifting his feet onto the bed and picking up a magazine.

"Come on," she said, grabbing his arm and pulling him off the bed. He opened his mouth to protest but she gave him a look.

"You said you only dig at night, Rob, so you've got some free time. Also, you'll have to help me find where you were digging."

Rob snorted. "It's not exactly difficult. Keep walking until you fall into the really big hole." Holly gave him another look. He put on his shoes, grumbling under his breath.

Holly found she was forced to agree with Rob's description of this corner of the South Downs National Park being particularly weed-ridden. Resilient, neck-high stinging nettles had refused to die down, despite the icy cold, and brambles tore at Holly's jeans. The only unusual thing was the tops of the nettles, which had been sheared off in a straight line.

"Rob, I believe you," she said when they passed a sapling - which was now little more than a stick with roots. Behind her, Rob muttered something about a lack of faith. Holly pressed onwards through the wild weeds and soon reached the clearing that Rob had spoken about.

She frowned when her eyes fell on the holes and she counted one, two, three.... four. In Rob's story, there had only been three holes dug. Had the men come back the next night and dug again? She walked forwards, immediately picking Rob's perfectly circular hole out from its jagged companions. The first two holes she looked into were empty. The third had a body in it.

Holly looked down at the decapitated corpse.

"Rob... would I be right to assume that you didn't report the attempt on your life to the police?" she said, already knowing the answer.

Rob joined her at the lip of the hole and shook his head. "No, the police are probably working with the government." Holly readjusted her view on Rob's paranoia levels.

"Then we have a problem," she observed.

FRIENDS REUNITED

"I don't believe it!" a familiar voice said.

Holly turned to see Detective Inspector Stephan Chittenden striding through the woods towards them. A cluster of police spread out through the clearing, taping off the area, while white-suited men inspected the body.

"What are you doing here?" Holly asked, not bothering with pleasantries - Chittenden never did.

"I'll ask the questions!" he barked back, spittle spraying from his lips. The silence stretched and Chittenden narrowed his piggy eyes. "What are you doing here?"

"We were just taking a nice stroll through the woods with Holly's dog - like normal people with dogs do - when all of a sudden, we saw the holes and found a body. It was all very unexpected," Rob said, completely unconvincingly.

Chittenden's eyes turned into slits when he examined Rob. "You were involved with the Amateur Archaeological Society murders." He sounded like he was accusing Rob of the crime itself.

Rob nodded enthusiastically. "Yes, and the Horn Hill House massacre. There was quite a good picture of me in the paper, although I'd never say so myself," he said, waving a hand. Chittenden's face might have been carved from marble, but it didn't seem to deter Rob. "Just to reiterate, we were walking through the woods when we happened upon the body and like the good citizens we are, we reported the crime to the police and hung around until you arrived - something which murderers don't tend to do," Rob added.

Holly wondered if anyone would notice if she jumped into one of the pits and kept digging until she reached Australia.

Chittenden's forehead creased as he struggled to comprehend Rob's humour, or perhaps he was just wondering which cell to throw him in. "You'll have to give statements and leave current contact details." He shot them both a withering look. "Not that it's any of your business, but I was transferred here due to my excellent past case record."

Holly opened her mouth to argue that she'd basically solved the two most recent cases he'd worked on but then thought better of it. She seemed to have an unfortunate knack for being at the scene when bodies turned up. She was lucky that, thus far, they'd found the people culpable for the crimes. Otherwise, she was fairly certain that Chittenden would have locked her up and thrown away the key.

"Well, what wonderful news. We should go for a drink to celebrate!" Rob said, not taking any of this seriously. Holly might have throttled him if they weren't at the scene of a murder and she was currently trying to come across as un-murdery as possible.

Chittenden looked like he might be physically sick. He finally turned away from Rob to go and look at the far less offensive corpse.

"I think we're bonding," Rob whispered. Holly jabbed him in the ribs.

Watson whined by her ankles and pulled on his lead. She

gave him some more slack and then followed when he seemed intent on walking on through the trees.

"This had better not be a squirrel…" she started to say but stopped speaking when they entered the next clearing.

There were holes everywhere.

Holly tried to count but the number was definitely upwards of twenty. Someone had been doing some serious digging.

"You can't just walk off!" Chittenden's voice bellowed through the woods before the man himself entered the clearing and stopped. His eyebrows shot up and then a frown creased his forehead, adding to the wrinkles that were already fixed there. "You're both coming with me to the station. I want to know exactly what is going on here!" he said and just waved a hand when Holly opened her mouth to protest that they'd simply been out walking Watson in the woods.

Even Chittenden wasn't that gullible.

"Do you get the feeling we're being used as bait, or is it just me?" Rob commented when they were finally released from the police station.

Holly glowered at the pavement as they walked towards the bus stop with Watson bouncing happily beside them.

"It's almost as if they expect us to get into trouble," Rob carried on. Holly ignored him.

After ascertaining that they hadn't decapitated the as yet unknown man, they'd been told they were free to go. The police's plan was pretty transparent. Holly didn't think she'd seen Chittenden smile before. She could also tell they hadn't bought Rob's story about the deadly drone. Even to Holly, it sounded like something from a sci-fi novel, but the severed weeds and the body in the hole suggested otherwise.

"I suppose it means we'll be being watched," Holly offered. "It could help keep us safe."

"That depends on whether they wait until after a crime has definitely been committed before running to help," Rob countered.

Holly sighed. They were on their own.

She noticed a car slowing down in her peripheral vision and turned slightly, wondering if they needed directions.

"Need a lift?" an overly cheerful voice asked.

That was the last thing Holly remembered.

She woke up in a room lit by a single bare light bulb. Normally, she'd have appreciated the irony, but her head was still swimming from whatever it was they'd used to knock her out.

That was right.

She'd been knocked out and kidnapped.

Holly blinked and tried to analyse her surroundings. It might mean the difference between life or death.

The walls and floor were all grey concrete with no windows at all. The only feature was the door and the chair she was sitting in. Watson was by her feet, asleep, which was something at least.

Two men dressed in suits walked into the room. Holly spared a thought for Rob, wondering where he was, before the men crossed their arms and stared at her.

"You're Holly Winter, a pianist, and more recently, a private detective," one of the men said.

There was a long pause.

"Should I be taking notes?" She couldn't resist having a dig. She'd been kidnapped, left in a tiny room, and now these two strange men were telling her they knew who she was and what she did. Big deal. What could they possibly want with her?

There was the sound of a scuffle outside of the room. Holly's heart lifted when she heard a familiar voice screaming about wanting a lawyer. The door burst open and two heavies half-threw, half-pushed Rob inside. Rob dusted himself down and walked over to stand next to Holly, facing down the two men.

"As I just said to your colleague, we're partners, so whatever you want, we're both involved," Rob said.

Holly didn't know whether to cheer or groan. Was Rob dragging her even deeper into this mess?

The two men exchanged a glance and then seemed to make a decision.

"We know you're looking for something, and we want to know when you find it. From now on, you're working for us," one man said.

"Will you pay us? Also, who are you?" Rob asked. Holly couldn't believe he was still joking around.

Another glance was exchanged. "No pay. We're the government. That's all you need to know," the other man said.

Rob shrugged. "I guess the lack of pay supports your claim, but have you got any ID on you?" The men made no move. "What… not even a company pen?"

"There are others looking for the same prize as you - people who we don't want to have that kind of power. When you find what you are looking for, you will let us know immediately. The other hunters may be dangerous," the man carried on.

"'May be dangerous'? Tell that to the headless corpse in

the hole," Rob muttered, shaking his head. "All of this over some old stolen coins." He sighed dramatically.

Holly bit her tongue right before she asked him what he was talking about.

The men exchanged another look.

Rob pretended to look confused. "You are looking for the horde, right? There's meant to be several million pounds worth of stolen gold buried around here, left by bank robbers in the twenties. Unfortunately, word has got out about it... Look, I've already found what I think might be a bit of it," Rob pulled a piece of gold, shaped like a coin, out of his pocket. Holly kept her facial muscles slack to hide any surprise.

"Mr Frost, we know you're looking for evidence of the Midastophian civilisation," one man said calmly, finally getting the word out in the open.

Rob shrugged. "You can believe what you want to. I'm on the lookout for stolen money. I'll let you know when I find it, the same as I always let the government know. I'm an honest man."

There wasn't much more that could be said after that. The men took them out to a back alley. Holly experienced a brief moment of panic when she wondered if they were going to be executed, before the men slammed the door shut behind them and left them alone in the street.

Holly waited until they were a few roads away before she broke the silence. "Stolen money?"

Rob grinned. "Yeah, too bad they didn't buy it." He took the gold piece out of his pocket and looked at it. "It really is stolen, too." Holly raised her eyebrows at him. "I stole it from a horde of gold coins I was meant to declare and hand over."

Holly snorted. "What was that you were saying about being an honest man?"

Rob's lips moved up, but his expression soon turned

stormy. "So, the government are sticking their noses in. I thought they might," he said, as they strode briskly down the streets. Watson was back to bouncing along, although Holly suspected their busy day might be sapping his energy.

"You think they're telling the truth about who they are?" Holly asked.

Rob nodded. "Let's just say I've had a few brushes with the government before. I know the kind of morons they employ. The old 'snatch and grab for no reason other than to intimidate' is exactly up their street."

Holly bit her lip and tried to take it all in. Rob was acting remarkably casual, considering they'd been kidnapped and told to hand over the very thing he'd been searching for his whole life.

"So... what do we do now?" Holly asked, thinking about having both the police and the government watching them. They wouldn't be able to sneeze without someone knowing it.

"We dig... we dig really obviously and in all of the wrong places," Rob said.

Holly opened her mouth to ask how he knew which places were wrong, when he hadn't found anything yet. She shut it again.

It wasn't worth it.

FIRE IN THE HOLE

Holly felt like she was in the film *Holes*. The only difference was, they were digging in sub-arctic temperatures and the ground was as hard as iron. She sighed and kept digging - still on her first hole while Rob had dug three. Although she couldn't see the police or the government officials, she sensed that they were being watched.

Her spade hit something and she felt a jolt of panic run through her. Oh no! She hadn't really found something had she? This was a disaster! She bent down and gently prised the item free from the earth. It shone a dull silver in the morning light.

"Er, Rob…" she said, not knowing how to be subtle about this. Was she holding something important, or was it just junk?

Rob walked over and slid into her hole, taking the item. "Hmmm looks like a Roman gold arm cuff, or something. I'll show you where to flog it later," he said and walked off again.

Holly felt strangely relieved. Any other time, she'd have been thrilled to make her first ever discovery, but if Rob really thought they were close to finding something that would prove the Midastophians really existed, every spadeful made her nervous.

"Pssst! The reason you found that is because we are digging right over the Roman settlement," he said from his hole next door. Holly finally figured out what he'd meant by saying that they would deliberately look in all of the wrong places.

It was an hour later when she decided her first hole was finished. She reached around for the grass to pull herself up and was surprised when a huge clod of earth, complete with its own patch of grass came loose. She looked at what was beneath it in horror and instinctively dropped the piece of earth back into place.

Oh no... she thought, realising what she'd just done. She threw herself out of her hole and into Rob's neighbouring pit, landing on him just as a violent explosion of rocks and dirt blew through the wall of Holly's dig. Holly suddenly realised she was straddling Rob and rolled off him, feeling the heat rise to her cheeks.

"What's wrong with digging a hole the normal way?" Rob asked, bemused.

"I found a landmine," Holly said. She'd learnt exactly what they looked like in the aftermath of the Horn Hill House massacre and had even known there was often a two second trigger. That was why she'd just had time to jump and had been lucky enough to be below the explosion when it went off. "I may have accidentally triggered it," she admitted.

Rob gifted her an incredibly sarcastic 'you don't say?' look.

They both hauled themselves out of the hole and sat on the grass of the field, not wanting to move.

"I was expecting more police and agents by now," Holly confessed when they were still sat there five minutes later.

Rob smirked. "Why do you think they tried to contract us? They don't have enough resources to do the dirty work themselves."

In the end, they figured out the way they'd walked into the field and carefully trod back. Holly was relieved that she'd left Watson back at the hotel, not wanting to risk having to sneak him in and out again.

She only hoped the hotel was still standing.

Rob pulled out his phone and called the police as soon as they were out of the mine field. Holly noticed a couple of about her age walking their way, carrying bunches of flowers.

"Hi, just to let you know, we found an unexploded land-mine. We're waiting for the police to come and check for more," Holly said, hoping they'd assume it was a freak mine left behind by some long gone military - and not attempted murder.

"Good luck getting the police around here to do anything that resembles work," the man said. He was sharply elbowed in his ribs by the lady.

Holly looked politely enquiring.

The woman sighed. "Sorry, we're not exactly in high spir-its. James' father died near here yesterday. All he was supposed to be doing was digging for Roman treasure, or something like that." She shook her head. "He was just a hobbyist. We don't understand how he could have died, and the police won't tell us anything. They haven't even let us know the cause of death yet," she explained while James looked sadly into the distance.

"They aren't doing anything. They're not even investigat-ing!" the man said, looking around the landscape for any evidence of police activity. Holly had to admit, there was absolutely no sign of life and any police officer in the area would surely have come running when she'd blown up the field.

"Look…" she began, wondering if she would regret this later. "I might know a bit about your father's death," she addressed James, feeling terrible about what had happened. The couple didn't know it, but the death definitely fell under the 'suspicious' category, and the lack of investigation was out of place. Either the police were secretly staking out the area, or, more plausibly - someone had told them to keep their noses clean.

Holly shivered when she thought about the creepy government men and wondered just how high up this whole thing went.

"Anything you can tell us, we'd really appreciate," the man said.

Holly took a deep breath before launching into an abridged and sensitive version of the story. She left out the Midastophians, the deadly drone, and the government organisation, but let them know how the man had met his end and where they'd found him. Without the additional information, the best she could do was to warn them to stay away from the woods if possible, or at least definitely only go there in daylight hours. The couple weren't stupid, she knew they could tell she was keeping things back, but they were grateful for any information at all.

"Please don't think me rude, but how are you involved in all of this?" the lady asked, and Holly had to think on her feet again.

"I'm a private detective. I've been looking into some unauthorised digging that's been going on around here," she said, hoping it didn't sound too lame.

The couple looked intrigued.

"You could work for us! We'd pay you to find out about dad's death," James said.

Holly felt a stab of guilt. "I have my suspicions that the case I'm working on and yours share the same answer, so I wouldn't take any money for it. I'll let you know if I find out anything," she said.

The woman scrabbled around in her bag for a business card. Holly pulled out her own newly pressed card and handed it over, feeling unusually professional.

"Oh... so here they are at last," James muttered when a police car pulled up, not even bothering to turn the emergency lights on - despite the threat of unexploded mines. Holly had expected a bomb squad at the very least. What was going on?

In between the distraught couple's ranting, Holly and Rob discovered that A - the police weren't going to do anything other than tape off the area (something that wouldn't even deter a determined amateur archaeologist from digging) and B - DI Chittenden had been called back to his original office. Holly guessed it was because he wasn't playing ball with his superiors and letting the case drop. She felt some grudging respect for that. Chittenden was an ass, but he was determined to go after criminals. His disappearance just made the situation look even more bleak.

Someone was manipulating the game and they didn't care if a few of the players were taken out.

"Surely there are other places to walk a dog in a national park?" Holly complained when she let Watson off the lead later that evening and hoped that the landmine planter hadn't spread their net too wide. They were walking just a few fields away from where they'd been digging that morning.

Watson tore off, eager to explore the new area and get into as much trouble as possible.

"Do you think even now, we're being watched?" she asked Rob.

His mouth smiled but his eyes remained hard. "Nope. I think you put that theory to the test pretty well with the landmine incident this morning. If anyone had been watching they would have come running - if only to see if you'd found anything good," he said, his tone dark.

"So what do we do now?" Holly asked, thinking aloud more than really asking the question.

"Keep looking and hope we find it before everyone else does. And when we do find it, we do our best to hide what we find," Rob answered.

They walked on in silence for a bit, both lost in thought, until Watson started barking.

They exchanged a glance and ran towards the sound.

The black and tan cross breed stood proudly by a fairly impressive hole of his own digging.

Rob let out a low whistle. "Looks like he's picked up a trick or two from the master!" he said with a grin.

Holly smiled, just glad it hadn't been another body. She walked over to inspect the hole and found that actually, there was something at the bottom of it.

"Rob…" she started to say. He appeared at her side, bending down before brushing the dirt off the smooth metal slab and reverently picking it up.

It looked like a smooth, silver, alien rock.

"Is that…?" Holly asked.

Rob nodded. "Something belonging to *them*. Yes, it is."

LOST IN TRANSLATION

"Stop," Rob said, just before they walked through some trees into a clearing. They were nearly back at the car and the hero of the hour, Watson, was back on his lead.

Holly tilted her head at Rob. He mouthed the word 'digging'. He went down on his belly and crawled forwards up a little bank, peering through the twilight. Holly strained her ears and could just about hear the sound of a spade being thrust into the earth. She shook her head. They must be a long way away. Why was Rob being so cautious?

He returned a few moments later, shaking his head.

"I don't know who they are, but they're digging near to where Watson found the item. It can't be a coincidence. Someone must have seen something…" he said, looking annoyed.

Holly didn't know what to say. She knew how devastated Rob would be if the proof he'd been looking for his whole life was discovered by someone else, and then just as quickly covered up.

"At least we have something," she said.

Rob's eyes darted around the woods, as if seeing the shadows of their enemies everywhere. "We'd better get back," he said. Holly didn't like his tone. It hinted that they were in grave danger.

She only breathed a sigh of relief when they made it back to the hotel without being beheaded or blown up. *Result.*

Rob had disappeared as soon as they'd returned to the room. Holly was left with a tuckered out Watson and nothing else to do. She sighed a few times, made herself a cup of limescale tea, and then got her laptop out to search for some new piano tune ideas.

When she was on the internet, she remembered the little blog she'd started. Holly smiled and thought about the adventures she'd had since the Enviable Emerald case. She needed to write up her two most recent cases. Her nose creased for a moment as she thought hard. *A Fatal Frost* and *Murder Beneath The Mistletoe* sounded like good names. She sipped her tea, regretted it, and then started to write.

It was gone midnight when the door to the hotel room was flung open and Rob bounced in, his eyes wide. He shut the door behind him, breathing heavily.

"What's wrong?" Holly asked, immediately jumping to her feet and getting ready to run, or fight.

"It's… it's the Midastophian artefact we found today. There's writing on it, which I translated. It talks about the demise of their society and exactly what it was that wiped them off the face of the planet."

Holly grinned. "That's great! Isn't that all the proof you wanted to find? They did exist and they did disappear mysteriously. Why did they disappear?"

Rob glanced down at the blank slab of metal again. Holly frowned. It was definitely blank.

Rob saw her look. "Before you ask - no, I'm not crazy. The Midastophians were very advanced and made this tablet so that the letters only show up at a specific temperature and with the addition of moonlight. I'm sure it was intentional, so that only the brightest and best of any society who uncovered their secrets would be able to read the message," he said airily.

Holly smirked. "Well it looks like they messed that up."

Rob spluttered indignantly before continuing.

"The language they use is actually very simple, which is curiously a sign of a technologically advanced people. Consider the way our own language is constantly being simplified and modified. Look at what the Americans have done to English... Anyway, the Midastophian text wasn't hard to decipher." He frowned again. "I almost wish I hadn't cracked it." He ran a hand through his dark hair.

"What the hell does it say, Rob?" Holly asked, itching to know what was making him so worried.

"The Midastophians wrote this: Our society is failing and there will be no survivors. The culprit is a disease, which we developed as a weapon to fight against others. The disease escaped, spread, and we have found no cure. All is lost," he quoted and took a deep breath. Holly realised there was more to it than that. "They also wrote that they preserved a vial of the disease and concealed it beneath the roots of their society for a better, more advanced civilisation than theirs to discover," he finished.

Holly felt the implication of his words sink in.

There was a sample of a disease that had wiped out an entire civilisation buried somewhere.

"That's bad," Holly said.

Rob nodded, rolling his eyes. "Yes it is. Now I can see why the government is so eager to get involved. I'm willing to bet they'd want to use the sample for the very same reason that the Midastophians developed the disease. Who knows? Perhaps they'd make the same mistake, and we'd all end up dead," he said. "Someone must have found something similar to the tablet and already be one step ahead of us," he concluded and then narrowed his eyes. "Or, they're just stuck on their coverup mission."

"We should assume the worst," Holly suggested.

Rob nodded. "You never know what someone could have dug up and sold on. Whoever was flying that drone and planting those landmines, they weren't from the government. Someone else is looking, and they're convinced that it's worth killing for." He paused. "That doesn't sound like your average history buff to me."

Holly inclined her head in agreement. "So, we're searching for an ancient biological agent, which may or may not be active, and may or may not have the power to kill everyone on the planet," she summed up.

"Maybe we could blow up the whole area?" Rob said, half seriously. She shot him a look, knowing his track record with explosives. He'd probably blow up the nearest three villages, too.

"Can't do it. It might release whatever it is that's hidden, and then we'd all be done for," she said, presuming the worst: that the disease was active, and that they had just as little resistance to it today as the Midastophians had experienced when they'd developed it.

"We could just tell the police, or the government people," she said, her gut already telling her that it was completely the wrong thing to do. Now it was Rob's turn to give her the look.

She groaned and ruffled Watson's ears, finding a distraction for a moment. "What the heck do we do?" Holly asked for what felt like the hundredth time.

Rob looked grim. "We make sure we find it first. I

suppose we'll figure the rest out after that."

Holly pulled a face. "That is the worst plan I've ever heard." She sighed. "I suppose it will have to do."

DOUBLE TROUBLE

Even though it was past midnight, they put on all of the warm clothes they could find and grabbed their spades. Holly tried not to think about the threat of decapitating drones and landmines. Instead, she focused on what might be their only opportunity to save the world. Her eyes grew misty as she thought about it. Perhaps she could add that to her business cards - private detective and saviour of the world. She rolled her eyes. It was too bad that if their mission succeeded, no one would ever find out just how close the planet might have come to another mass extinction.

"Oh no... I don't think I fed Watson!" she said and hurried back up the stairs before Rob could give an answer. The puppy would destroy the room if she left him without proper supplies. Not that it would be easy to notice the difference...

When she came down the stairs again, Rob was gone. She heard the revving of an engine and jumped back when a large, black van raced past her and then screeched to a halt. She sensed there was something familiar about the van.

Something sharp hit her arm and she blacked out.

When she woke up, she was in the small concrete room again.

"Can't you just pick up the phone?! What's with the kidnapping? It's not like I don't know the location. You made us walk back last time, remember?" Holly complained when the two suits entered the room. "Where's Rob? Get him in here now," she said, knowing that he'd be able to get them out again.

The suits exchanged one of their meaningful glances.

"We don't have him," one man said. "We thought you might know where he's gone."

"You're lying. You must have taken him, too," she said but noticed the uncomfortable stances of the two professionals. They'd messed up.

"Someone else has Mr Frost," they said.

Holly felt cold all over. It had to be the other group of hunters, right? The ones who liked killing people...

One of the men stepped forwards and handed her a piece of white paper. "We intercepted this after picking you up."

Holly was going to yell at him again about their different definitions of 'picking up' but what she read on the note stopped her.

It was addressed to her.

"Holly Winter, we have your partner. Find the answer and find us. It's the only way you'll save him," she read aloud.

The two men were staring at her. "Where are they?" they asked her, and she nearly laughed.

"How should I know?"

"Well, that letter suggests that you do."

She paused for a second, unsure of what to say. "Look, I don't know where Rob is. If I did, I obviously wouldn't have asked you where he was before you told me about the note, right?" she said, but the men didn't look convinced. "Maybe they thought I could figure it out?" she added, more thoughtfully. "But I really don't know - not now, anyway. I also don't know what the answer they're talking about is. That's all Rob's area of speciality. I was just here to investigate who was digging holes - other than Rob - and now I'm also looking into the murder of amateur archaeologist, Douglas Patterson - seeing as the police are doing nothing." She eyeballed the suits. They didn't flinch, although everyone in the room knew that nothing was being investigated on their say so.

"If these people find it first, we'll take them down. If you find it, bring it to us," one of the suits said.

She folded her arms at him. "How will that help Rob? From where I'm standing… the bad guys - if that's even what they are - are holding all the cards. Who am I more likely to hand this thing over to?" She was just as careful as the note writer had been to not reveal exactly what she knew. With Rob captured while presumably still carrying the artefact, it wouldn't be long before at least one of the other competing parties knew exactly what was hidden on the edge of the National Park.

The men looked at each other again before a thin smile lifted one of the men's lips. "Miss Winter, I think you'll find we can be very persuasive."

Holly just shook her head. "It's irrelevant, really. The other guys have the one you want. It's Rob who knows all of this stuff. I'm just a private detective. That's hardly a credible source for you to be relying on. The police will tell you just how much my input isn't usually wanted," she said with her own thin smile. *Take that!*

In the end, they let her go. Holly wasn't sure if it was because they believed her when she said she knew nothing, or if they'd finally figured out she was the useless one of the pair in this case. Holly was dropped off at the hotel by a silent driver and immediately went to check up on Watson, pleased to find him asleep on her bed despite everything. She almost wished he was a little bigger, so he could give them all a scare. She smiled at the sleeping puppy. It was silly to wish these days away. He'd never be a puppy again. He was already growing at an alarming rate and she knew she really had to work on some obedience training, or suffer the consequences when he was a full-grown dog.

She sighed and sat down on the lumpy bed, wondering where Rob was and if he was okay. The note had instructed her to find the answer and then find the people holding Rob. She hadn't a clue about how to do either of those things.

"I don't know what to do, Watson," she said before lying down on the bed and falling asleep fully clothed.

She woke up the next morning feeling panicky and with a dry mouth. What if someone had found the sample while she'd been asleep? What if it was all over for Rob? She shook herself awake, brushed her teeth, clipped a lead on Watson (grabbing his food on the way out), and raced to her car. Ten minutes later, she pulled up near the digging field.

As soon as she got out of the car, she knew something was wrong.

The usually silent surroundings were broken by the sound of many shovels digging. Holly wasn't willing to believe her ears and walked through the thin line of woods that divided the road from the field.

She was confronted with an extraordinary sight. Close to a couple of hundred people were digging in the field. She couldn't tell who was working for who, but there were the usual few amateur archaeologists who were scratching their heads as they tried to figure out what had got everyone so excited. Holly lowered her spade. Unless she got super lucky, she wasn't going to beat these diggers to the punch - not when she was guessing the same way they were. Even if she did, by some miracle, dig it up first, with all of these watching eyes, someone would see and she wouldn't have a chance to...

She bit her lip. She hadn't actually thought about what to do with the item if she did find it. She knew that Rob would tell her to go public, so that it was impossible for anyone to use the find politically or criminally (not that there was a huge difference between the two) but that would mean giving Rob a death sentence, and she knew she couldn't do that. Holly shook her head and vowed to think of something... right after she'd found the vial of disease.

Holly walked a little way up the hill, past the field. She had a lot to think about. She was going to make the assumption that the people who had taken Rob were the ones who'd flown the drone which had killed the amateur archaeologist, Douglas Patterson. If she figured out who and where they were, she'd be able to find Rob and hopefully bring the killers to justice. The note had said she'd be able to figure out how to find them. She snorted. Some of their lackeys were down in the field, weren't they? She'd found them easily enough, but somehow, she suspected they wouldn't be happy to tell her where they were keeping Rob. She chewed her lip, pausing to look out across the landscape from the side of the hill, her eyes sweeping over the diggers and the hilly fields beyond.

Her mind flashed up a piece of useless information - things were often buried at the top of hills, or mounds. She tilted her head and noted that the diggers were digging in a valley. But then, the same rules didn't necessarily apply to an ancient, but highly advanced, society. *A society who used moonlight to hide secret writing,* she silently reminded herself and wondered if they were closer to nature than most people were today.

She sighed, not feeling that she was getting anywhere. She wasn't an archaeologist. She didn't really have a clue what she was looking for and doubted she'd be able to gather any knowledge in the next 24 hours that would allow her to magically know the location of the Midastophian relic.

Sunlight flashed off metal and her eyes were drawn to the main car park for the National Park - the car park that all of the people digging had presumably used. She might not be an archaeologist, but she was a detective. It was time to put those skills to the test.

Watson darted around the car park, sniffing cars. Holly did the same - although without any actual sniffing and whilst acting as casually as possible. She was glad she had Watson there. It gave her a good excuse to be prowling around.

Think, Holly! Her eyes were drawn to a couple of vans. One of those would be big enough to hide a drone in, she realised and wandered over - first walking around the front to check that the vans were empty and then doing a complete circle.

The first van had rust spots all over it and years of dirt had accrued on its exterior. It was the sort of van you might see on any street corner. The second van was trying to look the same, but the sophisticated satellite tracking system and plush interior gave it away. Either the owner of this van was a very particular tradesman who loved technology, or she'd just hit the jackpot. She pulled her spy-supply lock-picking kit out of her pocket, having learnt a thing or two from YouTube. After a minute or so of sweating and fiddling with the lock, it clicked, letting her open the back door of the van.

Her jubilation was short-lived when the vehicle's alarm blared out, loud and piercing in the quiet country air. Holly swore under her breath and pulled both doors wide. The cold sunlight streamed into the van, giving her a perfect view of the killer drone. Holly sucked air between her teeth as she took in the sharpened rotating blades and noticed, with a sick feeling, that two of them were stained a rusty red.

The alarm was still screaming out its tune. Holly grabbed her phone and took a few photos, both of the drone and of the van, before shutting the back doors and legging it, with Watson panting happily beside her.

She wasn't a second too soon. The moment she'd reached the cover of trees, two men walked into the car park and went to inspect the van. Holly was suddenly horribly aware of the fingermarks she'd left in the dirt, but fortunately, one of the men put his hand right where hers had been and pulled open the back before shutting it again with a shrug.

"Guess you've got a faulty alarm. We'll have to get it sorted when we're back at The Grand. The boss won't like it," he said. The other one nodded before they walked back off in the direction of the digging field.

Holly stood up from her crouch and brushed herself free from leaf litter. The Grand... what could that mean? It sounded like a hotel to Holly, but she thought that would be an odd place for a load of criminals to hang out and plan operations. Perhaps she was being prejudiced. Bad people used hotels just as much as the good guys. She shook her head. Good and bad was all down to your perspective, anyway.

"That's a good lead, Watson. We might be able to find Rob after all." She ruffled the puppy's ears. "Now, I don't see any reason why those gentleman should be left to dig in peace, do you?"

She rang the police. At first, they didn't want to listen to her, but she made them give her an email address and then waited on the phone until they'd seen the pictures and agreed that at the very least - the drone was illegal, if not a murder weapon. Holly hung up with a frosty smile.

She hoped the couple she'd met would get some closure.

If only it was as easy to find the hidden vial! Holly sighed and started to walk back to her car. She was definitely searching for a needle in a haystack. *What if it's not even here?* she thought to herself and worried about that, too. Things didn't always stay buried. Someone could have found what they were searching for a long time ago and since lost it.

She rubbed her temples and got back into the car, deciding to spend the rest of the day reading about burial mounds and other points of interest. She supposed it would probably be a waste of time, but it was equally pointless digging with all those other people around. She planned to return that night when she hoped the flock would have thinned.

Holly glanced at the weather forecast on her phone and winced. She wouldn't be surprised if she were the only one crazy enough to do a little midnight digging. It was going to drop well below freezing and there was even snow forecast. At least she no longer had to worry about being decapitated by a deadly drone.

SOCIETY'S ROOTS

The night was silent when she walked through the wintery woods. She let Watson off the lead and hoped he'd let her know if any trouble was brewing. She felt rather ridiculous creeping around in the dark carrying a spade. If anyone saw her, she was sure they'd automatically assume she was up to no good. *Speaking of being up to no good,* she smiled a little when she thought back to earlier that evening when she'd received a call from James Patterson letting her know that both van men had been arrested, and the drone was currently being examined for evidence. At least one part of this case had been solved.

Unfortunately, she suspected the hard part was still to come. A thought had been nagging her all day. Even if she found the vial and handed it over to the lucky party of her choice, what was going to keep her alive? She'd put herself in the shoes of both and had concluded that things would be much simpler if she and Rob just... disappeared. So far, she hadn't figured out a way to alter the situation. She snorted. Some detective she was turning out to be!

Holly paused on the edge of what had once been a field.

She'd learned from Rob that the farmer didn't mind it being dug up as he was planning to plant crops there, but it looked like a war had taken place. Huge pits and heaps of earth mottled the area. Holly decided she definitely didn't want to go walking there in the dark. It was a recipe for a broken ankle and being a popsicle by morning.

Instead, she skirted the field and climbed the fence, looking for something - anything - to inspire her. She'd read a lot about ancient burial rituals earlier that day, but nothing felt relevant. Holly felt dismal as she walked, trailing her spade behind her. She supposed some kind of starting point was better than nothing.

"Come on... think!" she said aloud and tried to remember her last conversation with Rob. He'd said that the tablet read something about the vial being concealed beneath the roots of their society. She'd assumed that meant beneath where they used to live, but what if the word 'roots' was a clue?

"But no tree would still be alive after 5,000 years," she muttered, looking around at the woods and hills. There was a yew tree on a small hill in the next field. That afternoon, she'd read about yew trees and their symbolism to ancient societies. They also had one remarkable property - the ability to regenerate. There was actually no reason why a yew tree couldn't be immortal. Parts would die and perhaps rot back into itself, but the tree could continue to grow, with new life springing from the old.

She looked at the tree on the hill. It didn't look that old - not like the yews in churchyards that had been around since Roman times. But what if... what if it had always stood there - just dying down and coming back?

She took a deep breath and started walking in the direction of the tree-crested hill. It was as good a place to start as any.

Digging beneath tree roots turned out to not be such a great idea after all. When Holly dug, she constantly found her way blocked by roots that seemed as hard as iron and as thick as trunks. Technically, it boded well for her theory about the tree's longevity, but it was murder to dig through. In the end, Holly tried to go between, rather than through and ended up uncovering a web of roots which led down and down. She was on her stomach now, reaching to scrape dirt away with her hands, all the time thinking about Rob. If anyone saw her now, scratching through soil beneath a tree, they'd probably lock her up.

Holly dug down as deep as she could and then realised she would have to dig around the entire tree in the same fashion if she wanted to do a proper search. She shot a guilty look at the yew. Hopefully, it would be resilient enough to survive this indignity.

For once, luck was on her side, or with hindsight, maybe it was out to get her. Holly was only on her second big dig when her fingers brushed against something smooth - something that wasn't a tree root. With her heart jumping in her mouth, she gently pulled up what turned out to be a slim metal box, made from the same material as the tablet Watson had dug up. The box seemed not to have a lid, but when the bright moonlight caught it and Holly held the box against her skin, remembering what Rob had said about temperature, she felt something change. There was a little click as the lid came open. Holly silently prayed she hadn't just let some deadly disease walk free, before she peeked.

The interior of the box was lined with something soft, it felt like down, but artificially manufactured. Nestled at the centre of the box was a tube made of the same metal as all of the other artefacts. She felt her pulse quicken. The tube looked like it could quite feasibly contain a vial of something. Next to the tube was another metal tablet, which Holly slipped into her pocket, before gingerly closing the box again.

She sat down on a patch of undisturbed soil at the base of the tree. Watson rushed up to her, covering her in puppy kisses. She absentmindedly stroked him, wondering what the heck to do now. Two words echoed in her mind, *The Grand…* she'd done some research earlier, and while there was a local hotel with that name, there was also a casino - or rather, what had once been a casino - in the local tourist town of Entingbourne. It didn't look like anything had taken the casino's place, so in theory, all that was there was an empty building. It was the perfect place for a bad-guy HQ.

She took a deep breath and stood up, clipping Watson's lead on. Time to face the music.

The Grand Casino was a far cry from what its name inferred. The building had a faded, grey veneer of exhaust fumes all over it and four letters were missing from the casino sign. The front door and windows were boarded up, but it hadn't stopped people from writing graffiti all over the chipboard. Holly felt her heart sink when she took in the total dereliction and the boarded up entrances. It didn't look like anyone had been here for a long time. Had her hunch been wrong?

She got out her mobile phone and dialled a number she'd never imagined she would. A voice answered and she launched into preparing what she hoped would be a decent backup plan - if this was the right place after all. She sighed silently as she listened to what the other person was saying. One down, one to go. After the call, she tapped out a text message and pressed send. It was as good a plan as it got.

She decided to do a full sweep and walked down the side alley. Two men appeared from a concealed door and she ducked down behind a skip full of rubbish. The men walked past, both pulling out cigarettes, and Holly saw her opportunity. She tiptoed across the alley and silently pulled open the still-swinging door. It had no handle on the outside, which was probably why the men had left it ajar.

Once inside, the casino surprised her again. There was no smell of damp or decay. Instead, the carpet was a deep, lush red, and the walls were panelled with wood. It was a crime lord's den worthy of a *James Bond* film. Holly spared a moment to wish that she was *James Bond* and not a small town private detective, who'd been sucked too deep into a business that shouldn't have concerned her.

She shook her head. There was no time for that now. She had to find out all she could and then figure out how to get Rob out in one piece. The more knowledge she had, the more she would have to bargain with. She walked as silently as she could down the corridors, her heart jumping into her mouth at every corner. It was only when she approached a big set of double doors that she heard voices.

"...Doesn't look like she's coming. We'll have to do things another way. Looks like it's time to die, Mr Frost," a voice said.

Holly couldn't bear it any longer. She burst in, holding up the metal box. "Stop! I've got it!" she said, looking around a room full of bemused faces - but absent of Rob. She frowned, confused, until she saw the bank of televisions that were displaying the surveillance feeds from all over the building. *Oh.*

"Where is he?" she asked, hoping to bypass a 'you're so stupid' speech.

A man walked forwards, his lips curving up into a smile. He had oiled dark hair and an Italian or Portuguese look to him. When he spoke, his voice came out with a clipped British accent. "Mr Frost is otherwise engaged at the moment. Why don't you hand over what you've come to bring us?" the man said.

Holly thought about denying it for a second, but remembered she'd said she had it when she'd thought they'd been about to kill Rob. *What if he's already dead?* Her treacherous mind supplied. She shook it away. She still had a couple of cards left to play.

"You said if I found it, you'd give me Rob," she said, knowing she sounded like a petulant little girl.

The men all smirked.

"I've got some news for you... people lie. Hand it over." A gun appeared in the hand of one of the henchmen.

Holly ignored it, summoning all the brass she could. "Seeing as we're at the final showdown, would you mind spilling your master plan and letting me know who you are?" She deliberately looked down her nose at the men. A couple of men behind the leader exchanged a glance. Holly hid her smile. *Let them wonder why she was so confident!*

The leader laughed - the sound harsh and loud in the quiet surroundings. "It's not exactly lengthy, but sure, I bet Miranda would have wanted you to know," he said.

Holly's ears pricked up. The only Miranda she'd ever met had been the Miranda who'd turned out to be the mastermind behind the Horn Hill House massacre. She'd also been high up in the world of crime. The man read her expression.

"Yes... that Miranda," he confirmed. "We've been watching you ever since. At first, we all voted to send a sniper and end it that way, but then, because we were watching Rob Frost, too, we realised he was onto something - something that could be very profitable to us." He smiled nastily at her. "We took the chance that it actually existed and watched and waited. Now we have you, Mr Frost, and the destruction of humankind in our grasp. The right people will pay a lot for that."

Holly frowned. "I can see why someone would pay for that, but what if they actually decide to release it? You'd be just as dead as the Midastophians."

The leader's eyes flashed with amusement. "Did I say we were selling it? I just said people will pay a lot. They'll pay to stop us from letting it go. Who knows? Maybe one day we will release it... when our scientists have worked out an antidote and the world is desperate enough to give us anything we want in order to get it."

Holly's eyes scoured the room, looking for a way out while he spoke. There wasn't one. She'd just have to make her play and hope for the best.

The leader finished and the gun came up again.

"Wait!" Holly said, pulling the metal box out of her coat and holding it up in the air. "You don't know how to open it."

The leader rolled his eyes. "Actually, yes we do... Mr Frost was quite talkative once we got him going." Holly tried not to think about that but continued with her ploy.

"Sure... but I wasn't talking about the box, I was talking about the vial. You want it opened, right? The standard technique won't apply. The Midastophians were smart. Perhaps even more so than we are." She would have said definitely when considering her current company, but causing offence wouldn't be likely to work in her favour. "They won't have made it so that any fool can open the canister and retrieve the vial. Give it a try and let me know if I'm right," she said, pleased when her voice came out steady. She could feel beads of sweat starting at the base of her neck and was glad no one could see it beneath her dark-brown hair. She shut her mouth and waited. She waited to see if she would live through the next few seconds.

"Go get him," the leader barked. Holly's heart lifted,

praying they were talking about Rob. A few moments later, she breathed a sigh of relief when Rob was marched into the room flanked by two guards. He offered Holly a smile when he got in the room and she returned it, glad he was in one piece - despite the way the leader had been talking.

Her heart beat faster when she thought through their very limited options. She hoped that her backup plan would work out soon, or they were toast - but she had to let Rob know they needed to play for time.

"She says that it's not going to be simple to open the vial container up," the leader said to Rob, his eyes searching for a reaction.

Despite having been in their clutches for 24 hours, Rob shrugged and looked cool. "Holly's probably right. Give the usual method a try and see where it gets you," he said. For a second, Holly wished he didn't sound so confident… unless he really did know something. What if the darn thing just popped right open?

Rob gave her a look that said 'you do have a plan, right?' And she gave him a 'I'm not quite sure' look back. He shut his eyes for a second, but that was all the sign she got that he knew they were in deep trouble.

One of the henchmen walked over to her and grabbed the box. They opened a skylight and a shaft of moonlight shone into the room. Holly felt like cursing her luck for it being a clear night with a big, full moon. What were the chances of that happening in England mid-January?!

The henchman warmed the box and it popped open again, revealing the canister that probably contained a vial and potentially the demise of humankind.

He held the canister in the moonlight and warmed it, too, but to Holly's relief, it didn't open. Instead glowing writing flashed up and a grid of symbols appeared on the side of the canister.

"Looks like you need some kind of a code to get in," Rob commented, his eyes flashing with excitement.

"Then it's fortunate we've kept you alive so you can tell us what the code is," the leader said, his eyes dark with murder.

The henchman passed the canister over to Rob, who held it reverently. He was still staring at it when the leader cleared his throat. Rob shook himself, focusing on the symbols and their translation.

"Yeah, as I thought. The writing says something along the lines of: 'Only a society wise enough to learn from their mistakes will be able to access the secret'."

Holly tried not to groan at the irony. Here they were, with a bunch of people who wanted to blackmail the world with the contents of the tube. It was hardly what the Midastophians had intended.

"Open it," the leader pressed.

Rob frowned. "How? I don't know the password. Who knows what will happen if we enter it incorrectly too many times? It might lock up. It could even release the disease," Rob said, turning the canister, thoughtfully.

"Well, you'd better make sure you get it right!" the leader said. Rob smiled thinly. "Or what? Either the canister becomes useless, or we all die anyway. You've already said that you want us dead. Threats don't really matter anymore. How about this... we open the canister and you let us go without killing us and leave us alone forever?"

Holly privately agreed, but she couldn't figure out how they would be able to guarantee their safety.

The men in the room gathered into a huddle and words were exchanged before they grudgingly agreed, although a couple of men had wanted to torture the answer from them. Fortunately, they wanted the answer fast.

Luckily, Rob had watched far too many spy movies and had a great idea about how they would guarantee safety.

Two minutes later they were in a locked room - for some modicum of safety in case the disease was released. There was a CCTV camera trained on them. The idea was, they'd crack the code and then place the vial in a safe box, the combination to which Rob would set and be the only one to know. They'd walk out alive. Then, they'd get a call and hand over the code. It wasn't the greatest plan ever. Holly knew they might figure breaking into a safe was easier than letting them live, but there'd always be the possibility that the disease would break out if they used too much force. Perhaps that would be enough to keep them alive.

"If we do manage to get out of here, what will we do? It's not as if we'll be able to carry on our normal lives. This is bigger than anything we've ever been involved in and I don't know..." she said, thinking of Watson sitting outside in her car, waiting for her, or one of her backup plans, to turn up.

She hoped it would be her.

Rob nodded, his eyes on the tube and its glowing letters.

"We'll figure it out," was all he could think to say. Then he moved his head as close to her ear as possible. It would probably look like a lover's embrace to anyone watching. He whispered, barely audibly. "How long?"

Holly gave him what she hoped was a subtle half-shrug. She really had no idea. She didn't know who would come, or when they would arrive. It wasn't exactly ideal. Rob nodded and typed something into the grid of symbols. A beat passed and they all flashed red.

Wrong answer.

Rob blew out a breath and sat back on his haunches, his face lined with thought.

"Maybe it would be better to refuse to open it and sacrifice ourselves," Holly said, a little bitterly.

Rob just shook his head. "Someone will figure it out," was all he said. Holly hoped no one would listen and think it was a sign that they should be got rid of. She looked at the door they'd locked from the inside. It was a little insurance that they'd be able to get the vial into the safe before anyone busted in and shot them, but she still wasn't sold on whether or not they would be allowed to walk out unscathed.

"We'll be fine," Rob said through gritted teeth, although she wasn't sure if he was talking to himself or her.

Rob suddenly typed a few more symbols in and there was another pause before they flashed red. *Strike two,* Holly thought.

A bead of sweat slid down Rob's brow. What if the third wrong answer punished them by releasing the disease? A locked door would do nothing to stop an airborne pathogen!

"Take your time, Rob," she said, half-encouraging, half-warning. His fingers slipped on the canister and he rested it on the floor for a moment, running a hand through his hair. His eyes met Holly's and she was surprised to see they weren't stressed at all, Rob was ready and waiting.

They both heard the muffled rat-a-tat-tat of automatic gunfire and knew it was time to go.

RUN FOR IT

Rob shoved the canister into his pocket and unlocked the door. Holly was right behind him and Rob pushed open the door, fully expecting to find their way blocked by a couple of heavies.

The corridor was empty.

The sounds of shooting continued to their left. Holly wondered which task force had arrived. Judging by the wanton use of weapons, her money would be on the government. Who knew? They might even have blocked her instructions to her other backup party - although she doubted the man she'd contacted would listen, no matter how high up the orders came down from.

"Come on," Rob hissed. They walked in the opposite direction of the gunshots, hoping to find a way out of the rundown casino. They walked for a whole minute without seeing anyone. Holly wished they had some kind of weapon, but there was a whole load of nothing. Red carpet and wood panels were the grand sum of the casino. The lack of windows made her think they were in a basement of some sort. She wondered if there was a way out, or if there was only one set of stairs. She chewed her lip but kept silent, walking behind Rob.

A figure stumbled into view. Holly's eyes collided with those of the oily-haired leader. He was holding a gun.

"Where do you think you're going?" he growled.

They both raised their hands.

"We heard shots and thought we'd better get to safety. After all, our survival was the deal. When we looked out of the room to see what was going on, it didn't look like we were being looked after." Rob tried to look as self-righteous as possible, but Holly could tell the leader wasn't buying it.

"You're not leaving," he said flatly and kept the gun levelled at them.

"Like I said… we were just trying to find somewhere safe…" Rob said, carrying on with his spiel. A shot smashed through the wood panelling, next to Holly and Rob. The leader spun round to face a couple of men in black suits, who were running his way. He shot back and caught one of them in the shoulder. Holly's mouth fell open in horror, but Rob was already pulling her back the way they'd come.

"Come on! We've got to find the way out," he said. She tried to ignore the gunfire from behind, not wanting to know the outcome. It was highly probable that someone would be on their tail in seconds.

They burst into the main hall where the shootout had almost reached completion. Holly saw Rob bend down and scoop something up. She felt a little relief that he was now armed. She thought back, what felt like an age, to him talking about comparing 'toys' with the military detective who'd died at Horn Hill House and prayed Rob really did know how to use a gun.

He pulled her down behind an oak table, which had been flipped. They sat in silence, listening to the traded gunfire for a few moments. Somehow, they'd managed to get into the main room undetected. Holly tried not to look at the bodies on the ground. This was worse than anything she'd ever imagined!

"The only way out I can see from here is the front entrance, but it looks boarded up. Did you see it when you came in?" Rob asked.

Holly nodded, thinking back to what she'd observed. "It's just chipboard, but the door's probably locked, right?" she said, not feeling too hopeful.

Rob stifled a laugh. "Good thing I've got the key right here," he said, tilting the gun a little. "Now, when I give the word, we'll start sliding this table towards the door... as subtly as possible," he added. It now only sounded like one or two people were shooting, but it surely wouldn't be long before one side or the other received backup... or turned their attention to the missing fugitives. Holly didn't want to be caught by anyone.

The first few metres of sliding went without a hitch. Then somebody noticed that tables don't tend to move on their own. Two bullets punched through in-between Holly and Rob. They instinctively threw themselves flat.

Rob swore.

"Veneer?! Those cheapskates!" he muttered. Holly suddenly realised that the massive table had slid along the floor quite easily. They were hiding behind something about as bulletproof as cardboard. *Great.*

"We'd better make a run for it," Holly said, not feeling too hopeful. There was a pause in the fire. She figured that either the shooters were reloading, or, more likely, they were waiting for their targets to do something stupid... like running for the door.

"Hey, maybe they won't expect such a pathetically obvious attempt," Rob said sarcastically. His hand reached out and squeezed Holly's. She looked down in surprise before meeting his eyes. A silent apology flickered there, unsaid. She gave him what she hoped was a smile that told him not to worry about it. They were partners. This was what partners did. She felt a rush of regret in her stomach when she considered what if... what if they could have been more than just business partners? It didn't look as though she'd ever find out.

Rob took a deep breath. "Ready? On three... one... two..."

The boarded up door burst open. Two police officers holding a battering ram and wearing riot gear quickly pulled back. Shots whistled through the open doorway, proving that the shooters had been waiting. Their fire was returned until silence reigned and a man stepped into the breach. Holly looked up at the face of a person she'd never thought she'd be pleased to see.

"Detective Chittenden, I'm glad you could make it," she said, before Rob grabbed her arm and they bolted past the big policeman into the street outside. The DI led his small force into the building and the gunfire resumed. Holly felt a twinge of guilt for setting up the whole situation. If she hadn't called both the government and Chittenden, there wouldn't have been any shooting, and no one would be dead right now.

"You did the right thing. Better a few go down than the entire world," Rob said, answering her unspoken thoughts.

They took a moment to look around the street surrounding the casino. It was surprisingly empty. A few passersby had started to gather and were craning their necks at the sound of gunshots, but they didn't look particularly alarmed. The fight hadn't gone street level yet.

"Let's not look a gift horse in the mouth, but I think we've been forgotten," Rob commented.

Holly nodded. "My car's this way," she said and set off at a brisk walk, hoping they wouldn't draw any unwanted attention.

She only breathed normally again when they reached her car. Watson was yapping happily in the back. She opened the door and paused to give him a pat or two before getting into the driver's seat.

Holly drove out of town and across the countryside without a destination in mind. It was only when they stopped seeing the lights of buildings that she pulled into a lay-by and stopped the car.

"I can't believe we're alive. I can't believe we didn't get shot!" She stared through the windscreen at the starry sky and the full moon she'd so recently cursed.

"Yeah about that…" Rob said.

She looked across. He lifted his foot and peeled back the leather of his shoe. It came away red.

Holly considered it. "Did you shoot yourself in the foot?" she asked, unable to not grin.

"Shut up. No. It was a bad guy's bullet." He paused. "Probably."

"Ah well, at least you haven't lost any more fingers, and it's better than an arrow sticking out of your leg," she commented.

Rob frowned. "I'm starting to think working with you is bad for my health."

They wrapped up Rob's bullet wound (which turned out to only be a graze) and then sat in silence. Rob pulled the canister out of his pocket and considered it.

"Too bad you couldn't crack the code, although it's probably for the best," Holly said, resting a hand on Rob's shoulder. She knew this was what he'd worked his whole life for, and now, because of what it was that the Midastophians had left behind, he couldn't use this amazing find as evidence. It was too dangerous.

"Yeah, about that…" Rob typed a few symbols in and the tube popped open. Holly resisted the urge to dive out of the passenger window. Rob flipped the canister open and inspected the glass vial inside. "It's pretty well-sealed. I thought it would be. The Midastophians were careful, with the exception of their fatal mistake," he said casually. Holly was pleased to find that her heart was still beating normally after that shock.

"You… you knew how to open it?" she stuttered.

Rob nodded. "Yeah… I told you that once you get the gist of it, their language is pretty easy to decode. All that mumbo jumbo I said about the writing on the tube was exactly that - complete mumbo jumbo. What it actually says is something along the lines of: 'Change password from default setting of password'," he finished.

Holly stared at him. "You're telling me that the password for the canister was 'password'? You just said that the Midastophians were careful! What if they'd been as careless with the vial?" She eyed the dark liquid at the bottom of the vial with distrust.

Rob shrugged. "You know me, I like to take a chance," he said with a grin. Holly would have punched him if it hadn't been for the well-sealed, but breakable looking, glass vial in his hand.

"The question now is what do we do with it?" she said aloud. Rob sighed. She could tell he was thinking about the evidence of the Midastophians and how it would change everyone's view of the world's history. But then, if knowledge of the disease spread, there would be panic, and inevitably, more people who might choose to use it as a weapon. It wasn't safe in anyone's hands.

"I figured a few things out while I was waiting in my cell for you to come through and save my butt," Rob said with a slanted grin. "We can't let this thing get into anyone's hands.

It needs to be hidden again and never found." The smile slipped from his face. "The Midastophians... they'll stay a myth, or a suspected hoax, forever. We'll share something that looks just like the vial, but never the whole truth. The vial will almost certainly be found out as a hoax - even with the canister. But everything else must stay secret. This is just a smokescreen, something that will worry our hunters until we can get away," he finished with a sigh. Holly reached out and instinctively took his hand, knowing how hard it must be for him to say that after dedicating his whole life to finding real proof of the ancient population. "Where we're gonna hide the real deal though... I don't know."

Holly chewed her lip for a second before feeling a light bulb flash in her head. She grabbed her phone and typed out a text, not expecting a quick response. When her phone buzzed a moment later with a new message on the screen she was pleasantly surprised.

Madison Church, Little Green, Oakend

"What's that?" Rob asked, looking at the address. Holly typed the info into her sat nav.

"We're going to pay our last respects," she said.

LAST RESPECTS

"Grave digging? Is this what my lengthy career of crime fighting has come to?" Rob complained as he turned over a spadeful of earth. Holly didn't know why he was complaining so much. The grave had already been dug. They were just excavating it.

"If no one sees us, then this is a good idea," she said. Rob pulled a face, but he'd already grudgingly agreed that she had a point. Who'd think to look beneath a freshly dug grave for an ancient vial of deadly disease?

Holly paused to wipe the sweat from her forehead as their spades finally clunked against the wood of the coffin. This was the part she wasn't relishing.

"Ladies first…" Rob said. She glared at him before wedging a spade into the seam of the lid and levering upwards. She looked down at the pallid face of the deceased archaeologist, Douglas Patterson. A thick line of stitches showed where his head had been reattached for burial. She shook her head.

He shouldn't be dead.

"I know it's not much comfort, but you'll be keeping

something incredibly important safe for us," she said to the lifeless corpse. For once, Rob didn't make any jokes. He pulled the vial from his pocket, bending down and slipping it into the corpse's hand.

"May you rest in peace for a long, long time to come," he said.

Holly and Rob returned the lid and reburied the coffin. As the sky started to lighten in the east, the grave looked just as it had when they'd started - fresh, but professional. Holly was silently grateful for Rob's long digging career.

They walked back to the entrance of the graveyard with Watson playfully snapping at their heels.

"Things aren't going to be the same again, are they? We aren't just going to be let go," Holly said, knowing that sooner or later, one of the groups they'd crossed would come looking for the missing vial.

"Leave it to me… I'm a man with a plan," Rob said mysteriously. They made a stop at a 24 hour pharmacy and he returned to the car, his intentions still a secret. Holly watched as he coughed for a bit and than hacked up some phlegm.

"Eww, really?!" she complained when Rob gobbed into the glass tube he'd just bought.

"What? I've got a cold!" he said and then smirked. "It's the classic, isn't it? A vial of mysterious disease that wiped out an ancient, hyper-advanced civilisation is analysed - only to find that… dun dun daaaa… they were killed by the common cold. Case closed."

Holly rolled her eyes. "I think you've been listening to *The War Of The Worlds*. Also, no way is that going to fool anyone for long, right?" she said as Rob typed some coordinates into the sat nav.

He shrugged. "Well, it might not be far from the truth. Their civilisation died out, but some humans must have survived, or we wouldn't be here. It's possible that whatever is in that vial, we're resistant to it." He tilted his head. "Or, all the humans who survived were the dumb ones who lived far enough away from the smart population that they didn't catch the disease. It's probably that, but let's not dwell on it. Next stop... the local news!"

Holly drove off, wondering what they were going to do when they got there but couldn't ask Rob as he was on the phone.

"We're going to London, aren't we?" Holly said, glancing the estimated time of arrival and the postcode on the sat nav.

Rob shot her a grin in-between dialling numbers. "Yeah... the local news. It's time to go public with all of this," he said, picking up his disgustingly fresh vial of germs and popping it back into the metal tube. The case was still at the casino but they had the bits that mattered.

Holly nearly had to pinch herself to believe it. Just hours ago, she and Rob had been caught in the middle of a gunfight and now he was going live on the news to talk about the discovery of the Midastophian vial and to go public about both the government's and the underworld's intervention. The Twitter feed was already going nuts and Rob hadn't even dropped the bombshell about the potentially fatal disease he was carrying in the secret vial. She hoped he'd make that announcement sharpish, as she wouldn't put it past either of the big players they were up against to try and cut the news off... if that were even possible.

She breathed a sigh of relief when the interview concluded and the evidence was turned over - very publicly - to be analysed by top scientists who had already volunteered their services. It was just too bad that Rob had needed to lie about exactly when the society was and the extent of their technology. He'd likened them to Greeks or Romans, although it wouldn't be long before an analysis of the evidence threw up too many questions, and the whole thing was written off as a fraud. But for now, it bought them time.

"Won't they still come after us, despite all of this?" Holly said, ducking down as lights flashed in her face when she and Rob walked out of the studio. All too late, she remembered her self-promise that she would look super glamorous the next time she appeared in the news. Unfortunately, being caught up in a gunfight and pulling an all-nighter digging a grave did not equal a fresh face and a fashionable look. She had a strong feeling that she looked even worse than she had after Horn Hill House.

"Yeah, they'll come all right. Especially when they figure we did something with the real vial - which they will when they try to date the find and discover that the vial and the canister don't match," Rob said once they were beyond the rabid paparazzi.

"What will we do?" Holly pressed, thoughts of her cottage in Little Wemley and the surprisingly successful detective agency she'd set up flashing through her mind. They got in the car and Watson jumped over the seats, washing their faces eagerly. Holly realised he wanted breakfast and made a note to stop at the first shop they drove past. The poor puppy hadn't had the best 24 hours. *Neither have I*, Holly thought.

Her gaze drifted to Rob. She was disgusted to see that despite the mud, which stained the clothes that he'd worn for the past couple of days, he still looked great. His dark hair seemed to tousle itself naturally and the dirt just added to his rugged look. He might have walked straight off a calendar photoshoot.

It was so unfair.

Rob turned in his seat, noticing her stare and raised an eyebrow, his eyes flickering towards her mouth. His lips curved into his usual devilish smile.

"I've got a few ideas about what we can do together... but for starters, how about a company holiday?" He raised an eyebrow. Holly thought furiously, trying to ignore the seductive images of Rob lounging around on a sun bed, which seemed to be intent on distracting her.

"I can't leave Watson!" she said, thinking of the puppy above all else.

He nodded thoughtfully. "Yeah, I wasn't talking anywhere exotic. That would be way too predictable for two people on the run. We should go somewhere scenic, safe, and completely unexpected. How do you feel about..." he paused dramatically, "...Birmingham?"

A REVIEW IS WORTH ITS WEIGHT IN GOLD!

I really hope you enjoyed reading this story. I was wondering if you could spare a couple of moments to rate and review this book? As an indie author, one of the best ways you can help support my dream of being an author is to leave me a review on your favourite online book store, or even tell your friends.

Reviews help other readers, just like you, to take a chance on a new writer!

Thank you!
Ruby Loren

CPSIA information can be obtained
at www.ICGtesting.com
Printed in the USA
BVHW072051020420
576762BV00001B/230